Scripted

Maya Rock

Scripted

G. P. Putnam's Sons
An Imprint of Penguin Group (USA)

G. P. PUTNAM'S SONS
Published by the Penguin Group
Penguin Group (USA) LLC
375 Hudson Street
New York, NY 10014

USA | Canada | UK | Ireland | Australia
New Zealand | India | South Africa | China
penguin.com
A Penguin Random House Company

Library of Congress Cataloging-in-Publication Data
Rock, Maya. Scripted / Maya Rock. pages cm
Summary: "Nettie Starling has spent all her life on the set of a reality show, but as her
friends mysteriously get cut, she learns that her seemingly perfect world hides some
dangerous secrets"—Provided by publisher.
[1. Reality television programs—Fiction. 2. Popularity—Fiction. 3. Interpersonal
relations—Fiction. 4. Revolutions—Fiction. 5. Mystery and detective stories.] I. Title.
PZ7.R5876Scr 2015 [Fic]—dc23 2014015073

Printed in the United States of America.
ISBN 978-0-399-25733-9
10 9 8 7 6 5 4 3 2 1
Design by Annie Ericsson.
Text set in Plantin Std Light.

*To my mother, Gwendolyn Williams, my guiding light,
and my father, Anthony Rock, always in my heart.*

# Chapter 1

I like the hallway after lunch, when the sound of lingering Characters fills the space like a choir. Crickets with cameras on their shoulders weave through the crowd, searching for good scenes. Our lockers are right in the middle of it all, halfway between the school's entrance and the cafeteria. I watch everyone from here, but my eyes keep coming back to Callen.

"Selwyn, tell us *now*," Lia insists, pushing her flame-colored hair back as she kneels to rummage through the bottom of her locker.

Today, at lunch, Lincoln Grayson said he'd closed up with a girl at his parents' beach house last Saturday, after the Apocalypse (Lincoln likes his parties to have grandiose names) officially ended. We tried to guess who it was—Geraldine Spicer? Caren Trosser?—but he shook his head at each name we threw out.

Lia grumbled about the sin of secrets between friends, then accused him of making it up. Neither tactic got her a name. We left the cafeteria in a huddle, speculating feverishly, until Selwyn admitted that she knew the real story—"It's not like he said. I heard the girl's side."

"Who? Who?"

"I can't say anything else." Selwyn fidgets with her *liberato* beads. "I overheard her talking to her friends—Lincoln will kill me if I give it up." I'm worried about the audiotrack: Selwyn's voice is naturally soft, and with the noise in the hall, I can barely hear her. Last quarter's mark landed me on the E.L., so I need to make sure all my scenes are fit for broadcast. With a quick flick of my fingers (to the Audience it'll look as if I scratched my neck), I straighten the microphone pinned to my collar and step forward an inch, closing the gap between us.

"We'll keep our mouths shut, right, Nettie?" Still crouched down, Lia jabs my ankle with her elbow. Her eyes flit up to me, searching for support.

I always say what she needs to hear. "I won't tell anyone," I promise, tracking Callen as he moves away from his locker, accompanied by Rawls Talon, the Pigeons' second baseman. Callen's hair, so blond it's almost white, makes his path through the mass of Characters easy to follow. He ends up in front of the principal's office, checking out the poster tacked to the bulletin board.

I can't see it from here, but I know it by heart. I was with Lia when she wrote it.

APPRENTICESHIP ANNOUNCEMENT
SCHEDULE AND GUIDELINES

The Seventy-Third Apprenticeship Announcement
April 20

SCHEDULE

10 A.M. Mayor's Speech

10:15 A.M. Poem

10:30 A.M. Ceremony

DRESS CODE

Semiformal dresses for girls

Suits and ties for boys

Selwyn gazes intently at her *liberato* moccasins, until finally, she squares her tiny shoulders and coughs it up. "Mollie Silverine." She grins, relieved the pressure's off. The smile turns lopsided as she curls her lip down to conceal the chip on her upper left canine tooth. No one but her notices the flaw, but she's still self-conscious about it.

Lia smirks. "Mollie Silverine? You're kidding. I guess this won't make her gossip column." She's stopped rummaging, focused on our conversation.

"It's not like that. She was sleeping, and Lincoln tried to, like, nuzzle her," Selwyn goes on, "and she seriously thought he was the dog and pushed him away. Didn't sound like a close-up to me."

"Of course there was no close-up," Lia says scornfully. "I don't think Lincoln's ev—"

"Shhh, keep your voice down." Selwyn flaps her hand, eager to avoid the scrutiny of the Characters crowding the hall.

"Lincoln's never even kissed anyone," Lia whispers.

"He probably wanted her to play Spate with him," I joke, miming Lincoln briskly dealing cards, my tunic's clumsy bell-shaped sleeves fluttering in the air. Lincoln loves Spate. He's gotten so into games that he's knocked down glasses at our lunch table in his playing fervor.

"Lincoln and his Spate." Lia sighs. Selwyn giggles. I roll up the sleeves of the blouse. I can't wait for the motif change; I've about worn this shirt out. A smile lingers on Lia's face as she starts sifting through the junk in her locker again. She's one of those Characters whose smile transforms her. Without it, the even, defined lines of her face—high cheekbones, firm jaw, and hard green eyes—make her seem cold.

Selwyn moves closer to me and Lia, trying to seal us off from the rest of the hall. "Remember, it's a secret."

"We know." Lia doesn't look up. Old play programs and candy wrappers float down like autumn leaves. A pen clatters to the floor, and she snatches it up with a triumphant flourish. It's the slick red pen her dad gave her two seasons ago for her fourteenth birthday. She uses it when we work on the Diary of Destiny—she thinks it's lucky.

"Thank God. I need all the help I can get for the chemistry test," she says, standing up and shoving the pen in her pocket. She crushes the books and papers back into her locker and shoves the entire side of her body against the door to force it closed.

"You're as bad as Callen about that stuff. He sets his mitt underneath the oak tree in his backyard the night before every game for good luck," I say, cringing as soon as the words leave my mouth. Mentioning him to her is a pinch I can't resist giving myself.

The corner of Lia's mouth turns down, and she mutters, "Callen."

I can't let it go. "What do you mean? What about him?"

Selwyn hums, flipping the top buckle on her cello case up and down in an uneven rhythm. She's caught in a middle that Lia doesn't know about. Around us, the swirl of Characters intensifies as they move out of the hall toward classes.

"He did that with his mitt last year," Lia reports, "but I don't think he cares anymore. He actually forgot to bring his mitt to practice yesterday." She rolls her eyes. "That reminds me—I've got to talk to him about tonight. His parents are going to be out late. Maybe we'll *finally.*"

Nonono. I whip around and start twirling my combination with jittery fingers, getting it wrong on the first try. Lia just won't stop talking about how Callen won't close up with her.

"Why do *you* think he won't, Nettie?" she asks, smiling.

"Scared?" I suggest. At last, I hear the click and my locker opens. *Would he be scared with me?* I feel my skin heating up, and poke my head into the locker so no one can see my embarrassment.

"Poor Callen," Selwyn says behind me.

"Poor Callen?" Lia squawks. She leans her back against her locker, her face inches away from mine. She surveys the hall like a queen. "Poor *me.* Something's wrong with him. What could it be?"

I grab my math book and back out from the locker, calmer. "Maybe it's a ritual, like with the mitt." I think it's a reasonable guess. "Like if he closes up during baseball time, he'll lose games."

"Maybe," Lia says, drumming her fingers on her locker. "Whatever it is, he needs to get over it. I'm *ready*, you know what I mean?" Selwyn snorts with laughter, resorting to pressing her face against her arm to smother the sound.

I shrug. "Not really." She knows I've never closed up before.

Lia sighs. "Well, he better not cancel again. I want to get home late tonight anyway. Mom's been on a rampage." The drumming stops as she realizes she's said too much. Her eyes dart to the camera, risking a fine but hoping to make the footage unusable.

She succeeds in escaping the Audience, but not Selwyn.

"What rampage?" Selwyn asks hesitantly. Her inky black eyes are wide.

"Hmm? Oh, well, you know how mothers can be." Lia picks up the stylish straw bag she got for *liberato*, ready to make a run for it to escape the conversation. She's kept her mom's alcohol problem a secret from other Characters and tries to avoid talking about it on-camera, even though the Audience probably knows.

"My mom doesn—"

"Where's Callen?" Lia cranes her neck, scanning the hall. "This is the last chance I'll get to talk to him before practice."

"By the bulletin board, talking to Rawls," I report. They aren't looking at the poster anymore. Now Rawls is gabbing away, and Callen is listening, as usual.

"Okay, great." Her eyes flick past him and land on Mollie, the tall, coltish girl who spurned Lincoln, sauntering through the hall with her friend, brawny Thora Swan, Selwyn's apprenticeship rival. "Mollie really dodged a bullet," she muses. "She's so nice, and he's so Lincoln. What if we sent a blind item about it in to her column? She might not even realize it's about her, and he'd be so mad. What do you think?"

I shake my head.

"You're right," she says, adjusting the bag under her arm. "Too mean. Okay, I'm going to try to catch Callen. God, I should put a blind item in her column about *him*."

I play along. "What precocious pitcher . . . ," I begin while Selwyn starts fiddling with the buckle again, embarrassed.

"Can't close the real game," Lia finishes with a chuckle. "Bye." She rushes down the hall, hollering his name. He looks up, grins, and waits. I like the way he waits. When Callen is still, he reminds me of a river, fixed in space yet coursing with inner energy. Lia catches up with him, and their hands join. They don't look right together. Her purposeful stride, his loose glide.

What a nightmare.

"So weird and sad for you." Selwyn squeezes my shoulder. She has a light touch. She's like a doll come to life—her small, flat nose, inky black eyes, and wide face. Everything about her is mild and unthreatening, especially her girlish, whispery voice.

"Let's talk about something else." I wiggle free from her grasp and glance up at the clock across from our lockers. Ten minutes until class. "How's orchestra?"

Someone leaving the hall jostles her cello case, and she hugs it closer. It's almost as big as she is. "I'm practicing. A lot. Can you believe how close the Double A is?"

I stuff my math book into my book bag. "April twentieth is still a month away." The nearer we get to our Apprenticeship Announcement, the less excited I feel about what's supposed to be the most important day of my life.

Selwyn peers closely at me. "You're not excited?"

"I haven't been to Fincher's much lately," I confess. It's typical to put in a lot of hours at the apprenticeship you want before the Double A—like a pre-apprenticeship—so the Characters you'll be working with can get a feel for you. Mine, the repairman apprenticeship, would be at Fincher's Fix-Its, so I trudge down there every so often to tackle broken clocks and malfunctioning toasters. It's mind-numbingly boring. Imagining a life stuck in a dusty shop is depressing, but the alternative—getting anyassigned into some lame job no one wants—is worse. When I feel depressed, I try to remember that lots of people in the Sectors don't even have lifetime jobs. Compared to the Reals, I have it easy.

Selwyn glances over her shoulder to make sure no one's eavesdropping, then turns back to whisper, "Is it because of Witson?"

"No, not because—well, not *just* because of Witson." Unfortunately for me, Mr. Fincher is my ex's father, and Witson gets lurky whenever I'm there. But he *always* blows his own cover by stumbling over paint buckets and nail boxes, then stammering apologies while I watch him pick the stuff up, thinking, *I can't believe our lips ever touched.* "I'd be okay with Witson if I felt better about the apprenticeship."

"You feel bad about being a repairman?" Selwyn's cello case rocks, pushed by some geeky sophomore girls standing behind her, and she reaches out and steadies it. "It seems to fits you so well, though."

"Mom agrees with you. She thinks it's perfect because I like to build stuff. But the garage feels like a bat cave, and the work all seems the same after a while," I say. "It's too late to switch."

"Technically not *too* late to do something else." Selwyn purses her kitten lips and twists the buttons on her flowery cardigan as she thinks. "The apprenticeship lasts a year, but your profession is forever. You can write whatever you want on the Double A application . . . or leave it blank."

"If I put something new in, I'd be up against people who've already put in time. And blank means anyassigned, which would be a disaster. Face it, I'm stuck." I turn back to my locker, snagging the tunic sleeve on the handle. "Literally."

"Aw," Selwyn croons, rushing forward to help me untangle myself. Lia would have laughed.

I'll be wearing this tunic after school when I bike to the Center for my Show Physical. I'm so tired of billowy *liberato* fashions. Like I'm tired of Fincher's. Like I'm tired of Lia and Callen.

"Think of the positive. You get the parts you need for your own projects free, like that diode thing for the radio you're making," Selwyn says, running her hand through her long midnight-black hair.

"Yeah. Great." I gaze into the locker's void, then pull out my chemistry book. "That's nice, but it doesn't help when I'm in the garage, ready to claw my eyes out."

Selwyn sighs. "At least you know you'll probably get the repairman apprenticeship. I don't know if"—she lowers her voice—"if I can beat Thora Swan for the orchestra one. She practices constantly. She's a *beast*. I'm going to end up any-assigned to trash collection—"

Stomp. Stomp. Stomp. I dimly register the sound of footfalls, their rhythm regular, mechanized. Selwyn stiffens and complains about how her parents won't buy her a new cello. Then she stops talking, and so, I realize, has everyone else—the hall is silent except for those footfalls. I turn my head from my locker, dread fluttering through me, remembering my last ratings mark.

The Authority pass behind Selwyn, steps resounding loudly, and Characters move to the side to make room for them. They rush down the hall, a black blur. Five. Their guns jostle in their holsters.

"My cello sounds old—and out of—doesn't work right," Selwyn pulls at her necklace, which closes around her neck, tight as a noose. I recite in my head what Mik, my producer, told me: *Patriots are a natural part of life on the show.*

Selwyn's voice trembles as the Authority stampede out of the hall, into the cafeteria. The choir grows louder as everyone struggles to get back into show mode.

"You're more fun than Thora, though, and the orchestra

considers personality," I say, moving my chin so that my mouth is directly over my mic. Selwyn bobs her head, incapable of speech.

Lia finds me on the stairs. She's going down at the speed of a missile, her mouth tight, and I'm plodding up, on my way to calculus, my shoulders hunched, my ratings mark blaring in my head. Before I can say anything, she drags me over to the side, by the railing, forcing Characters to break around us as they hurry to their classes.

"What's up?" I say on-mic. I step up, and she bends down, and I let my hand fall over my mic. "Who was it?"

She straightens and taps her foot while she calculates how much time we have. Her catlike eyes sweep the space, on the lookout for crickets.

"Come with me to the bathroom," she says. "I need to redo my lipstick."

"Okay," I agree. We can frall safely about the cut there, since bathrooms are off-camera. She grabs my arm, and together, we jog up the stairs, barging into the bathroom at the end of the hall, interrupting Mollie Silverine, Thora Swan, and Terra Chiven, who are clustered outside the stalls.

"Hi." Mollie sniffles, twirling her long honey-blond hair around a finger, fat tears rolling down her wan cheeks. Her blue eyes seem to well up even more when she sees me. My breath catches in my throat; she's probably thinking, *Nettie will be next.*

Thora, the cellist built like a linebacker, grunts hello.

Terra, a senior, unlike the other two, and their chubby little leader, steps forward and glares. Mostly at me. As usual. "Shouldn't you be in class?" She sighs, knitting her thick eyebrows together. Her pigtails make her look a lot more innocent than she is. Terra's intense about everything she does, from managing her social life to maintaining her grueling doctor apprenticeship to being extravagantly rude to me because she thinks I'm into her crush, Scoop Cannery.

"Shouldn't *you* be in class?" Lia retorts. "I'm fixing up my makeup." She marches over to the window and plops her straw bag onto the windowsill.

"Nettie, have *you* thought of wearing makeup?" Terra purrs. "I hear Delton's is having a sale on starter kits. But I guess it might be a little expensive for you, even with the sale."

"Uh, no," I bumble, unable (as usual) to think of a plus-ten retort. Like Lia, Terra lives in Treasure Woods, one of the wealthiest neighborhoods on the island. The Arbor, where I live, is firmly middle class. I can't afford to buy *toothpicks* at Delton's. While I'm struggling to think of a comeback, Terra and her friends start mouthing to one another. Characters learn to lip-read from an early age so they can frall without getting fined. The trio peppers their conversation with decoy on-mic remarks about makeup and other Delton sales.

"She should check out the sale on Shake-It-Off," Lia murmurs to me when I join her by the mirror. Shake-It-Off is a popular weight-loss drink that comes in candy-cane-striped cans. Sometimes I see empty cans at Lia's house—she says her mom chugs them down before Show Physicals because her weight target is too low for her to achieve naturally. Which reminds me again that I have to go to the Center for my own Show Physical after school. Ugh. I want to just go home and forget about today.

"Shhhh," I hush Lia, worried Terra will overhear. It's funny but too mean. I actually do feel bad for Terra when I see how ruthlessly Scoop ignores her. I relate far too well to the torture of being infatuated with someone who's unattainable.

"She deserves it." Lia strides over to the sinks and turns on all the faucets. Then she returns to the window and heaves the sash up. Cars zoom outside. The idea is for Media1 to blame the cars and gushing water for the mashed audiotrack. She shoves aside her straw bag and sits on the windowsill, draping her long legs over the radiator.

"Belle," she mouths. "She turned sixteen two weeks ago. They got her in the cafeteria." She brushes radiator dust off her fawn-colored skirt while waiting for my response.

"Belle Cannery?" I mouth, stomach lurching. Scoop's sister. Slight and timid, with mousy brown hair that drooped onto oversized tortoiseshell glasses. I'd see Belle when I went to visit Mom at the library. "*Belle* is a Patriot?" No wonder Mollie is so upset; I've never heard of someone being cut so soon after they became eligible. It's rare for *anyone* who's still in school to be cut.

Lia tugs my tunic, grabbing my attention. "Let's do the Diary tomorrow morning, okay?" she says on-mic.

"Yeah, come by around ten." My gaze drifts behind her, toward the street with the cars and trucks and vans. Belle is probably inside one of the white Media1 vans right now, on her way to the Center.

"All right, great. Oh, it's on with Callen tonight." Lia coughs lightly to refocus me. I drag my gaze back to her, but seeing her eyes makes me want to crumble, so I stare at the peeling linoleum floor. Off-camera places are never as nice as sets. "His house," Lia continues, undaunted by my lack of response. "I'll give you all the dirty details tomorrow." It's a testament to how swerved off about Belle I am: these statements barely register. I keep my eyes on the sad, decrepit floor, in a fog.

Lia nudges my leg with her foot. I look up again, blinking.

"Are you okay?" she mouths briefly.

"Remember *my* last mark?" I mouth back. Media1 starts giving us ratings marks when we're ten. For twenty-four quarters, reduced payments are the only consequence for Characters whose marks fall 10 percent below their targets. But after we turn sixteen, if our marks are 10 percent below target, we end up on the E.L., the Eligibility List, and can be cut at any time until the next quarter starts—then the clock resets. I turned sixteen six months ago, and found out that I was on the E.L. at my most recent Character Report.

Lia nods briskly. "What was it again? One eighty-two?"

"One sixty-eight," I correct her. One hundred eighty-two is as low as Lia's mind can go, ratingswise. "My target was two thirty-two."

Her mouth twitches like she just got stung, then her eyes soften, and she mouths, "You're not going to be cut, you're imp—"

"I'm on the E.L., Lia. When the producers' circle was making their choice, my name was on the list, just like Belle's. I could be next. I could be a Patriot."

Just like my father.

"I get it, Nettie. You're on the E.L. But so are a ton of other Characters, and most of them aren't going to be cut. Especially not at our age. You're just scaring yourself," Lia mouths. "You'll be off in a few months." Her back is to the sun, and her face is shadowed, the swirl of freckles around her eyes just visible. She looks majestic with her chiseled cheekbones and long neck. Her green eyes are glittering, framed by long, light eyelashes. She looks like she believes what she's saying.

I wish I could.

I see my faint reflection in the window, my wavy, dark hair hanging behind me. I grew it out for *liberato,* and it just passes my shoulders now. My features are friendly: heart-shaped face with slight lips, and a small, rounded, upturned nose. It's a good face, but suddenly, desperately, I wish it were more. I wish it were enough to entrance the Audience.

"You don't know what will happen next quarter," I mouth, turning to the other girls to escape Lia's ineffective consolations.

"Belle didn't care enough about her ratings," Thora mouths, crossing her muscular arms.

Mollie wipes her eyes on her sleeve. "I wonder if Scoop knows."

"I'll be there for him," Terra mouths solemnly. As if a sacred duty has been placed in her hands.

Lia pokes me, and I glance back at her. "I think she's the youngest Patriot in seven seasons," she mouths. The bell rings, and the others trot out of the bathroom, laughing and talking about weekend plans as they get back on-camera. The door closes, and the noise from the hall slowly fades as everyone heads into classrooms.

Every year, around twenty-five Characters are cut. About two a month. The longer I live, the more likely I am to be one if my ratings don't improve.

Lia is watching me while she picks distractedly at the paint chipping off the windowsill. "Nettie, you're not like Belle," she whispers into my ear.

"*I* might not be like her, but my *ratings* are like hers. Lia, you're used to high ratings. It's never been easy for me. It wasn't easy for my father, either."

Lia's eyes glint with determination. "Listen. Belle's better off working for the company. You belong here, Nettie, not in the Sadtors, and *don't* talk about your dad."

Don't talk about your dad. When we were ten or eleven, I was obsessed with knowing where he was and what he was doing. What I really wanted was to know *him*, but that was impossible, so I tackled the where and what questions instead. Sometimes I try to solve *life*, like it's math or one of the toasters at Fincher's.

The Contract says "Patriots are enlisted in the service of Media1 and are given lodging and food provisions for their lifetimes." No more, no less. Still, rumors abound—I'd heard that Patriots become producers for the show, that they receive new identities and assimilate into the Sectors, or that they do grunt work for Media1—maintaining cables and building sets. I think I'd heard about seven rumors altogether, and investigated all of them, dragging Lia along with me.

I'd hover around the Center, hoping to catch glimpses of Patriots who had become producers. I'd shadow crickets, hoping to catch them talking about the Patriots. I'd pester Lia for ideas. Finally, sick of my obsession, she wrangled the truth out of our producer, Bek, who swore her to secrecy, then revealed that the Patriots work on publicity for Media1 in Zenta, the capitol of the Sectors. Writing about the show for magazines, creating posters and books for fans, giving interviews.

Not awful, but not for me.

"I just want to stay on the island," I mouth. "I don't want to watch you on television from the Sectors." The Sectors, the country the Originals fled from, where the Audience lives, is huge and varied, but there's no real stability like we have on Bliss: there are no guarantees about getting jobs or healthcare or even having a home.

Lia hops off the windowsill and puts her hands on her hips. "All we need are some exciting plotlines for you. Plotlines that would make you branch out more. Make new friends. Or new more-than-friends. You haven't so much as *looked* at anyone since Witson. A lifetime ago."

I've looked at Callen. But I can't say that. I've thought about milking my crush to get off the E.L.—best friends liking the same boy is a great plotline—but I don't want Lia to find out. So I confine myself to sneaking small glances and making little complaints to Selwyn.

"Four months since Witson, not a lifetime," I mouth, moving closer to the window, my jeans pressing against the radiator. Snowney covers the hill leading down to the street, sparkling in the sun. The lawn is usually a blinding green, enhanced by paint the crickets spray on. Commenting on the snowney would be a good bet if I want some scenes on the show. Even if Media1 doesn't have footage of me, they can still work my dialogue over picturesque scenes such as snowney-blanketed hills. But all I can think is, *Snowney machines kept me up late last night.* Fralling.

"Four months is more than a *whole* ratings quarter. I'll think up some plotlines tonight and we can talk about them when we do the Diary tomorrow." Lia bites her lower lip, a habit she slides into whenever she gets away from the cameras. "But you know what might really help—have you heard of the Initiative?"

"The Initials?"

"No." It's so rare for me to misread her. "The Initiative," she mouths again, more slowly. "Have you heard of it?"

"No, what is it?" Sounds like one of Lincoln's parties. I always hear about them through Lia. He never invites me directly.

"Um, never mind," she mouths. She whips out a pale pink lipstick, thrusts her face in front of the mirror, and deftly applies it. "We have to go to class. You have calculus, right? You should talk to Scoop."

"And say what?" Scoop and I are friendly, but we're not close.

"I guess, talk about whatever it is you two talk about—like, triangles?" Lia suggests, only half kidding, as she turns off the faucets. "The last Character he needs to see today is the Terror That Is Terra. She'll try too hard." She gives me a once-over. "You look really upset. Like, sickly. Crickets are right outside." Now that she mentions it, I do hear cameras buzzing behind the door.

"Do this." Lia pinches her cheeks.

I glimpse my pallid face in the mirror and obey Lia's direction, then flex my fingers and roll my neck. Like I'm about to step out into a brawl, but there's no enemy to prepare for. Just the Audience.

I walk into the classroom and slip into my seat next to Scoop. We've sat next to each other since the beginning of the school year. He started it—mostly so he could get me to help with his homework—but now we're sort of friends, strange as that might seem. He's this popular, charismatic, gorgeous senior, and in this class, I'm quiet, raising my head only to answer questions. A lot of my shyness is because I'm the only junior—save for the couple of days a month when my classmate Revere joins us, helping out Mr. Black in order to lock down the math teacher apprenticeship.

No charisma for Scoop today. He stares out the huge classroom windows that overlook the snowney-white lawn.

I'm not sure what to say, so I study my desk's surface until I find fresh graffiti scratched into it. *The Initiative Sux.* Lia didn't seem to think it was so sucky.

Mr. Black is always late, so Characters have spread across the room like an oil spill, talking and laughing *hard*, overcompensating for the shock about Belle.

"Let me know if you have any questions! I'm here to help!" Revere Yucann calls out in his singsongy voice. He's in a button-down plaid shirt and jeans that have been pressed flat—he always dresses well on his math-help days. Even his stringy hair is pulled back in a neater-than-usual ponytail. He flits from student to student, offering help with a dazzling smile. He winks as he passes me. We're not super-close, but Revere is one of the Characters I admire most. Always cheerful and generous with his time, even with the most duncelike seniors. He'll make a great math teacher.

A cloud moves outside, and sunlight warms my cheek. Okay. Conversation idea. I think this is the longest Scoop has ever gone without talking.

"It's so warm, you'd think it was summer," I say. Too late, I remember the Missive from a week ago that said we're supposed to pretend it's cold. Hence, the snowney. The company likes it if our weather roughly coincides with that of the most-populated regions of the Sectors; sometimes they manipulate the weather with chemicals, sometimes they have us pretend, sometimes both. Bottom line: my flub won't make broadcast.

Scoop turns his head, dubious, as if I've spoken in another

language. My pulse quickens. With high cheekbones, a cleft chin, and dark brown hair that swoops over his brow like an ocean wave, he qualifies as handsome in a universally acceptable sort of way. Girls kind of melt around him. I found it hard to look at him when he first started talking to me—Lia called it the Scoop Swoon. Sometimes she jokes about how we should date, even if the swoon wore off long ago.

"You must be running a fever or something, because it's freezing," Scoop says finally, unenthusiastically. I exhale, relieved. He points to the knitted hat on top of his book bag. "I actually had to wear the hat inside, at morning assembly. Side benefit: I couldn't hear Martin."

I laugh like it's the funniest thing I've heard all day. Martin Fennel, the senior class president with the paunch of a fifty-year-old, transforms weekly announcements into extended soliloquies. He's an odd one. He and Lia used to go out, and she'd chosen him to take her virginity ("dispose of her virginity" is how she put it). Afterward she reported that he'd fumbled through the whole thing and talked the entire time.

My laughter seems to energize Scoop, who grins. "Ninety-nine or a hundred?" he asks.

"What do you mean?" I smile back tentatively. He seems to be keeping it together.

"You're going to aim higher? Hundred and ten? Is that possible?" Scoop shifts sideways toward me.

"Do you mean the test? I think a hundred." Math is my best subject; it's always come easily to me.

He moves closer and glances at the cameras on the ceiling. I do the same. Only one is aimed at us.

He puts his hands around his mouth. "I'm worried about Belle. Where do you think your father is?"

Don't talk about your dad.

I remember my gloomy days about Dad all too well. I could save Scoop the gloom by telling him that they're doing publicity, but Lia swore me to secrecy, because she doesn't want to get Bek in trouble. I look down and start pushing the worn corner of my textbook back and forth, wishing we actually *could* just talk about triangles.

"Here, I'm here." Mr. Black bumbles in, wiggling his doughy torso to straighten the wire connecting his mic to its battery pack. As he contorts, we get a view of his ever-expanding bald spot, shiny as an egg. Everyone returns to their desks, moaning and groaning about the test. Mr. Black kicks haplessly at the doorstopper. Five tries later, the stopper is dislodged and the door swings shut. He's so awkward. A camera horror.

"Let me just, ergh—one second—um," he says, pulling out papers from his briefcase. He begins passing them out, squeezing down the aisles between desks. "Put away your book, Ella. Only prayer can help you now." He guffaws at his own joke.

Scoop gamely tilts his face to the camera-studded ceiling, closes his eyes, and joins his hands in mock-prayer. He and Belle have similar pillowy lips and hazel eyes. This is as close as I'll ever be to Belle Cannery again.

When he opens his eyes, he catches me staring at him, and

I blurt out, "I'm sorry." Everyone hears me practically fralling on-mic, and the Terror That Is Terra exchanges a look of disapproval with Mollie.

"That you didn't study for the test," I add hastily.

"Me too," Scoop says, tapping his pencil on his desk. Mr. Black passes out the tests, and I place my palms on the white sheet, trying to focus, but an uncomfortable feeling rises inside me, making my chest tight.

Belle didn't deserve this, even if the Originals did sign a Contract that allowed sixteen-year-olds to get cut. Even if Lia's right about Belle fitting in more in the Sadtors. Belle's too young to be torn away from her family.

I look sideways at Scoop. Should I tell him? He's jotting down answers—well, guesses—on his test. He feels my gaze, raises his head, and grins his fast, electric grin, and I think about how he may fool the Audience, but he can't fool me. I can't forget the worst days of obsessing about my father: the turmoil, the uncertainty, the questions that build a cage around you.

Chapter 2

I'm done with the test twenty minutes early. Mr. Black dismisses me, and I bolt down the hall, slowing by the history classroom. Lia's sitting at her desk near the front, next to Callen, her hand in her chin and her face relaxed. I'm sure she's stopped thinking about Belle. Lia gets over stuff fast. I wave. The gesture catches her eye, and she lifts up her hand, smiles, and mouths, "Everything's okay, okay?" fast as lightning. I nod, and she turns back to the map of the island hanging at the front of the classroom.

Bliss Island looks like a four-leaf clover surrounded by endless blue. Everyone knows that it's inaccurate, though. A chunk of the mainland Sectors, across from Avalon Beach, should be shown to the east. On the other side of the island, in the southwest, across from Eden Beach, should be at least some of Drowned Lands, an island chain, of which, strictly speaking, Bliss Island is part—I think Media1 leased the island from the Sectors government. The Drowned Lands, separated from the mainland by thousands of miles, are constantly causing problems for the rest of the Sectors by threatening secession.

But we just get the infinite blue because Media1 doesn't want us to think too much about what goes on out there.

I look away from the map and steal a glance at Callen. He's sitting next to Lia, in a faded red T-shirt and dark blue jeans, slumped back in his chair, his right arm dropped to his side, hand flexing unconsciously, a habit that began when he started pitching. I hear a long sigh echo through the empty hall and realize with horror that the sound came from me. *Time to get out of here.*

When I reach my locker, I stuff my books into my bag fast, as if they are hot coals. The more I think about Callen, the more I want him, and the more I want him, the farther away he seems. Which is absurd, because we actually live next door to each other; we used to sit on his porch and hang out—it was all so utterly normal. No foggy brain. No heart skipping. But our friendship got shaky once I became aware that I wanted more, then it collapsed completely when he started going out with Lia.

I got together with Witson to get Callen out of my head, but the main lesson I took from that relationship was that feelings can't be built—or dismantled—the same way clocks and radios can.

I lock my bike up in front of the Character Relations Building and hurry to the entrance, breezing past the display case containing the Contract and the season's Missives. I hear a buzzing sound undercut by a shrill whistle, and I lift my head to the sky—fighter jet. There have been a lot lately, crisscrossing our airspace on the way to and from the Drowned Lands. It's okay for me to look at them in the Center, since we're off-camera. In the past, when there'd be flurries of jet activity, I chalked it up to training. Nowadays . . . well, either they're training a lot or the Drowned Landers are causing serious trouble.

I type my code into the number pad next to the door. It unlocks, and I walk into the lobby, which is overflowing with loud, fast-talking, sloppy Reals.

No matter what the hour, they're always working, purple and green nylon jumpsuits scratching, sneakers pounding as they circulate, gibbering to one another. I keep my head down as I walk to the stairwell that's reserved for Characters. I won't get fined for acknowledging Reals in the Center, but that doesn't mean I *want* to interact with them. Lia says you can see a layer of grime on the Reals if you look close enough. It's probably because the Sadtors are such a mess. There's lots of sickness since they don't have mandatory vaccinations and consistent medical attention, plus there's tons of pollution.

I climb to the fourth floor, Show Physicals. The lights are low here, and a custodian pushes a mop down the floor. I sidestep him on my way to Dr. Kanavan's office near the end of the hall. My ears detect a low stream of sounds, and sure enough, when I reach the doorway, I can see that the television perched on her cabinet is on. I squint, taking in what I can of *Blissful Days*.

The Bliss Elementary playground, at recess. The sinuous slide, the pine tree scarred with initials, the creaky seesaw. Kids tumbling around and laughing.

Things were different then, I brood, watching the television. No fines, no payments, no ratings. No E.L.

Dr. Kanavan, springy blond curls piled on her head in a messy bun, glances at the television every few seconds, her head popping up like an overambitious cuckoo clock. My producer, Mik, says Reals are addicted to the show. I don't know how they do it—I get antsy a half hour into Lia's Drama Club productions. But Mik says the Reals can watch it for days on end, and Media1 gives them the opportunity to by broadcasting hour-long episodes back-to-back, twenty-four hours a day.

Dr. Kanavan doesn't spend all her leisure time on *Blissful Days*. She's a travel fiend, and in between glances at the television, she crosses off days on the calendar she's mounted above her desk. Countdown to her next furlough. The goal date box always has a new place in thick black marker. Today's is **Zenta!** In the past, there was **Kyliss! Misk!** She's an adventurer—in her clothing choices too. Free from following motifs, she has on a glittery green sequin top beneath her lab coat; it flashes and winks when she moves.

In the ten seasons I've been coming here, I've never seen Dr. Kanavan repeat a trip. The Sectors are a thousand times the size of Bliss, and she seems to want to visit every inch. I don't get why. I *like* the familiarity of the island. Thanks to great set designers, anything I could ever want to see—cliffs, waterfalls, plains, orchards, hills, valleys—are all less than an hour away.

My shoulders ache, and I slide off my book bag. Dr. Kanavan whirls around. "Nettie," she squeaks, rising and running over to the television, blond curls bouncing behind her. Her high heels—green satin to match her top—sound like rain hitting a tin roof. She turns the television off and taps over to me, shamefaced, as if it's the first time I've caught her with the television on.

Dr. Kanavan is cute for a Real, with her messy curls, ruddy cheeks, and button nose. Still, like most Reals, she'd look out of place on the island. All the Characters are better looking than the Reals, since the Originals were cast for their appearances.

Another difference is that Reals talk faster than Characters. But the ones used to conversing with us adapt, and I have no problems understanding Dr. Kanavan.

"Punctual as always," she says, ushering me away from the television. "You get that from your grandmother. On last night's seven o'clock episode, I saw that Violet showed up right on time for her weekly bingo game. Reminded me of you." Dr. Kanavan has always been more forthcoming talking about what she's seen on *Blissful Days* than Mik.

"Plus ten," I murmur, wincing a bit at the irony of my words. "Plus ten" comes from when a Character earns bonus money for getting more than 10 percent of their ratings mark—a situation that has never happened to me, but is Lia's ratings reality and probably Callen's, too, since he started baseball.

"Here you go." She passes me a pale green paper smock, and I go behind the screen to change. As I fold my tunic, a foghorn blares from the beach behind us, and the walls shiver. I wonder if Belle is on the sand now, being escorted onto a ship bound for the Sectors. Now I shiver. When I come out from behind the screen, I take off my shoes and socks, then step onto to the scale near the door. I clench my fists as I watch the electronic display make up its mind.

"You hit your weight target." Dr. Kanavan makes a note in my file.

"Great." I relax my fingers. If only it were all so simple. If I don't make my ratings target, the solution isn't as simple as cutting my candy intake. I can guess what the Audience wants to see, but I'll never know for sure. At my last Character Report, I asked Mik if he had any idea why my ratings had fallen, but he just clucked genially, patted my head, and reminded me of Clause 57, which limits how much the Reals can interfere with the show, the clause meant to keep *Blissful Days* natural and lifelike.

I sit on the metal table in the middle of the room and watch as Dr. Kanavan types out a code on a number pad next to a cabinet. She lifts the cabinet's cover and pulls out a tray of vaccination tubes, which she brings over and places on a table next to me. I stretch out my arm, and she preps the needle, then feels for a vein. I watch impassively as the needle slides under my skin, smooth as a diver slipping into water.

Selwyn claims her arm is sore for weeks after Media1 vaccines, but I don't feel much, and the red bumps the vaccinations leave behind vanish in a day or two. I turn my head and look at the thin sliver of sky the window shade leaves unconcealed, light blue with white undertones. It reminds me of Callen's eyes.

When I think about Callen, it's like I'm teetering.

"It's lovely, isn't it?" Dr. Kanavan says, following my gaze to the window.

But I never fall. I blink, returning to real life.

"So beautiful. The scripted sky," she continues.

This morning while I was in history, company helicopters thrumming outside had startled me out of my semislumber. The windows had fogged up with the chemicals they use to control the weather.

By this afternoon, the windows were clear, the clouds were gone, and what was left was the scripted sky.

"At home it never looks like that," Dr. Kanavan says, loading up another injection. "Always dirty because of pollution. The sky in Zenta will probably be pitch-black while I'm there."

"That's too bad." I shake my head, imagining Belle and my father stuck with a dark sky. Dr. Kanavan slides another needle in.

"Zenta wasn't my top pick," Dr. Kanavan murmurs. She keeps her eyes focused on the needle. "I wanted to go to the Drowned Lands. Everything's so cheap, the sky is clean, food is fresh, and I heard the water's clear as glass, but it's not like you can trust their hotels to be sanitary. So many dumpy places there, and I hear you get swarmed by beggar children. Not to mention the Drowned Lands aren't so safe for mainlanders right now." She draws back the syringe, and the needle slides out.

"I've heard the jets," I venture. I have to be careful not to act too interested.

"The secession movement has picked up strength, and the

government is having a lot of trouble stomping out all the rebel groups. They say some parts are secure, but I'm not going to risk it. I'll stick to the luxuries of Zenta," Dr. Kanavan says, gripping my arm firmly with her small hand and pressing in yet another needle. I avert my eyes and watch the custodian push his mop bucket down the hall through the open doorway. I wonder if Belle will visit the Drowned Lands when she's in the Sectors.

I flinch at a sudden pressure on my arm and turn back. Dr. Kanavan is twisting herself to the side to get a better angle on what's hopefully the last vaccine. Her new position makes the green sequins shimmer. "Almost done," she says. She wants to get back to her vacation daydreams and her television. She packs the vials back into the tray and returns them to the cabinet, on autopilot. While I wait, I draw circles in the air with my dangling feet, enjoying the sight of my painted toenails—Citrus Sensations nail polish borrowed from Lia.

Next, Dr. Kanavan listens to my heart with the stethoscope and tests my reflexes. She takes a blood sample. Media1 doctors are vigilant about disease control. Family Mapping hates the wild card illnesses can throw in—felling random Characters, skewing demographics.

Dr. Kanavan scrutinizes me, then clucks with disapproval. "Nettie, I can see that you're still not following your Skin Sequence." She's right. Most of the time, when choosing between more sleep or the fifteen minutes it takes to apply the Media1 lotions and exfoliants, I choose sleep.

"I know. I'll do better."

Dr. Kanavan raises her overly plucked eyebrows, and I feel a twinge of annoyance. Does she really think the Skin Sequence is going to help my ratings? I'll always have more of a sidekick's face than a star's.

"You might not see the point now, but when you're older, you'll get that being camperf is sometimes the key to keeping fans." She walks over to her cabinet and puts back the vaccines and my file. "You have a duty to the Audience—keep them happy by giving them something pleasing to look at."

"Okay, thanks." I hoist myself off the table. As I walk back to the changing screen in the corner, I glimpse a thick stack of magazines resting on a stand next to an eye chart. A lab coat lies over them, but about half of the cover of the top magazine is visible. I eagerly read it: "Ten Ways to Save on Groceries" . . . "I Was a Drowned Lands Hostage." Yikes. Seems like Zenta is definitely the right move for Dr. Kanavan.

I slip behind the metal changing screen and examine my blurry reflection in it, needing to assure myself my skin isn't that bad. Even, olive tone, like my grandmother's. Relatively smooth. But my hair seems worse than it was earlier. To put it bluntly, it looks like I stuck my fingers in an electric socket. If my ratings were good, sure, I could make the case that messy hair was an admirable quirk. But they're not, I'm on the E.L., and I need to do everything I can to get off. Which means setting the alarm early tomorrow so I have time to do the Skin Sequence before Lia comes over.

• • •

The setting sun turns the scripted sky fiery as I bike home. I keep thinking about Belle. She *was* out of place in her gregarious, glamorous family. Scoop's dad is a lawyer, known for his courtroom eloquence, and his mom is a photographer, always running around the island in a fedora and sunglasses, snapping pictures for newspapers and magazines. His aunt, my old history teacher, was pretty personable too, albeit somewhat eccentric.

Belle didn't fit.

The Cannerys live in the kind of house good ratings can buy. I bet Belle's ratings target was high, too, like mine. Media1 might not have expected her to be at the center of scenes, but they must have expected her to be a good foil for her brother and parents.

A tricky situation. I should know. My ratings targets used to be low, but crept up as Lia and I became closer. My marks, the actual number of Audience members who watched me every quarter, went up too, but sometimes it seemed like that didn't matter. To determine your ratings payment, Media1 doesn't only count the number of Reals watching you, but whether that number is more or less than the target their formula predicted.

Mik showed me the formula that generates targets. I saw all the variables, what Media1 takes into consideration to predict your mark. Number of Special Events Attended, Character Age, Previous Quarter's Screentime. Friends' Average Marks. That's the one that keeps mine high. There's one for Family's Average Marks. That's probably what doomed Belle. But who knows?

The formula is so complex. How does it go? X's, Y's, and Z's crowd my head.

I'm so busy recalling the formula that I don't see the figure in the blue jacket directly in my path on the stretch of road between Bliss High and the Arbor until it's too late. I twist the bike to the right, and it climbs halfway up the curb before the force of the abrupt turn topples it on its side, flinging me onto the grass.

I lie on my back, face-to-face with the sky, breath rapid and heart racing. I think I'm okay, but I'm too stunned to move.

"Nettie, are you all right?" Someone crouches next to me. I recognize the low voice and risk turning my neck. Okay. That worked. Sore, but functioning. I see white-striped blue sneakers. My eyes move up, all the way, to blue eyes under light blond hair. *Callen?*

"Callen?" I say aloud. He nods, searching my face, probably worried the fall scrambled my brains.

"Are you okay?" he repeats.

I take a deep breath, reenergizing myself. "I think so." I prop myself up on my elbows. "Just . . . shocked." I sit up, head spinning. I check my clothes—grass stains all over my jacket, but no rips, no blood.

"Yeah, that was . . . unexpected," he murmurs, with his typical understatement. He stands and holds out his hand, adding, "I should have been paying more attention. Thanks for not running me over."

I grab his hand, and he pulls me to my feet, and we stand

facing each other. My knees feel wobbly, and I can't tell if it's because I'm looking right at him or because of the fall. *Witson was too tall*, I think. Callen is medium height, and I don't have to crane to look into his eyes. Lia's always complaining because he's two inches shorter than she is, but for me, he's—

Lia.

We're still holding hands.

"Oh, oops." I pull my hand away and make a show of brushing off the grass and dirt on my jeans. But it's like I want to brush off his touch because it felt way too good and now I'm guilty. "No, it's my fault, not yours. Sorry, next time I'll watch where I'm going," I babble. He doesn't say anything.

I haul the bike up and wheel it to face forward while frantically trying to come up with more to say. It's been a while since Callen and I were alone together.

"Are you sure you can ride?" he asks, inspecting my face again. How dazed do I look? His scrutiny reminds me of my frizzy hair. It must look even worse. I try to seem casual as I run my hand through it.

"I'm fine." I summon up my best imitation of my mother's chastising-librarian voice. Still, the idea of getting back on the bike unsettles me.

"Are you headed home?" he asks, glancing down the street.

"Yeah."

"Me too. Let's walk together," he suggests, gesturing me forward on the concrete sidewalk.

"Okay," I agree quickly, glad for the excuse to stay off the bike, without having to admit that I'm scared. *Alone with Callen.* We're close to home, ten minutes give or take, but still.

Silence the first few steps. I'm sweating, partly out of nerves and partly because it's way too hot for this jacket. I'm only wearing it because of the Missive about the weather. I clear my throat. *Say something.*

"You're not at practice." I wince. I might as well have said, *I'm boring. Ignore me.*

"Coach was sick, so he called it off." On a route we could walk in our sleep, we wordlessly turn off the main road and enter the Arbor, stepping off the sidewalk and onto the mostly empty cobblestone streets. Squirrels scamper through the trees above us.

"Kind of brave to cancel practice when the game is so close." Our high school teams are facing off next week for the first game of their year, timed to coincide with the new season of *Blissful Days,* which will also, thankfully, bring a new motif. The game is a big deal, a Special Event, and held in the stadium usually reserved for our two professional baseball teams.

"Brave? Maybe." Slowing down his pace, he twists to dig into the back pocket of his jeans. It goes unsaid that Callen himself is probably the reason for his coach's confidence. He withdraws a pack of cigarettes and a lighter. I gape while he cups his hands together to light a cigarette.

"You smoke?" I ask, stopping in my tracks.

"Sometimes." He blows smoke to his right, away from me. "What? Oh, I should have offered you one?" He grins.

"No way." I widen the space between us and start walking again. I always thought smoking was dumb, a sign of weakness. Maybe partly because of Lia, who hates the habit even more than I do. Her mom used to chain smoke and stink up the house. A common game in the early days of our friendship was Flushing Mom's Cigarettes Down the Toilet.

"Isn't smoking bad for baseball?" I push my handlebars more forcefully as we go uphill.

"Maybe." There's a hint of defiance in his upturned chin. "But I like doing it. Everyone's allowed one vice. What's yours?"

You. "I don't think I have one," I say, getting caught up in watching the sun stripe the tanned planes of his face. He draws the cigarette to his lips and inhales. His very full, lush lips. Lia wouldn't stop talking about his lips when they first started dating.

"I believe it. You're pretty good," he says. We reach the top of the hill and turn onto Poplar Street, one of the less shady parts of the Arbor. Our houses are closer to the other end of the block, and I slow my pace, desperate to prolong my time with him.

"Except at Fincher's. I'm not so good there anymore. I was telling Selwyn today how stuck I feel. Too bad it's my best option." I look over at him, daring him to contradict me. He's watching the cigarette smoke curl up to the sky, with his dreamy look that Lia can't stand.

"That's what my parents keep telling me about baseball," he says, face still tilted toward the sky. "That it's my best option—"

"Well, it's something . . . something you can do well and—"

"And make a lot of money from," he finishes, dropping the cigarette to the ground and stubbing it out with his sneaker. "I know."

Not only will he get a good salary, he'll be guaranteed high ratings for seasons. He'll never have to think up plotlines to draw in more of the Audience. Great ratings and the payments that go along with them are just basically handed to you when you do something like that.

"You're lucky."

"I guess, but sometimes it seems like baseball came out of nowhere—sort of like how you did back there." He laughs.

"Well, it didn't come out of *nowhere*," I say, stopping at the end of the stone path leading to his house. My driveway is empty, so Mom isn't home yet. His is empty too, all sparkling white gravel. His parents are going to be home late, and Lia is supposed to come over, and they're supposed to close up.

"You weren't on any teams, but you were always—" I meant to say *graceful*, but I don't want him to know I've thought about how he moves. "Coordinated."

"Maybe, but I never liked sports. I miss free time," he says, sticking out his lower lip like a stubborn child. "I miss hiking in the Brambles and hanging out with Conor and Garrick. Even helping Mom with her garden. Now I'm too tired to do anything on the weekends. And then there's the tracs." He shakes his head and tugs at the bottom of his T-shirt. "I wore this just to screw with them, because it's red, and blue's our color." He chuckles.

"Heath, the captain, actually told me never to do it again. That's how easy it is to upset them."

"That's funny because they seem—" Screeching brakes interrupt me. Mom's fire-truck-red car pulls into our driveway a few feet away. Callen moves, like he's going inside, and I gesture for him to stay, hoping she won't notice us. She cuts the engine off and jumps out, her loaded key chain jangling loudly. She's probably heard about Belle by now. If so, she'll be on edge. She bends down to pick a microscopic piece of litter off the driveway, *tsk*ing under her breath, then strides up to our door, head high, gripping her tote bag full of books. When she reaches the door, she pauses and turns, her brown eyes, a few shades lighter than mine, sweeping the neighborhood and stopping when she spots us at the end of the path. She raises her eyebrows.

"Nettie, shouldn't you be at Fincher's?"

Worry lines groove her forehead. She pushes her square glasses up to the bridge of her aquiline nose. "Hi, Callen," she adds, in a tone that does not invite further conversation. Her voice, her nose, and most of all her hair, sheared right off at her chin, ensure that Mom pretty much always looks severe. Her plain wardrobe—today a black wool blazer and silk button-down blouse paired with a long black wool skirt—adds to the effect.

"No, not today." Mom *really* wants me to apprentice at Fincher's. She liked reading books, so she became a librarian. She figures that I like building gadgets, so I should become a repairman. She probably also thinks that doing something I'm good at will translate into plus-ten ratings. But I'm going about my tasks at Fincher's in such a cloud of misery that I suspect no one will want to watch me there for very long.

I haven't talked about my doubts with Mom. She and I never frall about ratings—never frall about anything, really. She stopped because I was so awful at it when I was young, slipping up on-mic all the time, saying things like *I'm tired of this motif* or *I don't care about that Special Event*. She might not want to talk to me about ratings, but I know she cares—a lot. More than once I've caught her fishing through my trash can after a Character Report.

"So, you'll go to Fincher's this weekend?" she persists. Her hand tightens around her tote bag. She has on a hemp bracelet, for *liberato*.

"Maybe." I cross my arms. I wish she would just go inside. I glance back at Callen. He's shuffling his feet and staring at the ground, pretending not to eavesdrop, but I see the small smile on his face.

"Nettie, you have to show them that you're interested," Mom says, putting the tote bag down on the doormat. "What if someone else applies and you end up anyassigned?" She takes a few steps down the porch stairs. Uh-oh. I don't want her coming here and embarrassing me more.

"I understand, Mom," I bite out. "I'll go tomorrow after Lia comes by."

She stops her march toward me, brown eyes flicking over

to Callen, gleaning that I want to be left alone. "Good. Okay, dinner will be ready soon, and then I need to draw up the volunteer schedule for work and do the reading for book club, so I better start cracking," she says, disappearing into the house. Mom is always busy—at work, cooking, book clubbing, or going to these unsexy singles dances. Still, it never seems like the busyness makes her happy, because she's always fretting about what could go wrong. What makes it even weirder is that I'm pretty sure she *thinks* she's happy as long as her ratings are on target.

I turn back to Callen. "Sorry about that. She can be . . . overbearing."

"She's worried," he says mildly. "And it seems like she worries a lot. Probably not that easy for either of you."

"Yeah, but I just wish she'd keep it to herself a little. The problem is she thinks we're alike." I kick at some of the snowney on his lawn.

"And you're not? Not even a little bit?" he teases. "I bet she'd be just as horrified about my smoking."

"I'm not horrified," I protest. Now he thinks I'm lame. He just raises his sandy eyebrows briefly. I've about run out of things to say, but the silence doesn't seem too bad, especially with the sun setting so spectacularly, the sky streaked in a million shades of pink, purple, and yellow.

"So pretty," I breathe. He tips his chin up in acknowledgment, and we watch it together for a few seconds until he bends down to retie his sneaker laces. I can't help but stare at his fingers, how deftly they move. He looks up and catches me watching him, and I start dusting off my jacket and jeans again, muttering about how Mom will kill me if I dirty up the house.

"Yeah, I better get inside too," he says, eyeing me. "Lia was supposed to be here by now."

Everything is so purposeful with him, and Lia is his purpose now.

"Oh, right, she told me you were, um, hanging out." Closing up. The sad and weird nightmare. Why can't I just like someone who likes me back?

Before I think about it, these bitchy words fall out of my mouth: "If you think I'm bad, well, Lia hates smoking."

"Lia hates a lot of stuff," Callen says, jaw clenching.

Is it my imagination, or does his mild voice have an edge to it? I linger, daring him to say more, but he just kind of does this half shrug. Irritation burns me. This is dumb. I'm reading too much into everything he says and does, because I want so much out of him.

"Yeah. Well, Lia's a passionate person." I grab my bike and stomp off toward our garage. "Um, I need to go. See you tomorrow."

Chapter 3

The scent of lavender disinfectant floats in the air. Mom probably went straight to the supply cabinet after talking to me and Callen. She's into extreme cleaning to begin with, and it always gets worse after Characters are cut. I hear her sweeping the kitchen downstairs. Her house, her rules. I smooth out the wrinkles on the hallway's long rug, then stand up and straighten my grandmother's oil landscapes on the walls.

A green light is blinking beneath my closed door at the end of the hall. I enter and walk to the flashing square screen embedded in the wall next to my desk.

Pots clang downstairs. In addition to going on cleaning sprees, Mom also prepares culinary masterpieces after cuts. I press the Missivor's silver button, and the screen turns white with green text.

Belle Cannery became a Patriot today under Clause 53, Item A, Unsatisfactory Ratings. As per the Contract, please refrain from mentioning Belle. As per the Contract, rid your personal sets of any reminders of Belle. Ratings mark: 168. Ratings target: 293.

I gasp on-mic, clamp my hand over my mouth, and then let it drop, trying to compose myself for the cameras. *Ratings mark: 168.*

Exactly the same as my mark.

I hit the silver button, and the Missivor turns off. We're only allowed a minute to read Missives since the scenes can't be broadcast. I turn and scan my small, sparse room, eyes crawling over its mostly bare white walls, the wooden desk, the low-lying bed, and the long shelves near the closet, searching for reminders.

The show's guiding ethos is that it's supposed to mimic real life, but there's no equivalent to Patriots in the Sectors. If there were, they wouldn't need to be mentioned in the Contract. Media1 doesn't want the Audience to think too hard about that discrepancy or it'll ruin *Blissful Days* viewings for them. So we're not allowed to mention the Patriots and we have to get rid of reminders that could spark memories of the departed Characters.

I comb through the shelves and closet, though I'm certain I don't have anything of Belle's. I get down on the floor and peer under the bed, discovering a turquoise ring that went missing a few weeks ago. I drop it into my largely empty jewelry box. Searching for reminders soothes me. Slowly, today's events are making sense. Except for her age and the fact that I knew her, there's nothing out of the ordinary about Belle's cut, really.

She is a Clause 53, Item A, cut, like most Patriots. Item B—Risk to the Show—cuts are for Characters who crisp, or break the fourth wall in a particularly egregious way. There's only been one in my lifetime—Lynne Thrush, who lost it at her son's

Double A ceremony, complaining that Media1 played favorites in assigning. I wasn't there—the Double A is a Special Event, and attendance is optional, though encouraged. Lia had gone, of course—there aren't many Special Events she misses—and had later told me how the Authority rushed in out of nowhere and seized Lynne while she ranted.

It's only when Characters are getting cut that the Authority interact with us. I've heard the Authority are Sectors military or maybe ex-military, hired by Media1 to maintain the peace. They're like police for the Reals and mostly deal with them. Except when it comes to Patriots.

Sometimes I wonder why the Reals don't send crickets to escort the Patriots, instead of big men with guns. I've never heard of anyone resisting. Why would they? Becoming a Patriot is in the Contract.

"Rawls was running laps." I hear Lia outside now, her voice soaring over the sound of Mom's cooking. I go to the window behind my desk and peek out at the Herrons' porch. Below me, Lia and Callen are standing next to the porch swing, facing each other.

"So?" Callen backs away from her, raking his hand through his hair. The equivalent of a full-blown temper tantrum for him.

"So, don't you have to stay in shape too?" she says, scowling. She takes a step forward, and he moves back farther, trapping himself in the corner of the porch.

"I don't understand why you care so much," he grumbles.

"We're *so* close to the Apprenticeship Announcement," she

sighs. She kisses him on the cheek, her hair concealing the point of contact from me, like a stage curtain. Lia's *liberato* outfit looks so much better than mine. Her short-sleeved white blouse with little flowers embroidered at the collar is tucked into her tight fawn-colored skirt, which stops right above her knees. She's wearing her chunky clogs, which put her a head above Callen.

Their voices get lower, unintelligible. I back away from the window and sit on my bed, pushing off my sneakers with my feet. Five months ago, I was sitting here while Lia was at my desk saying she thought Callen was a possibility.

I think that's how she phrased it too. *A possibility.* She'd used the same word when casting last semester's Drama Club play. She ticked off Callen's good qualities one by one, as if she were contemplating an expensive purchase. *Excellent at baseball. Nice hair. Sometimes funny.* She'd even fralled something like, *Probably good for my ratings too.*

I remember watching her and thinking, *Maybe I should say something.* But then, in the next moment, *What's there to say? I have feelings that are going nowhere?* I tried to convince myself it wasn't that bad. Lia had dated and dropped a series of boys after Martin. I assumed her relationship with Callen would be the same, measured in days rather than months.

Four and a half agonizing months.

The worst part is that, even after spending so much time with him, she still doesn't know him. Not the way I do. Maybe that just comes with the territory of being obsessed, or maybe I'm obsessed because I see these things. Chicken or egg deal. I see that his aloofness covers up his sensitivity. I see how he distances himself from all of us at lunch and I know that he still thinks of himself as someone who's on the outskirts of every social situation, even though his sports success has made the opposite true. He didn't have to tell me he was tired of baseball. I see him flinch when the other tracs get too rowdy. I know he doesn't feel like one of them. That he isn't one of them.

The Herrons' screen door slams shut. They're inside now. I get up and jerk the cord on the blinds, ignoring Media1's encouragement to keep our windows unshaded. I can't risk seeing them close up. It's bad enough that Lia's going to share every detail when she comes over tomorrow. She's going to be thrilled, and not just because they did it. When she started closing up with Martin, her already high ratings skyrocketed, and she's sure that's why. Yet another way in which her desires coincide with what the Audience wants to see.

As I walk away from the window, my elbow knocks against an empty blue bottle that stands next to the old telephone receiver I'm using for the radio. My breath catches as the bottle wobbles precipitously. I reach out and still it. *Rid your personal sets of any reminders of Belle.*

Belle gave me the bottle in sixth grade.

We'd taken a field trip to Avalon Beach, playing tag on the shore. I'd broken off from Selwyn and Geraldine Spicer and scrambled onto a jetty, hunting for seashells. But Belle had beaten me there and was bent down, spidery-legged, pulling out a bottle wedged between the rocks.

"What's that?" I asked.

She gasped, surprised, and stammered in her faltering voice, "Sorry, I thought—I didn't hear you. Um, I just—it's a bottle."

I came closer. "It's nice," I said.

She glanced at it and back at me, calming, her hazel eyes assessing me. It was one of the few times I'd seen her without her glasses, and she almost looked pretty, her stringy hair wet and clinging to her cheeks.

"You think so?" She didn't wait for me to answer, just stood and thrust her hand out at me. "Here, take it."

"Oh, okay, thanks," I said, cradling it. She was already scurrying back over the rocks to the shore. The deal was done.

I haven't thought of her connection to the bottle in seasons.

I want to keep it.

I wonder if Mom had struggled with letting go of my father's reminders. If she hadn't given them up willingly, Media1 would have taken them and fined her. I wouldn't know if they'd missed any. He was cut a long time ago, and I don't have any memories of him. Sometimes my grandmother Violet rambles about him as if he's still on the island. From what I've pieced together from her accidental reveals, he was shy. He liked the rain. He disliked the sound of markers scrawling on paper.

"I have to do something," I mumble to myself. I'm sick of thinking, so I decide to work on the radio. Everyone's so impressed I can build stuff, make things, figure out how electricity and levers and pulleys and transistors work, but it's easy to do when the reward for working on a project is *peace*. I never get that feeling at Fincher's, where I'm pressured to hurry up and fix; it's totally different from slowing down and creating.

I'm in the final stages. I have all the materials I need—now it's time to put them together. I use an old pen to poke four holes into a used-up hydrogen peroxide bottle that I snagged from the chemistry classroom and then carefully weave green insulated wire through the holes. I'm following the instructions from an electronics book I borrowed from Fincher's. Then I coil the wire around the outside of the bottle. I tape the wires to the germanium diode and connect the other end of the diode to the copper foil beneath the stripped telephone cord wires with alligator clips. I hold the receiver to my ear and move an alligator clip to different points on the wire wrapped around the bottle until I hear faint noise. The volume wavers.

One station is especially loud—oldies, playing the jingly frenetic music from season sixty-eight, *gaudacious*. I touch another loop of wire and hear Nelly and George, popular evening talk show hosts, bantering about next Sunday's baseball game.

"My money's on the Pigeons," chortles George. He's from the Arbor, so he *has* to root for them.

"I'm with you, George," Nelly coos. "It's not going to be easy for the Ants, going up against Callen Herron."

I just can't escape Callen today. A burst of static makes me move the alligator clip farther down the wire. Static scratches in my ear again, then I hear muffled voices.

"Did you see the show?"

"My mom said it was scary." More scratchiness, then an

unintelligible string of syllables. I hear something that sounds like *srastle*. Sounds like Reals. *Blissful Days*–obsessed Reals, like Dr. Kanavan. I press my ear harder into the receiver. I think I've tapped into one of their walkie-talkie transmissions.

"Sandcastle." I pull out from the garble. Not srastle, sandcastle. Probably having fun on Eden beach. The whole transmission dissolves into static, and after a couple of minutes, I give up.

Chapter 4

I smear the pink lotion from Media1's Skin Sequence onto my face and let my skin soak it up while I go over to the bathroom's porthole window. The snowney has melted, and the flowers in the Herrons' backyard are all opening, welcoming the morning sun. When Media1 really wants to push the fake weather, they'll raze the plants, but the garden's been spared so far. Callen's mother must be happy about that.

I wash the lotion off, thinking about the day ahead. Lia should be here soon, for the Diary of Destiny. Afterward I'll go to Fincher's. A normal day. With Belle gone. The one thought shifts everything, and next thing I know, I'm looking at my face in the mirror, wondering if Belle did her Skin Sequence yesterday morning.

She'd thought it was a normal day, and she had been wrong.

The reflection of my face takes on a greenish tinge, catching light from the Missivor blinking in my room. Clutching my towel around me, I go to check it.

Product Promotion: Consider the benefits of fruit of all kinds.
Oranges, apples, grapes, bananas. Fruit is delicious and healthy.
Talk to your friends and family about how much you like fruit.
Weather: Please refer and react to the weather as you deem
appropriate.

First good news in ages. I turn the Missivor off and walk to my closet, pulling out a lime-green tank top and the jean shorts that I frayed for *liberato*. I'm taking underwear from the dresser drawer when the phone rings. I dash over to my night table and pick it up while trying to maintain a grip on my towel and clothes.

"Nettie, I'm having an emergency." Selwyn's wispy voice flutters through the receiver. "I saw a roach by the stove, and I'm calling you from the counter where I've taken refuge."

"You're where? On the counter?" I tuck the phone between my chin and shoulder. Selwyn's kitchen isn't very big, and their counters are always junked up with pans and dishes and cereal boxes and potato chip bags.

"Yeah, there's room next to the toaster and the napkin holder. The second I saw it—well, first I heard it, this *sound*, like someone dropped a bunch of pins—I screamed and jumped up here. I haven't eaten yet, and I was going to boil an egg, but now I'm too scared to do anything."

"You're a prisoner." I wiggle into my clothes, then fall back on the bed and stare at the motionless cameras on the ceiling. They rarely swivel when I talk to Selwyn.

She sighs. "Distract me. Did Lia and Callen close up?"

"I don't know, and it's killing me," I report, voice thick with misery.

"They probably didn't," she says. "Lia would have called you if they had. Heck, she'd have come over afterward. You know Lia. She likes talking about it more than doing it."

It. "Ugh, stop." I shut my eyes, trying to block the images whirling through my mind. "I don't even want to—"

Selwyn shrieks, and I hold the receiver away from my ear.

"I thought I heard the roach," she wheezes. "But it was just the fridge making noises."

"Your parents are at work?"

"Yeah," Selwyn confirms. Her parents often spend weekends and nights in the hospital, where they hold administrative positions. They were anyassigned into the apprenticeships that led to those professions. The Bakers rarely make school functions, and when they do, they seem scattered and have dark circles around their eyes.

"Okay, enough," I say, pushing my mind into problem-solving mode. "You gotta get out of there. Forget the egg. Grab some bread and leave the kitchen."

"All right." She forces herself to slow her breathing. "I'm putting my foot on the floor . . . ," she narrates, her voice taut. I listen as she describes her four-step trip to the bread box, the untying of the bread bag, withdrawing of two slices, and retying of the bag. "I'm going to take it upstairs," she says rapidly. I hear her scurrying up the Bakers' carpeted stairs and running down the hall to her closet-sized bedroom.

"You can do it," I call encouragingly.

"Made it," she declares a few seconds later. "So scary." I hear the sound of her bedroom door slamming shut.

"I know. Good for you," I say. Lia gets impatient with Selwyn's sensitivity, but Selwyn and I have been friends since kindergarten—far longer than Lia and I. I trust her completely, even though she is a little high-strung. These days she's crucial, since she's sympathetic about me and Callen. Which reminds me.

"Selwyn, I almost sent Callen to the hospital yesterday," I announce.

"Really?" she gasps.

I recount the whole walk to her, joking darkly, "If only I had really hit him. Disabled him before close-up time." Above me, the cameras swivel.

Lia arrives while I'm fiddling with the radio, trying to catch the Reals' transmission again, and I hear Mom, probably up since dawn, go to the door to let her in. Mom adores Lia because she keeps the Audience watching me.

"Hey, Ms. Egretine, how are you? I saw the new reading space in the library with those plush cushions. Soooo cute." Lia sounds upbeat. Like she got what she wanted last night.

While she and Mom talk, I go over to the mirror hanging from my closet door and practice looking normal, a little smile to show that I'm happy to see her.

After a few more minutes of chitchat with my mother, Lia

comes up, pushing my door wide open with her hip, and I hear the tinny sounds of cameras rotating and shifting.

"Diary time," she sings, taking off her jacket and sniffing it. "This reeks. Of smoke. Did I tell you Callen started smoking? I saw him, what, over twelve hours ago, and I can still smell it. It's all over my body. Mom still smokes when . . ." She trails off. "I just hate it."

"Callen smokes? Really?" I squeak, not looking her in the eye.

"I told him he's going to be a haggard old man, but he doesn't listen. He's so stubborn. I say go right, he's, like, *left*." She stalks the room, searching for a place to put her coat. I'm still standing by the mirror, watching her. "Not just left, but, like, *left, now and always*. The coach got sick yesterday and called off practice, but most of the Pigeons stayed anyway. Not Callen. He's so lazy."

"We can all be lazy." Would she be so irritated with him if they'd closed up last night?

"Hmm, speak for yourself." She flings the coat over the back of my desk chair. She's in jeans and another *liberato* tunic. Hers is nicer than mine, though, gauzy and pink with lace embroidery at the sleeves. It even has some shape because she put on a belt. She settles onto the bed, mouth curled petulantly. "Do you think I'm too mean to him?"

"I don't know," I say, the total truth. I can't take it anymore. "So, last night." I study my fingernails.

"Last night," she repeats, puzzled. She twirls her braid around her finger. "What do you mean?"

I swallow the lump in my throat. "You and Callen."

"Me and Callen, what?" But then she bursts out laughing. "Just kidding. I know what you mean. It didn't happen."

Relief pours through me. "Oh, no—why not?"

"We're, like, on the couch, and I reach down, and I'm going to, like, unzip his jeans, and I open my eyes, and Nettie, he has his I'm-barely-here stare." Lia does an expert imitation of Callen's faraway look. "We're making out, and his arms aren't even around me. They're at his sides, like I'm so hard to touch. God, I felt like I had to pry his mouth open—like, am I your dentist? I couldn't go through with it."

"Ew, weird." I sit down next to her, shaking my head. From here I have a clear view of the coat she threw on my chair. I resist the urge to put it in the closet. Lia hates it when I clean up after her.

"I don't even know if he has before. I assumed all the tracs had, but maybe I was wrong. What if he's a virgin?" Her eyes bulge out.

"I don't know." I giggle nervously. She waits for me to say more, but soon gives up, pulling her lucky pen out of her straw bag. "Never mind. I want to come up with some plus-ten Vows for this week. Like we talked about?" She stares at me significantly, and it takes me a second to recall her saying she'd think up juicier plotlines for me.

"Yeah, I remember."

"March twenty-third," she declares, writing the date. A glint of light catches her eye. She looks over to the window and inhales sharply. Uh-oh. She pushes her hair forward, obscuring her mouth from the cameras. "You have to get rid of the bottle."

I put my chin in my hand and curl my fingers around my lips. "Does it matter? They won't notice."

"Nettie, just do it. You don't want to get fined for keeping a dirty old bottle."

I stare at the bottle, glowing in the early morning sun. "The whole thing is depressing," I mouth, remembering Scoop's stricken face and then his questions. She's gone, but she's not, still in his head and mine.

"Yes, Nettie, I know it's depressing, but you have to throw that bottle out," Lia mouths, putting her hand on my arm.

"I don't want to," I mouth back stubbornly. "I think it's nice, and it's been seasons since Belle even touched it." I hang my head.

Lia snaps her fingers in front of my face. "Stop. You're being melodramatic. I already told you, Belle is probably happier doing publicity in the Sadtors. You are still on the show. Act like it."

She's right. The company's still taking care of Belle. I cling to that knowledge like it's a precious jewel, and my doubts begin to fade.

"What were your Good Things this week?" I say, taking the notebook and pen from Lia.

"I got an A on my literature test," she declares, lying on her back, entirely exposed to the cameras on the ceiling. "Nice picture," she says, noticing the framed photo of a conch shell next to my shelves behind us. Lia's been on me for seasons to decorate, saying my bone-white walls need the help, so I knew she'd approve of this photo I scored at a Four Corners tag sale. She stretches her arms out above her head and arches like a gymnast, then lifts her legs up until her toes touch the slanted ceiling above my bed. "Yippee," she crows before letting her legs fall flat. I sense her relief that we've stopped fralling, her natural ease in front of the cameras taking over. She's like a lightbulb with multiple wattages, and she's on High now. I write down her grade.

"Also, Ms. Pepperidge likes the play."

"Plus ten."

"Yeah, I know. It'll definitely set me apart from the other Blisslet applicants." Lia wants to apprentice as an actress in the island theater troupe. There are four slots and nine girls interested. But she's Lia—she's going to get it.

She sits up abruptly and turns, positioning her face so at least four cameras have a good shot of her.

"I actually made a major change in the play," she confides. "Instead of cheating on the chemistry test, the Mia character is going to embezzle funds from her dad's bank."

"Yeah?" I like listening to Lia talk about her play stuff. My mind just doesn't work like hers—I'm all about cut-and-dried logic.

"Yup, and I even might have her go to jail. What do you think?"

"Well, I—"

"I know, I know," she says, playing with her braid again. "Now people might just end up hating her. But I think I can still show her vulnerability." She takes the notebook from me. "Okay, your Good Things."

I have one—yesterday's math test.

Lia writes it down, sighing, "Already time for Bad Things." She hums as she thinks. "Well, obvious, no close-up, and—" She hesitates, then scrawls a lowercase *m* on a line by itself. Tiny *m*'s are scattered all through this volume of the Diary.

"Mom again?" I say.

She nods, ducking out of view of the cameras and motioning me to come closer. "She got so plastered on Monday that she tripped down the stairs and sprained her ankle. Dad just hid out in his study." Lia's father is really into his job, adult education. He's sort of an absentminded professor most of the time, only ever speaking up, it seems, to admonish Lia if her grades aren't up to par. Grades don't matter if you want to become a Blisslet, but he wants her to be like him.

I bite my lip, trying to figure out how to respond to the stuff about her mom. "Sorry about that," I say on-mic, inching backward. It's all I can think of, and with my ratings the way they are, I need to stay on-camera, which means cutting down on the fralling.

"Yup, it sucks," she says bluntly, reaching for the Diary again. "Hey, I came up with one—did you finish your radio? That would be a Good Thing."

"Yeah, I did." I look over at the completed radio on my desk. I'm about to tell her what I heard on Media1's walkie-talkie channel, but she's off and running before I have a chance.

"How are we going to get you out of Fincher's?" Lia says. She nibbles at the top of the lucky pen. "Maybe you should ask Mr. Black about the math teacher apprenticeship. That could be your Vow for next week." She pokes my knee with the pen, arching her eyebrows, like, *See?* This is it. Her attempt to get me off the E.L.

"But Revere's been working for the slot since they were announced. I won't be able to catch up," I protest, curling up on my side across from her.

"The Double A is in a month. There's still time." Lia begins writing in the notebook. "I think you'd be a great teacher." She can't say it on-mic, but I hear the unspoken reason: maybe my ratings would be better if I were in an apprenticeship I liked.

But . . . Revere. "I'd feel awful if I got it, though. Revere would be pissed if he ended up anyassigned."

"Oh, come on. Revere's incapable of being mad. Listen, it can't hurt to ask," Lia says. She puts the pen down next to her leg, and I discreetly pick it up, not wanting red marks on my comforter. She reads what she wrote out loud. "Vows. Nettie Starling vows to quit moping around and ask Mr. Black about her chances of getting the available high school math teacher apprenticeship slot." She blocks her face from the camera and quickly mouths, "The Audience will love it if there's conflict between you and Revere."

I nod slowly. Coming up with plus-ten plotlines comes so naturally to Lia. I imagine storming past Revere to the front of the classroom and demanding a chance from Mr. Black, the Audience cheering me on.

"I'll think about it," I say.

"Ask him. Monday."

"All right," I agree. I look over at the clock on my night table. "I gotta get going."

Lia claps the journal shut. "Okay, maybe I'll visit Callen. Stuff ended not so plus ten last night after No Arms." She picks up her book bag. "Which means we argued as much as Callen *can* argue. It's, like, different shades of silence. I-hate-you silence, I'm-hurt silence, I'm-tired-of-this-silence silence."

I give her some silence of my own. Like, I-would-love-it-if-he-never-spoke-to-you-again silence. I smooth out wrinkles in my comforter. "I hope you make up," I say finally.

I take the really long way to Fincher's, riding down the eastern coast, gliding past Avalon beach houses, including Lincoln's. A blue sheen radiates from the distance. The aquarium. Scoop works there every weekend as part of his apprenticeship. Thinking about him grieving while cleaning out tank filters makes me want to tell him *something* about the Patriots.

If I move fast, I can find him, say what I have to say, and still make it to Fincher's on time. I get a ticket, lock my bike to a camerapole, and join the crowds churning through the halls. The air in here is sharp and pure, with a vacuumed, institutional quality to it. I haven't been to the aquarium since I was a kid, and I find myself almost hypnotized by the octopi and squid, lobsters and eels, salmon and sharks.

Lots of entrancing sea creatures, but no Scoop. I take a break from my search to get an ice cream from the concession stand. I'm peering over the cartons, trying to choose a flavor, when I remember the morning's propro Missive.

"Do you have any fruit?" I ask the elderly man with a flourishing mustache.

He shuffles over to a carton of apples and hands one over. "Half a cetek," he says crankily. He was probably anyassigned.

Apple in hand, I sit on a concrete bench across from the jellyfish tank and bite in. Juicy and sweet. Must be from the Granary. The best fruit is grown there—a cluster of farms and orchards at the southern tip of the island. I let the apple lie in my lap, resting my head against the wall and closing my eyes. What if Callen were with me, watching the jellyfish, their transparent, filmy skins undulating through the water like silk scarves fluttering in the air. Then I imagine us on the Herrons' living room couch, his arms around me. *Eagerly* around me.

I'm so transfixed by my daydreams that Scoop manages to sneak up on me.

"You're watching that tank almost as intensely as you watch Callen during lunch." He grins, waiting for my response.

Ugh, how? I've never breathed a word about how I feel about Callen to any Character but Selwyn. Scoop doesn't even sit at our lunch table that much—he kind of rotates tables—and his figuring this out jolts me. He's in the standard aquarium worker uniform—dorky aquamarine nylon pants that are far too baggy, a coral-colored polyester polo shirt, and an aquamarine Windbreaker with a dolphin silhouette stitched over the heart. Somehow his dreamboat face, with the razor-sharp cheekbones, overpowers all the ridiculousness and makes it look good.

"I don't—I don't know what you mean," I stutter unconvincingly.

"If you say so." He has an apple too, and he chomps it loudly. "Kiel Apples are the best. Juicy."

"Kiel Apples give me energy," I reply. Other Characters have to have noticed if he did. Maybe even Callen. Well, it's not the important thing now. "I need to talk to you, Scoop. *Not* about Callen," I say, scanning the hall. We're so exposed in this position. A cube-shaped ventilator with hoses snaking into the tank seems promising, humming loudly enough to cover up whispers.

"Come here." I stand and guide him to the ventilator, then crouch down and gesture toward a crumbling replica reef. "I think I see a seahorse," I say loudly. I check above me: the cameras can't see our faces as long as we stay kneeling and looking down. Scoop follows my example.

"This is a secret, so you can't tell anyone," I whisper. "The Patriots do publicity for Media1 in Zenta. You know, writing ads, answering fan letters. Belle's going to be fine."

Scoop grabs my wrist with his other hand, pulling me in

closer. All the joking is over. I can see his eyes are bloodshot, like he spent the whole night crying. "Where did you hear that? I don't believe it."

I feel myself flushing. "I can't say who told me, exactly, but it's a Media1 source. A reliable one."

He zips up his Windbreaker. "I have another, equally reliable source—"

"Weneedtopauseforreenactment," a voice says behind us. My pulse quickens and my throat goes dry as we slowly look up. A male cricket. Did he hear us fralling? I cannot afford a fine, not with the motif change coming up.

The cricket has a nose like a boxer's, crooked, as if it had been broken and healed wrong. His eyes are small and dark like olive pits. He's ugly, even for a Real, and his voice is raspy. "Pauseforreenactment," he repeats.

"Hmm?" I say, rising to my feet. "What—what did you say?"

"Where do you want us to start?" Scoop says, next to me. He straightens out his Windbreaker cuffs and unzips it again. "He said 'pause for reenactment.'" A reenactment. My breathing slows to normal—it's okay. They just want the propro. I'm safe.

"Go back to the bench," says a younger female Real with a high ponytail, a camera balanced on her shoulder. I straighten the straps on my tank top and return to the bench. Glad I did the Skin Sequence this morning. I rarely have reenactments—and when I have in the past, they're usually silent or sidekick parts in scenes with Lia. Reenactments almost guarantee a scene will be broadcast.

We wait as the cricket struggles to mount the heavy camera on her shoulder.

Actually, they don't want the propro. The male recites our lines to us several times, and we repeat them back, starting with "You're watching that tank almost as hard as you watch Callen during lunch," which makes me wince, ruining several takes. It's exciting that the Audience might be interested, but I don't want any of the Characters in the hall to overhear. Someone might tell Lia.

The reenactment goes up to and through the propro for Kiel Apples. They don't seem to have noticed any of the fralling afterward.

The male cricket murmurs to the female as they look over the footage on the camera. I hope they like what they see. I hear one word over and over. *Pipits*. The stern-faced Real looks over at us, and what I think is a smile creases his rough face. "We have what we need."

"What was that word they kept saying, *pipits*?" I whisper to Scoop as they leave.

"*Puppets*," he whispers back. "That's what the crew calls us."

"Really?" I mouth. I've always felt superior to the Reals, and in the back of my mind, I assumed they agreed. But *puppets* needles at me.

Scoop's mouth quirks up. "Don't let it pull your strings. Besides, what do you expect? They're not our friends."

"Yeah, but they—" I strive for the right words. "They care about us. Without us, they'd have to live in the Sectors. They might not even have jobs if the show didn't exist," I remember

Dr. Kanavan once lamenting how a childhood friend of hers, a nurse, couldn't find any work in the Sectors.

"The Audience cares, maybe. But Media1 doesn't," Scoop whispers. He shrugs off his Windbreaker, revealing arms that are pretty muscular for someone who doesn't do sports. Scoop isn't gangly tall like Witson, or scary large like some tracs. He has just enough heft to make you feel protected but not threatened. Belle was lucky to have him as a big brother.

But he's not my brother. We're not even close friends, and I get the feeling if I stick around here longer, he's going to try to frall with me about her again. We were already way too close to getting caught. I clamp my hand over my mic. "I have to go. I'm supposed to help out at Mr. Fincher's."

"Wait," he says. "Do you know what the Sandcastle is?"

I step back, a chill running through me. I rub my arms, wondering if I should tell him that I heard the word on my radio's Media1 channel.

"You've heard of it, haven't you?" he whispers, closing the space between us. "I think it's where they keep the Patriots. I don't think they make it to the Sectors."

"I—I have to go," I declare, turning and walking down the hall as fast as I can without breaking into a run. I can't let myself get too bogged down in thoughts about Patriots again, not while I'm on the E.L.

Chapter 5

I start dozing off on my bed Sunday evening while reading *The Player in the Attic*. I'm dangerously close to drooling on the cover when the phone shrieks.

"Nettie. It's me," Lia announces.

"You woke me up," I greet her groggily. "Trying to read the book. Can you just tell me what happens?"

"Sure. But can you come meet me at the playground now?" She throws out the request like a dart to a board. "It's important."

She's upset—I can tell by her clipped tone. "Okay. Be there soon." I shove my sneakers on and leave the house, quickly covering the short distance to the playground that divides the Arbor from Treasure Woods. We used to frall here, swinging side by side so the cameras couldn't get a good view of us. Lia's waiting for me, hunched on a swing, hands gripped high on the chains. When she sees me, she smiles weakly. Her eyes are puffy.

Still, she looks more beautiful than ever. She's wearing a long white sleeveless dress and the *liberato* beads she bought with Selwyn on a post-ratings-payment shopping spree. Up close, I discern eyeliner tracing the lids of her cat eyes and mascara turning her light brown eyelashes black. Media1's been inviting her to private Sessions at the Center; they're offered to high-ratings Characters on how to be more camperf.

"Hey." I drop into the swing next to hers, feeling underdressed in my frayed jean shorts, same ones from yesterday.

"Callen and I broke up," she says flatly, staring straight ahead.

My mind splinters, jagged cracks radiating from the words *Callen and I broke up.* I wet my lips nervously, feeling like I'd better say something, but Lia keeps going without even glancing at me.

"Yesterday, after the Diary, I went over to his house. To apologize about the night before. It was like he was waiting. Like he'd been waiting for weeks, for the right moment." She glances over at me quickly, checking to make sure I'm listening, and I nod. "He said we want different things. That's true." She laughs bitterly. "*He's* not even sure about the baseball apprenticeship. *I* have goals."

I draw circles in the dirt with my sneakers, trying to come up with the thoughts that belong to the trustworthy friend she needs. Not the boyfriend-coveting one she has.

"You do have goals," I summon up. "Your ambition is one of the best things about you." I mean it. She's so certain about what she wants and how to get it, in every area of her life.

While I float around, aimless, just like Callen.

"I've been in shock since yesterday," she says, dipping back in the swing and kicking at the air like a temperamental baby. "I thought things were fine," she cries out, sitting up again. "I know we were arguing, but God. I completely misread him."

"I thought everything was okay too," I say, though now the slight edge he had when talking about her on Friday seems much more significant. "I never saw it coming." But Callen would make sure we didn't; he's so controlled.

I'll never have to watch them hold hands again, I realize. Never have to hear about potential close-ups again. No more spied-on kisses to drive spikes into my heart. *The torture is over.*

"Let's walk," she says, jumping off the swing. We leave the playground and head down Elm Street. A buzzing noise cuts in underneath birdsong, and I glance up. Another fighter jet.

"I knew I'd get bored of him eventually," Lia reflects, picking a leaf off a hedge. "Callen isn't the best conversationalist. You know what I mean?" She tears the leaf apart, scattering the pieces on the ground, like she's making a trail to help us find our way back.

"Yeah, he's quiet," I say. We pass house after house with Saturday-night family scenes on view. I see a father and a daughter bent over a board game in one house. At another, a family with three kids—a real rarity on the island—gobbles down sundaes at a mahogany dining room table.

"But I would have stayed with him longer," she allows, increasing her pace. The longer we walk, the faster she goes. "If it had been my choice."

If it had been my choice. "So many things are like that," I say. "And it almost never is."

Lia frowns, her forehead creasing. "Nettie, God. Don't bleak me out more."

"Sorry." We start down the wide road that leads out of the Arbor, passing the spot where I was thrown off the bike. No more houses, only trees and traffic lights and us strolling down the sidewalk, jolted by the occasional car speeding by. We pass the high school and cross into downtown.

"Where should we go?" Lia says as we pass a string of closed shops, including Delton's, the luxury department store Terra mocked me about. Restaurants and bars are open, and since the weather is nice, Characters are dining outside, laughing softly and sipping wine. The crickets changed the downtown public spaces for *liberato,* so everything is in beiges and tans, all the benches are wicker, and all the signs are in a loosey-goosey typeface, like drunk Gothic lettering.

We get caught up in a small crowd waiting to get inside the Game Palace. Last time we went, Selwyn stood by the Spate table for hours, mesmerized. She can't handle playing—says her heart starts pounding way too fast—but she loves to watch.

Lia pushes her way through and bumps into a burly senior whose name I can't remember. "Look where you're going," she chides him.

When he recognizes her, he falls into conciliatory mode. "Oops, my fault," he says, putting his hands up. "I wasn't paying attention."

"No kidding," she says, surging past him. I sneak a look back and see that he's still watching her, enthralled. Lia's always been liked, admired—feared, even. But something changed when we were sophomores, after she dated Martin, grew three inches, and got the starring role in last season's play. Even the freckles around her eyes turned sexy.

"A lot of boys will be glad Callen's out of the way," I offer as she pulls me down a short alley between the Game Palace and Music Maven.

"Maybe," she mutters, picking up her pace again when we emerge back onto the street. She points up to a set of bay windows with flower boxes above an ice cream shop. "We should live in those apartments after graduation," she says, arms stretched out, balancing on the curb like it's a tightrope. "It's near the Blisslet Theater and all the most plus-ten restaurants on the island. I'll be able to walk to the theater for rehearsals and performances. You'll be able to walk to work too." She glances over at me mischievously. "To your work as a math teacher at Bliss High."

"Don't jinx me." I give her a gentle push, and she pauses and teeters, but her feet stay planted on the curb, and soon she starts walking it again, even faster. "Living here would be fun," I say, catching up with her. A lie—downtown is too noisy for me—but I want to keep her mind off Callen.

I'm not really sure where on the island I want to end up after graduation. If I saved enough, I could apply for a beach house, like Lincoln's family has. But my ratings would have to be higher for Media1 to give it to me—as with apprenticeships, housing is a joint decision between Media1 and the Character owners.

"Let's scope out the plaza for the Double A." Lia hops off

the curb in front of the town hall and rounds the corner of the building, me right behind her. We emerge onto the plaza, which is blazing with light from the dozens of lamps Media1 installs on all important sets. Lia sits down on the fountain's ledge and bops a mermaid's hollow bronze tail.

"He won't be sitting with us at lunch anymore," she announces as I walk over toward her.

"Yeah, that'd be strange," I say, dipping my fingers into the fountain's cool water. Coins glimmer at the bottom; all those swallowed-up wishes. I want to prove my support. "I don't even want to talk to him after what he did to you." I cringe. I can hear the lie loud and clear, but Lia seems so caught up in her own thoughts that she doesn't notice.

"Thanks," she says. "He doesn't deserve me, and he doesn't deserve my friends. Let him have all the tracs he says he doesn't fit in with."

"Yeah." I sit on the ledge next to her. "I hate that he hurt you."

"Me too." Lia's shoulders droop, her earlier gloom returning. "I always wanted us to be closer. I don't mean like the close-up, I mean, like, with feelings, and I hoped one day we would get there, but . . ." Her voice trails off, and she studies her shoes, subdued.

"It seems like Callen just wasn't right for you," I say, putting my arm around her. She doesn't respond, so I change the subject. "I went to the aquarium yesterday."

Lia raises her head, grinning. "You went to see Scoop? Give in already, you two were meant for each other. He's tall, exactly your type." She claps her hands.

"No, no, that . . ." I suddenly want to be honest with her, like I can cancel out my lie about not wanting to talk to Callen with this unrelated truth. I push my hair forward to block my mouth from the cameras on the mermaids. "Yeah, I went to see him, but there was no love stuff. I told him how the Patriots are doing publicity in Zenta, to cheer him up about Belle." Lia's jaw drops open, and I rush to reassure her. "But don't worry—I didn't tell him the information came from you or Bek."

She clamps her hands on her temples, aghast. "Nettie, that was a secret."

"What's the harm?" I whisper back. "No one can trace it back to you. Besides, you were the one who said I should talk to him."

"I said *get his mind off it,* not *reveal what I swore you to secrecy about.* We could get in big trouble," she hisses. She draws back, squinting at the night sky and thinking, before diving forward, pushing her hair in front of her face again to block the cameras. "The real problem is—why do you care so much?" she whispers. "You weren't even friends with her. Let Scoop deal with it and move on, like everyone else on this island whose relatives get cut."

"I'm not caught up in—"

Before I can finish, Lia grips my arm. "You know what? Never mind. Just don't do it again, okay? And throw out that dirty bottle." She leaps up and runs down the terrace steps before I can tell her I have no intention of throwing out the bottle.

"There's a lot of work to be done here before the Double A," she shouts over her shoulder to me, back on-mic. "You don't know how slow the planning committee is. Sometimes I wish

I could just run the whole ceremony on my own." A squirrel pokes its head out of a trash can, then scampers off when it sees us. Lia frowns. "Gross. I wonder if we could get trash cans with lids for the ceremony."

"I'm sure you can," I say, descending the terrace steps. "It's going to be great, Lia. We're lucky you're in charge of so much of it." I pause at the bottom step, imagining what it will feel like to be sitting here, listening to Mayor Cardinal's opening remarks and the traditional poem about our futures, waiting for the apprenticeships to be called out.

When mine is, I'll march up to the podium and shake hands with the mayor as I receive my assignment and smile for the pictures. At last I'll know. My future will be set. But the vision feels hazy and dissipates quickly. What's left is a mostly empty plaza and my present, which is all uncertainty.

We get back to the Arbor around eight. Lia seems to have regained her confidence. She walks me to my door, rolling her eyes at Callen's house while I scrounge in my pockets for the keys.

"Growing a real jungle over there," she sneers.

I actually think the Herrons' yard is plus ten—it's cool they're not scared to distinguish themselves from the tame lawns around them. "Yeah," I say, shrugging. "The mosquitoes go wild in the summer."

"Ick," she says and falls silent. I find the key and make a point of taking it out slowly, not wanting her to feel like I'm eager to leave.

She spends a while retying a ribbon at the neckline of her dress, glancing up twice, before saying, "At least my next boyfriend won't be scared of closing up. Or holding me."

"You're so better off. *Onward through the turmoil*," I say, quoting a line from a Drama Club play that we always mock, about a girl cheating on a biology test with tragic results. It was that mediocre play that convinced Lia she could write her own.

"*Tomorrow beckons*," she quotes back. "Speaking of tomorrow, don't change your mind about Mr. Black, okay?" She claps her hand over my shoulder, like we're tracs getting pumped for a game.

I nod. "I won't. Fincher's was awful yesterday. Five hours spent on a defective music box."

"Black's your ticket out. See you later." She leaves, and I go inside, hoping to catch the Reals on the radio again. But the idea drops away when I see the green light from the Missivor. I approach my room cautiously, dreading hearing about another Patriot.

Nettie Starling: Please go to the Center at 8 a.m. Saturday for a rescheduled Character Report, during which you will learn about the Initiative.

The Initiative. I press the off button hard, pick up *The Player in the Attic*, and flip pages for the cameras. Not reading. I can't concentrate. Lia had been pretty positive about the Initiative, but I still remember the graffiti scrawled on my math desk.

Chapter 6

I carry a block of plastic-wrapped clay from the back of the room to the table Selwyn and I share for art, our first class on Monday. I end up taking a circuitous route, avoiding Rawls and Callen's table but unable to resist casting a look back. Callen doesn't see me—he's concentrating on unwrapping the plastic. I can't believe I told Lia I wouldn't talk to him anymore. How long until she stops caring?

My path takes me past Belle's old seat, which she shared with Shar Corone, a shy hulk with massive shoulders and a soft voice. Belle's stool is gone, and Shar has spread out all his materials to further the illusion that he's always sat there alone. Selwyn and I sit near the front. I heave the block onto our table, and it lands with an enormous thump.

"Yay, what took you so long?" Selwyn smiles as she ties on her smock. She reclips the barrettes pulling her long black hair off her face and then gets down to business, grabbing the block of clay and stripping off the plastic wrap like it's a present. She claws out a chunk and begins expertly rolling out coils for her bowl—before she decided on the cello, Selwyn considered an art-related apprenticeship.

I eye the clay as if it's an enemy, certain to defeat my attempts to control it.

"Nettie, get started," Ms. Shade—our young art teacher with the Mohawk and single hoop earring—orders as she roams the room, snapping peppermint gum. "Clay won't bite."

"Okay," I say, clumsily tearing off a piece. Art perplexes me, because there's never an end goal. Like when I built the radio, I knew I was making an object identical to the one in the book. What am I making now? Ms. Shade made an example bowl but insisted we "form our own interpretations of what a coil bowl should be."

I roll out a coil, but instead of coming out smooth and firm like Selwyn's, mine remains lumpy and then, to my horror, the ends start to disintegrate. I survey the room—no one else's is doing that. Ms. Shade comes over when she sees what's happening and puts her hands around mine, guiding me to put more pressure on the clay.

"You have to control the clay, Belle—Nettie," she catches herself, but it's too late. Selwyn gasps, bringing her hand to her tiny lips, and Ms. Shade releases my hands and runs off to another table, mumbling, "Good luck." The back of her neck is red. Even her shaved head is red. I didn't realize heads could blush.

"Um, I saw Lia," Selwyn chirps, flicking long strands of escaped hair out of her face.

"How is she?"

"She told me what happened this weekend," she whispers. Not quietly enough. Out of the corner of my eye, I see well-lipsticked Ayana Lemon and leggy Caren Trosser tilting toward us from across the aisle.

"Shhhh." I motion to Selwyn to keep her voice down. "You mean the breakup?"

"Yeah. Last night she tore up all the pictures of them and mailed him the scraps."

"Whoa." It might be a while before she stops caring. I'm glad Witson never pulled that kind of stunt. It sounds kind of psycho. Caren Trosser falls off her stool in her attempt to eavesdrop, and a few boys snort with laughter. I huddle closer to Selwyn, recalling how Media1 had wanted that line about Callen for the aquarium reenactment and how the cameras had been interested when I told her about our near collision. I can't talk *to* him, but I have a hunch it'll help my ratings if I keep talking *about* him. "Selwyn, how long do you think before she gets over him?"

"Two weeks. Are you excited? Isn't this your *chance*?"

"Maybe?" I cast a quick glance behind us to make sure he's not listening. "But Lia would hate it. She doesn't even want us talking as friends, so I think—I need to forget about him. Besides, Callen doesn't—he's not interested."

"You always say that, but you've never tried." Selwyn loops her latest coil around and up, then steps back and cocks her head from side to side, assessing it. "Maybe write him a note."

"No way." I lower my voice. "Lia's going to hate him forever because he dumped her. I can't do anything."

"If you say so. Hey," she says, reshaping the bowl, "how do you feel about tattoos?"

I abandon my coiling. "Selwyn, you almost fainted when you got your ears pierced. Do you think you can handle a tattoo needle?"

"It'll be worth it," she sniffs. "I was thinking of music notes with wings. Or a cello wrapped in rainbows. That would show the orchestra I'm more committed than Thora."

"I don't know, Selwyn. Rainbows?" She has on a flirty ruffled yellow summer dress underneath the smock, and now that she's mentioned tattoos, all the exposed skin around her neckline seems vulnerable.

She fidgets with her beads fiercely again, just as she did in the hall on Friday, and avoids meeting my eyes. "Well, I haven't made up my mind."

"Starving," Lia sighs as we get on the lunch line. "We're out of food at home," she whispers. "I had *sugar cubes* for breakfast. I am *not* a horse. It's because Mom needs, like, half a bottle of wine to tackle grocery shopping. She loses her list most of the time."

I don't understand why Lia's mother can't get herself together—her life seems so easy. It's almost like she creates problems because she doesn't have any real ones. I give Lia a hug. "So lame."

She nods and pulls a banana from an overflowing fruit basket.

"A banana, just what I needed." She smiles at the nearest camera.

"Yum," I say, summoning up some fake enthusiasm for pro-pro. While I fill my glass up with Cherry Kofasip, she casts a critical eye at the cafeteria. "I think this place is too nice to just be a cafeteria. Look at those big, beautiful windows, the high ceilings, the polished floors. We should have a dance here one day. What do you think?"

I sip my drink. "Maybe? Decorations—sparkling cutlery?"

She laughs. "Right, and then everyone can dance on top of the tables and the tracs will start a food fight." We head toward our table in the center of the cafeteria. For Lia, our walk away from the lunch line is more of a strut. Her long red braid swings like a whip across her back and she holds her head high. "Did you see Callen this morning at art? You know what—never mind, I don't want to know."

I'm a step behind her. Today she's wearing equestrian-style boots that go over her jeans and nearly reach her knees, along with a sleeveless white linen top. Freshmen and sophomores steal glances at us as we pass, faces full of envy and longing. Next, a table of junior wallflowers, girls I was friends with a long time ago. Lia calls them the Pastels because they're sort of dull. "Better than pencils, less than paints" is what she says.

Tracs are at the back of the cafeteria, loud and rambunctious, like caged elephants. The floor beneath them is always littered with food and napkins and errant silverware. Callen's there too, smiling and talking to his teammates as if he's always eaten at that table.

The light from the window makes him seem kind of angelic.

"Keep moving." Lia bumps me with the edge of her tray. I hadn't realized I'd stopped, and I press forward, blushing and hoping she didn't notice why I stopped.

"Play Spate with me, Lia," Lincoln Grayson whines as soon as Lia sets her tray down. I sit between her and Selwyn, who's pecking at a pile of grapes. Lincoln stretches across the table like a snake, waving his deck of cards in Lia's face. The handkerchief in his shirt pocket is a spritely green today, with "LG" printed in black all over it. "Please," he begs, his almond-shaped eyes wide as he implores her.

"I'm busy being miserable." Lia peels her banana. "Didn't you hear? I was dumped by an albino baseball player."

Lincoln cackles and settles back in his chair. "At least you're joking about it. I thought you'd be, like, rending your garments." Lia's been friends with Lincoln forever; they live near each other in Treasure Woods. He's so rich that the Audience watches him just to gawk at his luxuries, like the spiffy gold watch on his wrist or his old-man monogrammed handkerchiefs.

"I have Drama Club and the Double A Planning Committee to lead. No time to feel sorry for myself." She waves her hand in front of her, showing off her long, aristocratic fingers, as if being dumped is a pesky fly she can brush away.

Lincoln only half hears her. He's distracted by Revere strolling up to the table, whistling. "Spate, now!" he says.

"Definitely," Revere trills. Revere and Lincoln are so different. Revere is tall and pale with a messy ponytail, a large, pointy nose, and gray eyes. Lincoln is snub-nosed, has dark skin, tightly curled hair, and his best feature: velvety brown eyes that he doesn't seem worthy of. Revere can't help but be nice, and Lincoln . . . well, he's Lincoln. You're forever on the verge of slapping him.

What cements their friendship, I think, is that Revere is *always* willing to play Spate. He even bought Lincoln this special deck of cards for his birthday, one with sleek cars on the backs—car collecting is a favorite Grayson family pastime.

Lincoln pushes his tray to the side and spreads the cards out in the game's starting pyramid formation. Spate has never really interested me, but Selwyn is quickly absorbed and brings her knuckles to her mouth to muffle her anxious gasps and squeals.

"Oooh!" she bleats as Revere lays a two of spades over the nine of hearts. "Oh no, Lincoln, what are you going to do?"

"Selwyn, you should just play," Lincoln says, scratching his head as he plots his next move.

"Competition makes me too nervous." She puts her hand over her eyes. "Make your move already! The suspense is killing me."

Lia elbows me and whispers loud enough for the mics, but low enough so no one but me hears her, "You're talking to Mr. Black today, right?"

I hesitate, watching Revere. He seems even nicer than usual today, playing Spate with Lincoln, his tongue at the corner of his mouth as he concentrates. But I *have* to get off the E.L. He wins the round and sweeps up the cards.

"For sure," I whisper back. Lia smiles and nods approvingly.

"I want a tattoo," Selwyn announces, lifting her hair and patting the bare expanse of skin on her back. "Here. Thoughts?"

Revere and Lincoln stop playing, and Lia gapes.

"Adventurous," Lincoln pronounces admiringly.

Lia recovers. "Selwyn, is this about getting closer to Garrick?" she asks, a sliver of exasperation in her voice.

"*No,*" Selwyn yelps, flustered. Her expression plus the yellow dress makes her look like a fussy baby chick. "Garrick has nothing to do with it."

"Oh, no, not Garrick," I groan. Garrick is a friend of Callen's, who graduated last season and now works at a tattoo parlor downtown. Selwyn adored him. I have no idea why. He had this lunatic glint in his eyes and was mostly known for charging people to see a private insect trove he named the Krazy Kollection. He made out with Selwyn at parties, but treated her like she was a distant acquaintance the rest of the time.

"You'd have to live with a tattoo for the rest of your life," Lia says, pinning Selwyn with a sharp schoolmarm stare.

"I *know* that, Lia," Selwyn says. Lincoln leans over and mouths *Initiative* to Revere. So they're in this too?

"Whatever makes you happy," Revere pipes up, shuffling and reshuffling the cards for a new round of Spate. "I think a tattooed cellist would be cool."

"*If* I get the apprenticeship," Selwyn sighs.

"You'll get it," Lia assures her. "Henna and I are designing the program for the Double A this week. Any ideas?"

I look over to where Henna sits with the misfits. She's got hot-pink streaks in her hair and a red plaid shirt over the zebra leggings she's worn every day for the last month. Peacock feather earrings are her only concession to *liberato*. Callen's old friend Conor is there too, probably forcing one of his morose poems on them. Belle used to sit at the corner of that table, up against the window, crouched over a book, her mousy hair falling over her glasses.

"Hey, dreamer." Lia pokes her knee into mine. "What are you thinking about?" She follows the direction of my gaze and says, "Oh," sagely. She takes a sip of her water. "It'll take a while to feel back to normal, and that's okay, okay?"

"Got it," I answer, turning my attention back to my food. "Thanks," I add.

Scoop slouches back in his chair, talking to Terra Chiven, who is hovering over him, her fingers grazing his desk. With her peachy complexion enhanced by the warm smile she reserves just for him, she looks prettier than usual. As soon as I sit down, he turns away from her. "Nettie, I wanted to—finish our conversation from Friday," he says. "Can you leave us alone, Terra?" The transformation to the Terror is immediate. Terra glowers at me before stomping off to the back of the room and her seat next to Mollie.

"After school," I say absently, sliding into my seat. I can't think about Patriots now. I need to prepare for my conversation with Mr. Black. I straighten up, pretending I'm Lia, a trick I use when I'm nervous. Neck high, chin up. By the time the bell rings for the end of class, my body is aching.

I wait until the room has emptied, clear my throat, and walk up to Mr. Black's desk. He's going over the homework already, his bald spot gleaming, aimed right at me.

"Mr. Black?"

He looks up from his work. "What's up, Nettie?"

I fiddle with the straps on my book bag. "I know . . . it's a little late." His polka-dot tie is on crooked. He adjusts it while I talk, his fingers as plump as sausages. I struggle to remember my speech, but can barely hear my thoughts over the pounding of my heart. "If I were to apply, do you think I'd have any chance at getting the math teacher apprenticeship?"

Mr. Black's face contorts like a squeezed balloon. "Well, I don't know, Nettie. Most people started preparing for their apprenticeships a while back," he says. "It has nothing to do with your talents."

He keeps going, and I stand and nod, disappointment trickling through me. I know Lia said that even *trying* would pull in the Audience, but nothing about this feels good. Mr. Black is still talking, but I mumble good-bye and flee the classroom.

I'd tried to keep my hopes in check about the apprenticeship, but I can't deny how happy the idea of a future *not* at Fincher's made me. I'm midway to my locker when I feel dampness on my cheeks and realize I'm crying. Startled, I wipe my eyes against my sleeves and take a detour to the bathroom to wash my face.

In between splashes of cold water, I see my blotchy skin and swollen eyes in the mirror, the proof of my distress.

I'm going to be miserable my whole life, like Selwyn's parents, and then I'll be cut and shipped to the Sectors, separated from my friends and family, and forced to endure all the things the Originals wanted to escape. My sadness turns into anger at myself for waiting so long, and I kick a lead pipe curving under the sink.

"Ow," I say into my mic, reaching down to massage my foot. I hear a familiar buzzing and turn my head up to the ceiling, only to see half a dozen cameras. Aimed away from the stalls, but in the *bathroom*. There are four more: against the walls, on the radiator, near the mirror. I don't like it; I want *some* privacy. And I don't like being forced to do a job I hate because of rules the Originals agreed to almost a hundred seasons ago. I blame Media1; they just control so much in my life, and there's nothing I can do to stop them.

The school is mostly cleared out when I finally leave the bathroom. I turn the corner and frown when I see a lone figure. At *my* locker. Scoop.

"Hi," I say, opening up my locker and piling books into my bag.

"So I might be wrong about what I said at the aquarium," he says, a smile tugging at the corners of his lips.

"You probably are." Glad he's dropping whatever story he's been weaving about the Sandcastle. It's just some beach games.

"You probably stare at a lot of people." He grins, a dimple showing. He leans against Lia's locker. His light green sweater matches his eyes. "Not just Callen."

I pause for a second. I fell right into that. Whatever. I don't have time for this. I quickly pack my book bag, zip it up, hoist it over my shoulders, and push past him. "I have to go home."

"Isn't it all right now, since he and Lia are broken up?" He follows me, matching my stride and waiting for my answer.

I glance over at him, weighing how much I should say. *Who cares? He already knows.*

"She doesn't want me to talk to him." We pass through the double doors and out into the sunshine. Two boys are tossing a football, while a couple of Pastels look over at us with undisguised curiosity. I start up the hill to the parking lot where the bike rack is, and Scoop increases his pace to keep up.

"Why'd you stay after math, anyway?"

"I asked Mr. Black about the math teacher apprenticeship, and he basically said I wouldn't get it." I surprise myself again with my own bluntness.

"I thought you were set for Fincher's?" Scoop asks, managing to maintain eye contact while walking.

"I am. I just thought maybe I'd be . . . happier teaching math." His hazel eyes seem bottomless suddenly. Still handsome, but less sexy and more kind and approachable. Who knew he could be such a good listener? "But I'll be fine at the shop." My voice rises higher at the last part. I don't know if I believe it. I stop at the bike rack.

"Are you sure?" he prods. "It doesn't sound like that's what you want."

"Does what I want matter?" I bend down to unlock my bike, grab the handlebars, and begin walking it downhill, since Scoop doesn't seem in any hurry to leave.

"It's the only thing that matters," Scoop counters quickly.

"How'd you get so confident?" I try to keep the bitterness out of my voice. It must be the ratings thing. If what I wanted always coincided with what the Audience wanted, life might seem easy for me too.

"I think it's all the extraordinary fruit we have here on Bliss Island." He smiles again, his hazel eyes dazzling in the afternoon sun, and I imagine the Audience swooning.

"No, really, how did you?" I insist. I want what he has, what Lia has. That way of going through life at ease. Fearless. Scoop raises his eyebrows, puzzled, like it's something so taken for granted that he can't begin to explain. But he tries to answer my question, voice tentative.

"I guess—I'm not afraid of people, a lot?" His long face tightens, and for once, the smile disappears. "Do you remember my aunt, the fifth-grade history teacher?"

"Yes, of course," I say, my voice softening at the memory. She passed away a couple of seasons ago. The only funeral I've ever been to.

"Aunt Dana used to question *everything*. She and my dad would get into huge debates. Like which lollipop flavor lasts longest or what the highest point on the island is—or more important things, like how to discipline children. She'd never just let him win. She'd research day and night until she got the answer, to prove she was right."

"She was pretty plus ten," I say, averting my eyes, feeling awkward talking about someone who's, well, dead.

"I always wanted to be like her." His lips twitch as if he's trying to stop himself from saying something. We reach the bottom of the hill and turn right, in the opposite direction from a bunch of kids going downtown to hang out. "Maybe the question is, how did you get so *un*confident?"

Where to begin? Asking about my father on-mic when I was five and having my mother freak out? Never seeming to be able to choose the right things, like friends, or boyfriends, or apprenticeships? Landing on the E.L. as soon as I turned sixteen? It just seems like I do everything wrong.

"Disappointments." I swerve my bike around a deep crevice in the sidewalk. "I just wish there was more than one slot, so Revere and I could both get the apprenticeship."

"Yeah, sometimes the rules seem unfair," Scoop agrees, kicking a pebble down the hill ahead of us. "You can get any-assigned, though, if you really don't want to be at Fincher's."

"I know." We quiet down as we pass crickets, their noses and mouths swaddled in surgeon's masks as they douse grass with green paint. When we're a safe distance away, Scoop whispers, "My aunt discovered that the Patriot—"

I knew he wasn't done talking about this. I don't want to hear it. Whatever her discovery was, his aunt was only a Character, and my information came from a Real, someone who actually knows about the world outside of Bliss Island.

I'm shaking my head and stepping back just as a voice calls out behind us, "Nettie, how'd it go?" I turn around. Lia, sprinting down the hill, her braid bouncing behind her.

"What'd Mr. Black say?" she asks as she catches up with us. "Hi, Scoop," Lia tosses off, then pivots to me. "What happened? What'd he say?"

Scoop takes one look at her, her eyes practically feverish with excitement, and decides to take off. "I'm going to catch the Tram. See you later."

"Well? Well?" Lia grabs my arm.

Best to just get it over with, like ripping off a Band-Aid.

"Mr. Black said more or less that it's Revere's."

Lia's shoulders slump. "That sucks, Nettie," she says, putting her arm around me and pulling me close. But I don't feel comforted.

"I don't really want to talk about it," I say, loosening myself from her grip. "How are you? How's life after Callen?"

"Life after Callen." She laughs and fills me in on her day as we walk to the Arbor together. Apparently there was a moment in history when she and Callen stood by their desks, not wanting to sit next to each other, but unwilling to surrender their usual spots.

"After a minute, I just sat down and Callen had to go back by the window." She giggles. "Where he can stare at the sky more easily, which is all he ever wants to do anyway. Loser."

"Good for you." At this rate, she'll be over it in a couple weeks, and I'll be able to talk to him again.

"Small victories." Lia flicks her mic up to make sure the Audience can hear every word. "So, I decided that in the play, Mia embezzles from her father's bank."

She told me this on Saturday. It's not like Lia to repeat herself. I pretend I haven't already heard, and she keeps chattering about the play all the way to the Arbor.

Lia changes subjects abruptly as we near the Arbor and empty fields give way to its small, well-maintained houses. "What were you and Scoop talking about?" she says, looking at me closely. "You seem to have a lot to say to him lately."

"Apprenticeship stuff."

"Hmm." She sighs and fixes her gaze in the distance, like she might find a solution to my problems there. But no luck. "Well, even if it didn't work out with Mr. Black, I'm glad you took the initiative, Nettie."

Initiative. As we cross onto the Arbor cobblestones, I quickly mouth, "Last night, I got a Missive, rescheduling my Character Report for Saturday. They're going to introduce the Initiative to me."

The sun falls on her face and her green eyes glitter. "Good," she mouths, smiling. "My rescheduled Report was last week. Some new stuff they're trying out. It's a little different."

"How?" I mouth uneasily. "How different?"

"Don't worry, StressNett. Just do what they say."

Chapter 7

The first difference I notice when I step into Mik's narrow office on Saturday is the brightness. The shade at the back of the office is up for the first time. I take in the view—a stone building wedged into the hill that runs down to Eden Beach—then scan the office's newly luminous interior.

Mom would approve: it's spick-and-span. There's a Missivor screen instead of the still life of tomatoes and teacups, a floor lamp where there used to be a precarious tower of yellowing papers, and a sleek leather couch instead of the fraying checkered one. The white walls are aggressively bright, and the smell of fresh paint curls through the air. The massive oak desk that seemed like an outgrowth of the dusty floorboards has vanished. In its place stands one of light pine, its surface crowded with unidentifiable electronic gizmos. Wires coil through, under, and around the desk like vines.

There's one more difference that trumps all the rest. Grandfatherly Mik, my producer for the past six seasons, is *gone*. In his place is a man no more than ten years older than I am, with a narrow face and curly brown hair long enough to brush his navy-blue collar. The shirt is paired with crimson corduroy pants.

"Who are you?" I stride into this updated, modern office, the new paint making me sneeze.

The man leaps to his feet, and a notepad tumbles off his lap. "Hi, Nettie. I'm Luz. I'm so glad to meet you," he says, bending down to retrieve the notepad. He's making an effort to talk slowly, but still speaks faster than Mik. "I'll be handling your Character Report from now on. Sit down, please." As the man gestures me toward the couch, his dark curls sway like wildflowers in the wind.

"Where's Mik?" I sit on the couch, doing my best to not reveal how swerved off I am by all the changes. I cross my legs and rest my hands demurely on the plaid jumper I found at the bottom of the closet. Underneath it, I put a plain white shirt. I just wanted to look as normal and harmless as possible for whatever the Initiative is. At the last minute, I borrowed Mom's hemp bracelet for a *liberato* touch. Today, I want to be as good as a Character with lousy ratings can be.

My palms are sweaty.

"On a furlough, fishing at Lake Inok. Happy, happy," Luz answers from behind his fancy desk. He puts down the notepad and trains his eyes on me. His smile bares yellowish teeth, not too unusual with Reals. I force myself not to recoil.

"Lake Inok," I repeat. Sectors names always sound absurdly

plain, as if a butcher took some juicy cut of meat and stripped it to the bone. "What's going on? Am I getting a ratings mark?"

"No. Today you're getting much more." He twirls a pen like a cheerleader's baton. "Nettie, welcome to the Initiative."

"Um, thanks." I shrink back into the couch, meek as a Pastel at a party.

"The Initiative was created to increase and retain the Audience." He lays down his pen and puts his arms behind his head. "The Audience needs *Blissful Days* more than ever. Yet they're watching the show less."

"I don't understand." I inch forward.

"Partly it's because of the Drowned Lands. This latest attempt at secession has been harder to put down than past ones. There are entire Drowned Lands islands that are actually under rebel control now," Luz explains, propping his legs on his desk. "Along with the usual uncertainties and vicissitudes of Real life, the fighting has taken a toll on the Audience. They want entertainment, desperately, but *Blissful Days* doesn't have the excitement and rawness necessary to fully engage today's viewers, to alleviate their distress over political realities. That's where the Initiative comes in.

"The Initiative gives the Audience what they need. A select group of Characters has weekly Reports in which they'll receive, along with their ratings marks, suggestions on how to provide the Audience with the captivating entertainment it craves."

"Suggestions," I repeat slowly, frowning. "Do you mean I'll have, like, chores to perform?"

Luz laughs. "No, you'll *want* to do your suggestions—they'll align with your actual desires. That's what makes them so effective. Here's your first." Luz drops his hands, removes his legs from his desk, and sits up, clearing his throat. "Flirt with Callen Herron. Just once, and your ratings will skyrocket."

I'm not sure what to say for a few seconds. The thought of spending time with Callen thrills me. But there's a serious problem. "I told Lia I wouldn't talk to him."

"Forget Lia. The Audience likes hearing you confide in Selwyn about your tortured feelings. But they want more, need more, to be able to invest in you. Now is the time to take action."

"I don't know." I'd sometimes wished Mik would give me hints about how to improve my ratings, but this feels different. "Doesn't the Initiative break the noninterference clause of the Contract?"

"Everything's been cleared by the legal department. Outside, you'll find an addendum to the Contract, which goes into more detail about the Initiative, if you're curious. Remember, these are *suggestions,* not orders. You don't have to take them, but why wouldn't you?" Luz jumps up and paces the narrow aisle between his window and his desk. He's skinny and short, full of kinetic energy. "I saved the best part for last. Initiative suggestions come with rewards. If you complete this suggestion, you'll get the high school math apprenticeship."

I gulp. "You could do that? Mr. Black said—"

"I know what he said. Don't worry about it. Fincher's is not for you. You need to be challenged. Flirt with Callen, and you'll never have to set foot in Fincher's again. The extra time you spent at Fincher's during the past few months is probably what put you on the E.L."

"That's what I thought." I settle back and recross my legs, satisfied that someone else is confirming what I've guessed. The legal department must have done some tricky maneuvering to make the Initiative okay, but if it'll get me better ratings and out of Fincher's, it's worth it.

Flirting with Callen. Probably I should explain to Lia ahead of time, so she'll see that I have no choice. Excitement builds in me. I can talk to him again, maybe even touch him. Of course, he'll have to *want* to.

"Wait, is Callen in the Initiative, too? Did you tell him to flirt with *me*?"

"That's confidential, sorry," Luz says briskly. I start to protest, but he cuts me off with a wave of his hand. "What do you think about the Initiative? About getting the apprenticeship? And making your ratings soar?"

I sigh. "Even if I do exactly what you say, you can't force the Audience to watch. You don't *know* that my ratings will improve."

Luz sits on the edge of the desk, drumming against it with his heels. The laces of his squat leather boots are undone, and the ends hit the desk. He screws his face up, deep in thought. As I wait for his answer, I realize that I want him to tell me I'm wrong. I want that math apprenticeship. I want to believe that Luz can keep me off the E.L. I *want* to flirt with Callen.

"You're right. I can't guarantee your ratings." Luz breaks his silence. "But I know the Characters, and I know the Audience. Media1 trusts me, and you should too." The light shifts in the room, landing on a splash of purple in the corner—the jumpsuit he's not wearing. He sees me looking at it and shrugs. "Makes me itch."

"How long have you worked for Media1?" I never would have dared ask Mik such a private question, but Luz talks to me like we're equals. He doesn't wear the jumpsuit—he seems to be a different kind of Real.

"Only a few seasons," he says, straightening his back. "But that's exactly why the board in Zenta values me—producers who've been on the island too long lose their perspective. I have fresh eyes. Many Media1 employees see this as a job, but I'm a fan first. I'm especially a fan of *yours*." He stabs a finger in the air at me when he says *yours*. "I might be designing Initiatives for several Characters, but you're who I wanted to meet with one-on-one. You're special, and I can make the Audience see that."

After the Report, I stop by the public display of the Contract outside of Character Relations, needing to read it alone, without Luz's spin. First, the most fundamental.

CLAUSE 1, CHARACTERS.

Item A: Characters are bound to the territory of Bliss Island for the duration of their lives.

The only way to leave the island alive is as a Patriot. I move farther down along the display outside the Character Relations Building.

Clause 53, Patriots.

Item A: Unsatisfactory Ratings. Characters who fall 10 percent below their ratings mark are eligible to become Patriots during the subsequent ratings quarter.

Item B: Risk to the Show. Characters who constitute a risk to the show *Blissful Days* are eligible to become Patriots.

Item C: Reference on Show. Reference to Patriots by Characters is not permitted and falls under Clause 56.

Item D: Patriots are enlisted in the service of Media1 and are given lodging and food provisions for their lifetimes.

Close by, Clause 56:

Clause 56, Breaking the Fourth Wall.

Fralling. Forty-two examples of what constitutes breaking the fourth wall follow, a handful of which I commit regularly— things like deliberately obscuring the audiotrack or avoiding cameras.

Next, Clause 57, Noninterference with the Show. The clause I brought up to Luz.

> **Media1 will not impede, control, or manipulate Characters on *Blissful Days*. Characters on *Blissful Days* retain autonomy over their lives.**

At the end of the display of the Contract is the addendum, two paragraphs on pale green paper. I read it swiftly. The Initiative encompasses much more than Luz revealed during the Report. Several aspects of the Initiative will affect the entire cast: *Stricter enforcement of Clause 56 . . . Increased camera coverage . . . Selected Characters from the fifty-eighth to seventieth birth seasons will have a redesigned ratings schedule . . . Suggestions to increase ratings . . . Introductions of mobile cameras.*

Mobile cameras? Does that mean there will be fewer crickets slinking around? *Increased camera coverage* would explain the cameras in the school bathrooms. I groan aloud. I hope they don't install them at home too.

I sign the leather-bound Hidehall visitor's register. Under Visitee, I write my grandmother's name, Violet Starling. It's so nice that we share the last name, unlike Mom and I. Media1 has some algorithm they use to distribute last names around the island, so it's not uncommon for parents and children to have different ones.

"I'll let Violet know you're here," Tula the receptionist says.

She picks up the telephone and rings my grandmother, tilting her mouth from the receiver so her dark red lipstick stays untouched. "She's ready." Tula gestures toward the hall on her left.

"Thanks." I swing my arms as I walk through the mansion. Here there's no pressure. Smooth, slow, serene Hidehall. Pressed flowers and photographs of the island line the dark-wood-paneled walls. Expansive windows look out onto the long, still lake and the brown-green sliver of the Brambles in the distance. Orderlies float by, dressed in the *liberato* uniform: puffy blouses and flowing skirts for the women and light linen pants for men.

"Nettie, my most beloved grandchild," Violet cries from her royal-purple velvet armchair as I step inside her apartment at the corner of the first floor.

"Your *only* grandchild." I smile, sadness twinging me. She used to be able to get up to greet me. As I bend and hug her, I can feel her fragility. Time has stamped her: it's in her sunken cheeks and the wrinkles of her moon-shaped face. But her jet-black ringlets, dyed religiously, are the same as ever, as is the bright scoop-necked dress that displays her cleavage. No *liberato* for her. Hidehall arranges bused shopping excursions downtown around the motif change time, but Violet never gets on.

Her dress is on the ostentatious side, and so is her room. Paintings, most by Violet herself, crowd the walls. Each piece of furniture is upholstered in velvets and chenilles. Knickknacks compete for space on the white lacquered shelves. Sometimes it's hard for me to believe that someone with her opulent—some might say garish—sense of style ever made a living as a portrait painter, but she's assured me that she knew how to "tone it down for customers."

"Only and most beloved grandchild," she says as I sit in the hard-backed chair across from her and next to an open window. "How's your mother? Are you looking forward to the game tomorrow?"

"She's fine. Yeah, a little." A lot. I loved watching Callen pitch the opening game last season, and I can't wait to have an excuse to look at him again.

"How's the apprenticeship?"

"The same." I've told her about my problems at Fincher's, but I don't want to hash it out again, so I just leave it at that. I stare up at the intricate ceiling moldings, wishing I could tell Violet about the Character Report but not wanting to risk the chance that her mind will start wandering and she'll talk about it on-mic. We used to frall a lot, but it's become too dangerous.

"Did you get your dress for the Double A yet?"

"No, Selwyn and I are going to go shopping soon." Thinking about Selwyn reminds me of Lincoln whispering *Initiative* to Revere at lunch when she brought up the tattoo. My skin prickles. Selwyn would never do something like that on her own. The tattoo might be a suggestion. She'd do anything for the cello apprenticeship.

"Fantastic. That girl has great taste." She scans me up and down, but doesn't say anything. She doesn't need to. I know my jumper is way too subdued for her. "Any boys around? Since Witson?"

"No, no one new." I never told Violet about Callen because I knew she'd just urge me to, like, seduce him behind Lia's back. I spot a new watercolor on the wall behind her chair, depicting a cardinal and a bluebird at the feeder located right outside the window next to me. "This one's plus ten."

"Yes, I think that painting came out well," she says, poking her head up over the chair to look at it with me. "Birds are hard to get right, because they're so quick. Even a tiny painting takes so many studies."

Something looks off about the painting, though, and it takes me a second to figure it out.

"Wait, would a cardinal and a bluebird share a feeder?" I ask, sitting back down. "Aren't bluebirds really shy?" Because of all the trees, the Arbor's full of birds, so I've done some casual bird-watching at home. I've seen bluebirds flit away at the sight of a shadow.

Violet bursts out laughing across from me, her shoulders quivering against her chair's plump cushions.

"What?" I say, stung.

"You notice all the details no one else sees, Nettie," she says softly, reaching over and patting my knee with her bejeweled hand. A few seconds pass, and her brown eyes glaze and lose focus. I tense.

"Hart's the same way," she says.

I keep a stiff smile on my face. "Do you want me to make some tea? You have honey here, right?" I hurry to the small kitchenette.

"Where is Hart?" she asks behind me.

I ignore her, moving faster and humming, hoping to mash the audiotrack. I yank open a cabinet just as a cricket barges into the room. Startled, I back into the wall, still clutching the kettle.

Youngish, with pimples clouding his cheeks, the cricket storms over to my grandmother and glares down at her.

"You can't talk about Patriots," he growls. "That's breaking Clause 56. You're getting a fine."

"I don't understand," Violet says. "Is something wrong with Hart?" She looks up at the cricket, begging him to answer.

The cricket grabs her shoulder. "Stop talking. You're making the fine worse."

I put the kettle down and run over. "Stop! She's not doing it on purpose, she's just—she's not all there anymore." I pray she doesn't get a fine. She can't afford one. It's not like Hidehall denizens are impoverished—Media1 pays most of their housing and food costs, and they have savings and ratings payments, but they still don't make as much as people with jobs.

The cricket doesn't look at me, but he releases her shoulder. Violet slumps as if he's squeezed the life out of her.

"Do you understand?" he spits. His face is flushed, and his eyes are burning into her.

"What?" Violet lifts her head, but her pupils are unfocused, and she's speaking out into space.

"Do you understand?" the cricket repeats, placing his hand on the arm of her chair and lunging forward so he's less than an inch away from her face.

"Yes." She squints, and I know she's surfacing again. "Oh, dear," she says. "Nettie?"

"I'm here. It's okay," I say from behind the cricket, but she doesn't seem to hear me. Thankfully, he marches out the room, and Violet seems frozen. The only sign of life is her wrinkled hand clenching the arm of her chair.

"I'm going to make the tea." I shakily walk over to the stove. I've only actually seen crickets break into scenes to stop Characters from fralling once or twice in my life.

Violet remains quiet, and her eyes have gone distant again. My hands tremble slightly as I turn the burner on.

"What kind do you want?" I call out over my shoulder. She doesn't reply. "Lemon it is!" I declare brightly. I watch her as I fetch the tea bags from the cabinet. She gazes blankly at my empty chair for a minute or two, then a scuffling sound from outside rouses her—birds at the feeder. She blinks, once, twice, tilting her head toward the window, then calling over her shoulder to me.

"Nettie?" she says in a muddled sort of way. "Did I? Oh, my. Another fuzzy moment."

"Yeah, I think so," I say lightly. The kettle goes off, and I quickly prepare the tray, eager to bring some normalcy back to the scene.

When I reenter the room, she's gotten up and is peering out the window at the feeder. "Tula bought me a charming book on local wildlife. Take a look." She points to a book on her bureau, then waddles back to her chair.

I set the tray down and fetch the book, *Blissful Nature*, while she sits and pours the tea.

"Pretty," I say, flopping back onto the chair and looking at the book's line drawings of island flora and fauna. The truth is I can hardly pay attention. I'm overwhelmed by guilt and anger because of what just happened. I wish I'd told Violet to stop talking when she brought up my father's name. Why had the cricket been so mean to her? Was that part of the Initiative?

When we're done with the tea, I leave, taking the book with me at Violet's insistence. I walk down the hall and see the pimply cricket with three others, outside a bathroom that's being rewired for cameras. I have to ball my hands into fists to stop them from shaking.

"Can't read the Contract," he says. Maybe it's because I had to listen to Luz talk fast this morning, but I can understand him clearly as he speedmurmurs to his friends, a smug smile on his face. The anger in me amplifies. I try staring at the floor, not wanting to look at them, and I see keys, wallets, and sunglasses spilled out next to a toolbox.

"Stupid puppets," a different one says, with a deeper voice.

Crack. I tread on the sunglasses, hard. The crickets fall silent, and I wish I could turn around and see their astonished faces, but that would be against the Contract, so I keep walking, smiling to myself.

Chapter 8

"We'll reach the stadium faster if we cut across the field,"
I say, climbing over the wooden fence before Lia can protest.
She follows me, breaking away from the scores of Characters
streaming from the Tram station to the stadium.

I survey the field, a vacant plot of land in the Granary, near
the stadium. Camerapoles shoot up every dozen feet or so, and
it takes me a few seconds to spot a patch of grass out of their
range. "Let me show you this . . . flower." I pull Lia over to the
spot. Once I've moved us out of view, she scours the grass, intent
on finding the nonexistent flower, until I nudge her sneaker—
red-laced, in honor of the Ants—and she looks up.

"I had the rescheduled Report, yesterday morning. It's official. I'm in the Initiative now," I mouth.

She smiles and mouths, "Awesome. This is just what you
needed."

"Yeah, it's good, definitely," I say, struggling to come up with
the right way to word this, knowing I can't spend too much time
off-camera and off-mic. "But Luz asked me to—"

"You spoke with the Real in charge of the Initiative? What

was he like?" Lia cocks her head to the side like she did while trying to coax Mollie's name out of Lincoln.

"Well. He's sort of nerdy." She's paying close attention, and I draw it out, enjoying lording my insider's knowledge over her. "Young. Enthusiastic."

"Wow, you spent a lot of time with him." Lia crosses her arms, ruffled. "Bek said that Luz wasn't meeting with any Characters one-on-one."

"Yeah, he said I was the only one. Because he's a fan of mine," I say. Seeing her expression curdle stops me. "But his first suggestion, it's odd."

"Spit it out," Lia commands, her face hard and her arms still folded.

"He wants me to flirt with Callen," I say, shrugging apologetically. "They'll give me the math apprenticeship if I do." I feel a lump in my throat, the same one I get when I lie. But it's not a lie, I argue to myself.

"Flirt with Callen?" Lia repeats. She twines her braid in her hand. "The way Bek explained the suggestions to me, they're supposed to be things we *want* to do," she mouths, the braid slipping over her wrist like a handcuff. "But you don't want to flirt with Callen, and it's not like he *wants* to be flirted with, by you or anyone else. All he wants to do is smoke cigarettes alone and feel sorry for himself."

"I don't even want to have to *see* him after what he did to you." Now, that's a lie, and it comes out effortlessly. Of course I want to see him. But I would never have dared without the

Initiative. "It's just—I really want the math apprenticeship. Have your suggestions been things you actually wanted?"

"I didn't think about it before, but I guess not. I've only had one. Remember how I changed the play? Bek said if I did it, my reward would be a private acting lesson with a top Blisslet. Actually, I didn't really want to—I thought my ending was better," she says, frowning. "And this week's, ugh. I'm supposed to bring up my mother's, you know, alcohol issues. In public, on-camera. In exchange for a B-plus in chemistry, to get Dad off my back."

"Have you thought about *not* doing it?" I ask. "Dropping out of the Initiative?"

"No. Is that an option?" Lia adjusts her red T-shirt, getting ready for all the cameras in the stadium. Not that there's much to adjust. She cut off the bottom half, baring a good two inches of her stomach. I haven't really mentioned it—must have had something to do with showing up Callen on his big day. "Media1 knows what's right for the Audience."

The image of the cricket bullying Violet flashes in my mind. "But what about us?" I mouth. "Do they know what's right for *us*?"

"It's the same thing. Listen, without Media1, what would we be?" she mouths.

Her question hovers in the air. I know the emptiness in my mind isn't the right answer, except, maybe it is. Nothing. We'd be nothing.

Lia glances over her shoulder, toward the stadium. "We should get going."

I tug her arm, stopping her. "So you agree that I should just go ahead and flirt with Callen?"

"Well . . ." She stubs the ground with the toe of her sneaker. "I'm not happy about it, but obviously, I want you off the E.L., and the math apprenticeship would be amazing."

"Ants attack! Ants attack! Ants attack!" Three younger boys scream, vaulting over the fence and sprinting across the pasture, a red blur, kicking up mud and grass and splattering Lia's jeans.

"Brats." Lia scowls as she brushes the dirt off her jeans. "Let's go." We follow their path, climb back over the fence, and merge with the crowd moving toward the stadium. "Selwyn's probably there already."

Which reminds me. "I think Selwyn is in the Initiative," I whisper to her. "I bet they told her to get the tattoo."

"I figured, but I haven't actually fralled about the Initiative with anyone but Callen. He hates the whole idea. He's not in it." She plunges forward, deftly weaving through the crowd.

"He's not in it," I repeat, a thrill going through me. So his reaction to my flirting will be genuine.

I fall behind Lia in the crowd, and she reaches back for me. "Come on," she says, pulling me toward her. She whispers into my ear when I'm next to her, "Let's tell Selwyn we're in it too. We should all be honest about what they're asking us to do. Otherwise it might lead to misunderstandings."

We're on the third level of seven. A decent view. Selwyn's already at our seats, in a periwinkle-blue dress with a patent-leather black belt around the waist and big blue-rimmed sunglasses that cover half her face. I glance down at my jeans—dark blue—and tank top—faded blue—and feel uncreative. Selwyn even has a pigeon finger painted on her cheek. She pops up as she sees us sidling down the aisle. She's brandishing a pigeon pennant, and it looks like she's about to leap out of her skin; she's effervescent, her lustrous black hair reflecting the sunlight like pavement slick with rain. It's not like she loves baseball, but she's easily excited and gets swept up by the tumult around us.

"You're late," she shouts over the din. The blue dress has a wide, square neckline, and I don't see any traces of a tattoo.

"It was a slow walk from the Tram, with all the people coming here." I hug her, then sit down between her and Lia and—*screeeeek*. I gasp. A device attached to the seat back directly in front of us springs out like a jack-in-the-box. After a couple of stunned seconds, I recognize the lens and the red light, and my heart slows down to a normal rate.

A camera. The mobile camera the Initiative posting at the Center had mentioned. Lia doesn't react to it at all, and Selwyn just pats my knee. They must have seen them before.

I move back in my seat, and the camera stretches forward, like a reflection.

"No Callen, no pretending I care about sports." Lia takes a stack of papers out of her straw bag, like she's in study hall instead of at one of the biggest Special Events of the seasons. "I'm going to work on the play." The new camera screeks over to her, its movements straighter than the swerve and sway of the ones the crickets carry. I relax, pleased to have it off me.

"Plus ten," I murmur.

"Yeah, without Callen, I have time to focus on stuff I really care about. I'm thinking of getting Mom help." Lia tilts her head to give the camera a flattering three-quarter view of her face.

"Is something wrong with your mom, Lia?" Selwyn asks, taking a break from her fervent pennant-waving.

Lia pauses and looks from one of us to the other several times before taking a deep breath. "I think she may have a real problem. She stays up all night guzzling white wine, and then she starts screaming at me and Dad. Last night, she tore apart her closet, looking for a necklace her mother gave her, and when she couldn't find it, she came to my room and went on and on about how I had stolen it."

"Guzzling white wine?" Selwyn puts the pennant down in her lap and leans over me so she can make eye contact with Lia. "Are you saying she's an alcoholic?"

"That's what I want her to figure out," Lia says, flipping her braid behind her and turning her attention to the field.

"Lia, that is so terrible. I'm here for you, if you ever want to talk about it," Selwyn says, wringing her hands.

Lia is cringing, like she wants to run away and hide, but she manages a "thanks," raising her voice so the mic can hear her over the stadium noise.

The organ player works the crowd into a feverish pitch

around us, and Selwyn leans back into her seat, shaking her head and murmuring, "I had no idea." It's the perfect time to frall. "She wanted her mom's problems to be a secret," I mouth to Selwyn, "but she had to bring them up because of the Initiative. We're both in it. You're part of it too, right?"

Her eyes widen. "How'd you know?" she mouths, shifting closer to me, making it harder for the moving camera to see us.

"I knew you'd never want a tattoo. They told you to get one, right?"

"Yes, but I didn't have to. They just wanted me to say I wanted it. And look, my reward was getting my tooth fixed!" She lifts her lip so I can see her restored canine tooth. "And my ratings bumped up."

"Neat," I say, glad for her. The Initiative worked for Selwyn, and maybe it'll work for me too. Off the E.L., in a plus-ten apprenticeship, and whatever flirting with Callen leads to.

The organ plays a few notes, signaling us to stand. Cheering gets louder, becoming a roar, and Selwyn and I get up to do the Pigeon chant—"Cooooooo! Coooooo!"—ignoring the Ant fans shooting nasty looks at us. I sit down again, but she keeps standing, cheering. Unlike hers, my enthusiasm is fake, mostly for the Audience's sake. The camera snakes forward, real close, then retracts, and Lia leans over. "I heard Characters calling them '*biles*," she whispers. "Short for mobile cameras."

"They are sort of bile-inducing," I whisper back. "Do they need to be so close to our faces?"

"I know." Lia rolls her eyes. "Thank God for these makeup

techniques from the Sessions." She bats her eyelashes comically. But she does look better with whatever tricks they showed her at the Center, and I feel a pinch of jealousy.

Selwyn pokes my shoulder, blocks her mouth with her pennant and hand, and mouths, "What's your suggestion?" My skin grows hot.

"Flirt with Callen." I keep my eyes fixed on the still-empty field.

The pigeon on her cheek crinkles with her smile. "So. Plus. Ten," she says on-mic, forgetting to hide the fralling. "That your radio works!"

I whisper, "I'm only doing it because they said so. Probably nothing's going to happen."

"They must have you doing it for a reason. They want you to go out, and they think you have a chance!" she mouths, smiling. I can't help smiling back. I'm too scared to say it aloud, but it's great hearing her voice my biggest dream.

She turns back to the game. "Where are they?" she shouts down to the field. I touch my face while she's looking away. Between Lia's makeup and Selwyn's perfect smile, I can't help but feel drab, and I remember Dr. Kanavan chastising me at my Show Physical. Will better Initiative plotlines even work if the Audience doesn't like my face?

Lia passes me the binoculars. "Your mom's across the field, to the right." I twist around and zoom in. There she is, with her book club brigade, their eyeglasses glinting in the sun. I don't think baseball is their thing, but they know how to fake enthusiasm for a Special Event; they're all waving pennants and cheering.

I turn the binoculars to closer targets. Lincoln is a few rows down, next to Revere. Farther down the row is Scoop, eating popcorn and chatting with his friends, including Terra, who's fanning herself with a souvenir red palm, her hair in two pigtails tied with red ribbons.

She touches his shoulder and asks something, gesturing toward the field. He points at home base, then at the outfield, pausing to make sure she understands. She nods and runs her tongue along her lips, and I laugh aloud. Maybe I should use that move on Callen.

"Welcome to the opening game for your high school, Ants vs. Pigeons!" the announcer booms.

The crowd's in a frenzy by the time Callen saunters to the mound, his easy gait at odds with the frenetic energy in the stands and on the field. Selwyn jabs me, grinning, and I ignore her, staring straight ahead, my breath caught in my throat.

He's so beautiful.

The crowd roars, and the 'bile in front of us retracts. The game starts. The first Ant hitter saunters up, brushing off dust on home plate with his sneaker, then loosening up his arms like a dog shaking off rain. Selwyn jumps up and down as the hitter settles into batting position, facing Callen.

I imagine flirting with him. I'm not good at that. Compliment him? What nice hair you have . . . I bury my head in my hands. I can't even talk to him without blushing.

Lia puts down her pen and elbows me. "What's going on with you?" she says gruffly.

"Just . . ." I don't want to drag her into the suggestion anymore, but her eyebrows furrow in that way that I know means she's reading my mind.

She looks for the 'bile, then turns so her body blocks it and whispers in my ear, "Don't agonize about Callen. He'll probably just walk away from you. I don't think he wants anything to do with any of us. Once Media1 sees that, they'll give you new suggestions." At *us*, she makes a sweeping gesture that covers me, Selwyn, Revere, and Lincoln, and even seems to include some random Drama Club members sitting nearby. The message is clear: she has the bigger team, and Callen stands alone. I grin, like it's hilarious and true, but my stomach turns because I hear another message too.

She thinks he'd never notice me. I know I don't have long, expertly mascaraed eyelashes or finely cut cheekbones, or whatever it is that makes the Audience—and the boys at school—so into her, but it's not like I'm invisible either.

Ratings mark: 168. Still—that doesn't make me a leper, just a low ratings earner. Maybe that's how she sees me: a low ratings Character she's taken under her wing.

"Are you all right?" she asks on-mic as the crack of the bat reverberates throughout the stadium and Characters angle their necks, following the arc of the ball.

"Fine." Selwyn jumps back on her feet to celebrate the foul ball, cooing again. "So, we were right about Selwyn," I whisper.

I explain to Lia about the tattoo, and Lia nods, but she's pre-occupied with her play.

So I watch the game, zeroing in on Callen. He's pretty far away, a blue stick figure from here, but my imagination fills in the rest. I've spent so long looking at him.

The catcher signals the pitches to Callen, and I get an idea. What if we had a signal for the Initiative? Something that would help us communicate what Media1 had asked us to do.

I whisper my idea to Lia. "Anytime we're doing something for the Initiative, how about we go like this?" I scratch behind my ear.

Lia blinks, confused—I broke her concentration—and her eyes dart up to the hand on my ear. Then she brings her hand to her own ear. "Got it," she mouths. "Neat idea."

"What are you talking about?" Selwyn nudges me. I explain the signal to her, and she murmurs, "Smart." And then, smiling coyly, she scratches behind her ear and says on-mic, "Wanna hang out after school with me tomorrow? I have fun plans."

"Yeah, sure," I say, mirroring her ear scratch so she knows I understand.

Chapter 9

"Are you ready?" Selwyn asks, bending down and unzipping the bulging nylon bag she hauled all the way from school. She has a ton of energy somehow. I'm exhausted. Last night, after the Pigeons won, everyone in the Arbor congregated on the streets, celebrating until past two a.m., even Mom. Callen had been off at some private baseball bash, so there was no chance to flirt. I'd shuffled through the day like a zombie.

"I guess," I say, half yawning. We're in an abandoned underground passageway that goes beneath the Tram tracks. The tunnel is blocked on both ends by decaying wooden boards. We'd squeezed through a jagged hole in one board, wriggling to avoid the splintering wood.

I poke my head out of the hole and look in both directions. Some Tram passengers are going upstairs to the platform, a dozen feet away. No one notices us. Good. This is part of the Initiative, but that doesn't mean police or parents wouldn't be swerved off to find us here. I gulp down the fresh air before turning back to the damp, mossy tunnel. Selwyn props a flashlight up on the ground, so at least it's not pitch-black anymore.

The tunnel still makes me claustrophobic, but I ignore the fear crawling through me and move deeper inside, toward Selwyn, in her pool of light.

My sneakers crunch over beer bottle remains. With the flashlight on, I can make out the graffiti sprawling across the curved walls, and the only cameras I see are older models, all dead, no red lights on. Why would she bring us here if it's for the Initiative?

I mouth as much to her and she shrugs, mouthing back, "I'm just doing what they said." She paws through the bag, and clanking echoes throughout the tunnel. I squat next to her and check out what's inside. Dozens of gleaming spray paint canisters.

"I'm going to use blue, white, and silver," she says, scooping out three canisters.

Bam. I jump to my feet, and Selwyn drops a canister. Someone, someone large, kicked at a wooden board, trying, and failing, to widen the hole. He squeezes into the tunnel, and all I can think is, *Mom is going to kill me.* Relief floods me when the figure steps closer to the light: a cricket. Another one follows him, a camera on his shoulder. I avert my eyes, my heart slowing. Better crickets than police.

"Choose a color, Nettie," Selwyn says, turning her back to them.

The crickets draw near, stopping about two feet away, and I turn my back to them. Yeah, they're not going to arrest me or tell my mother, but I don't feel like seeing them. The memory of what happened to Violet is still fresh in my mind.

"I'll go with yellow." I pick up the yellow canister and stand next to her.

"Where to tag?" she ponders, shining the flashlight.

"It seems like every inch of this place is covered."

"Maybe here." Selwyn approaches a wall plastered in graffiti: Character names, obscene stick figures, enigmatic symbols. There are a couple that break Clause 56, like *All for the Audience* and *Drowned Bliss Island* above a drawing of the island covered in ratings cards.

"Not enough room." Selwyn pulls me past the fralling graffiti down toward the end of the tunnel, beaming the flashlight at the walls, trying to find free space. The crickets and I trail her. Her walk is full of new swagger, and I can't tell if it's genuine. She's in jeans and an old T-shirt, a departure from her usual ultragirly frocks. I wonder if the wardrobe change was part of the suggestion too.

"Here," she declares, reaching a free space, right up against the tunnel's end, at the corner between the wooden boards and the wall. She moves the flashlight around to get a fuller look, and spiders scramble across their webs, fleeing the light.

"What do you think?" She beams.

"Yeah, plus ten," I say, checking discreetly over my shoulder. The crickets are still behind us, their faces impassive, the hum of their cameras audible in the quiet tunnel. Selwyn presses the nozzle down and shrieks as paint jets out.

"It stinks," she wails, pinching her nose. But she goes on,

soon wielding two cans with ease, her hands moving like they've been choreographed. Paint coats the wall. Staying a safe distance away, I tilt my head left, right, trying to discern what she's making, the swoop of silver stirring up a faint memory.

When she starts in with the blue, adding white streaks, it clicks: the fountain in the plaza behind town hall. The blue and white are the water under sunlight; the silver, the steel fountain. She asks to borrow my yellow, the closest she has to bronze, I guess, and does the mermaids. The crickets tiptoe closer, the hum of their cameras blending in with the sound of pressed air.

"Selwyn, that's amazing," I say, coming closer when she's finished. "You're so talented. My grandma always said your stuff was plus ten."

Selwyn sighs. "Yeah, sometimes I wish I had gone for an art apprenticeship. But too much competition." She backs away from the wall, grinning, and pokes me. "Your turn, Nettie."

It's the same pressure I feel during art class. Make something pretty. Right now, all I can think is, *What do I do? What do I do?* The crickets huddle behind me. They don't have the answer. But Selwyn does. She pulls me away and stops about midway to the other end of the tunnel.

"Check it out," she says mischievously, shining the light on the wall. "Add to that list." I step closer to inspect what she's pointing out. "Garrick told me about it," Selwyn says behind me. "The Love List." It's mostly names, tons of names—names I recognize, names I don't recognize, names that sound fake, names that are blurred out or chipped away or overlap other names. Delfine + Morgan, ME + YOU, Teressa + Nicolet, Looks + Brains. There are columns and columns of names.

"Do it." Selwyn shoves me closer to the wall, scratching behind her ear. The Initiative signal. She's right: it's not flirting, but if Media1 wants to tease the Audience with the idea of me and Callen, they'll love this scene. It'll fit into the whole plotline they're building.

"Okay," I say, holding up the can and standing on my tiptoes so my tag goes right underneath Looks + Brains. I begin my *N*, my hand wobbling, part nerves, part throttle. Soon I get into the rhythm, even adding little curlicues to my letters. I think about how Selwyn's suggestion is so easy and the reward is so nice: Selwyn's producer said they'll give her parents fewer shifts at the hospital, lighten those dark rings around their eyes.

Mine isn't quite so easy. I had one chance today, in art class. Callen was at the sink, washing his hands, but when I tried to force my feet to get up and go, they turned into anvils.

Five more days.

I start the *C*, and by now I'm a pro. It helps that I'm used to writing Callen's name in my notebooks whenever I'm bored in class.

"Well done," Selwyn says. Her wide face, illuminated only in brief sections by the flashlight, looks moonlike. "Okay, okay, enough of this. Let's go before we get in trouble." She gathers up the canisters and packs the bag. I snatch up my book bag, and together we leave the tunnel and emerge into the daylight, squinting at the sudden onslaught of sun.

The crickets are behind us as we walk to the train platform. I gesture to Selwyn to hurry up, hoping that they'll lose interest when we join the rest of the commuters and become harder to film.

Sure enough, the camera buzz is gone by the time we reach the crowd climbing up to the steps to the Tram platform.

Selwyn flashes her paint-smudged hands at me as we walk up the stairs.

"Yuck," she declares.

"It'll come off. Unlike a tattoo."

"So happy I didn't do that." She shudders.

A crack of thunder overhead, and the sky turns into a swamp of gray. Rain slams down, hard and loud. Neither of us has an umbrella, and the small glass waiting room at the Tram stop is packed. We huddle up under a narrow overhang, shoulder to shoulder with the rest of the unfortunate umbrellaless.

We tuck our mics into our shirts to protect them from the rain, and Selwyn takes the opportunity to frall. "Do you think I'll get the reward?" she whispers.

"Yes! We could have gotten *arrested*. The Audience will love it."

"Good. Now it's your turn. You should call Callen up and arrange to meet him at midnight. Ro-man-tic," she mouths.

"Really?" I mouth, glancing around to make sure no one's watching. I put my hand up to shield my mouth from the nearest camera. "I'm just—I'm not even sure what I should do. Witson was always sort of around, and one day he, like, *declared* his affections, and then we were a couple. I'm not even sure I *can* flirt."

"You can," Selwyn asserts. "Garrick had no clue who I was, so I'd sit next to him at parties and scoot over until our legs were touching, just a little. So it looked like an accident. Eventually he noticed me."

I refrain from reminding her how ridiculous the chain of party make-outs that constituted their relationship was. "Yeah, I need the right opport—"

The rain interrupts me, coming down in even heavier torrents and splashing us. Selwyn shrieks. The Tram pulls up, thankfully, full of the businesspeople who work on the outskirts of downtown. Pushing through them, aware of raised eyebrows and disapproving glares, I feel every inch an island rebel, in sodden clothes, with the fumes of spray paint lingering on me.

There are no seats left, so we stand in the tight compartment at the end of the car, wedged up against the doors. Selwyn clutches the nylon bag with the cans in front of her with both hands.

"Want me to hold that for a bit?" I ask.

"Thanks," she says, passing me the bag. "It's heavier than I thought it would be."

"No problem," I murmur, watching a new pair of crickets stumble into the crowded car, two men again. One has a distracting mole right under his nose. They're speaking low, but it's quiet enough to hear them.

"I read there might be a draft," Mole growls. "Take care of the drownclowns once and for all."

The other replies in a hoarse voice, the kind Media1 will fine you for having because it messes with the audiotrack: "Before they do that, they should up the adventures." His eyes scan the car, meeting mine. I drop my gaze to my sneakers.

The Arbor stop comes up a few minutes later, and I hand the bag back to Selwyn and get off fast, glad to be cricket-free. The rain has tapered to a drizzle, and the sun is breaking out from the clouds. A figure on the Herrons' porch catches my eye. Turns out there's no need for a midnight meeting. Callen's sitting on his porch swing. No baseball, I realize. Rained out.

But what do I say? Forget flirting—even a simple hello seems out of reach at this moment, I'm so tongue-tied. My stomach is in knots, but I remember being in Luz's office, and his total confidence that flirting was what the Audience wanted. I can do this.

"Callen, guess where I just came from?" I approach the house, but hesitate at the bottom of the steps.

"Not school," he says, pushing back the mop of blond hair that's fallen in front of his eyes.

"Nope. I was spray painting with Selwyn, in an abandoned passageway at the Granary stop. Do you know about it?"

"Really?" he says, waving me up. I scramble up the stairs and sit on the porch swing with him. "I've heard about it, but I've never been there. What'd you do?"

"Selwyn spray painted a *masterpiece*. The town hall plaza fountain. It looked so real—she chose just the right colors, and, well, I couldn't begin to do something like that . . ." I trail off, realizing what I'm leading up to.

"Well, what did you do?" he prompts.

I keep my lie short and simple. "My name. Then we got

out fast. I thought the police might catch us or something. But the only thing that caught us was the rain." I lift up my soaked sneakers ruefully.

"Spring rain is the best," he says. I love how the skin around his eyes crinkles when he smiles. "It gives me my afternoons back."

I'm barely listening, my mind whirling as I try to figure out how to flirt. Between us, lying on the swing, is a baseball. I pick it up, using the movement as an excuse to edge closer to him. Flirting. I need to say something that's coy, but not too subtle. Channel my inner Terra.

"You did such a plus-ten job yesterday." I spin the baseball in my hands.

"Thanks," he says, pushing back on the floor with his feet so the swing rocks a little. "It's scary being in the stadium. So many people there. Much more than the bleachers at school can hold. Nerve-racking." He glances at me, then quickly looks away. By his standards, that was probably a huge admission.

What would Terra say? "I couldn't tell at all, you looked so calm," I say, unable to meet his eyes, but I make sure my head is positioned so my voice will reach the mic.

"So tell me about the tunnel. Garrick told me they'd nailed it shut. How'd you get in?" he says after a moment. The sun fills his eyes with light, and I almost forget to reply.

"Someone had broken through the boards on one end. Still, it wasn't easy." I show him the scratches on my arms.

"I wish I could have been with you," he says. I feel myself blush, and I'm glad my skin hides it better than Lia's.

"Do you miss Lia?" I wince. That's the furthest thing from flirting I could have said. But it just came out.

"I'm all right." He shrugs. Back to the inscrutable face I'm used to seeing on him, eyelids at half-mast, looking off in the distance. I put the baseball down and flatten my hand on the swing. Only a few inches from his. My stomach churns with nerves. Hands touching. That would be undeniable flirting. Actually, putting my hand over his would seem more like *harassment* than flirting.

I become aware and then slightly mortified that I can *smell* him. Soapy. Fresh. He must have showered after practice was canceled. His hand seems so close, so warm, callused fingers splayed slightly on the wood, and I move mine nearer, in small motions, like an inchworm, start stop, start stop.

"Seems like it was best for both of you." The closer my hand gets to his, the more still and fixed the rest of my body becomes. Focused.

"The thing with Lia was that she wanted me to be someone I wasn't," he says, staring straight ahead at the street. "Someone who loves baseball. Someone who talks more."

"She means well," I say, thinking of Lia charging into my room, the Diary of Destiny swinging in her hand, full of ideas about what's best for me. I need her around, being her pushy self. Without her ideas, my mark would be way lower than 168. But Callen doesn't need her in that way.

"I know," Callen says. "I hope she's not too hurt." I make my hand close those last couple of inches. Our pinky fingers are touching, and he turns and looks directly at me, finally.

"I think there's spray paint in your hair," he says. He reaches over and touches a strand lying against my cheek. His fingers graze my skin and stay there. My heart slows, and the world around me—the cars and cobblestones of Poplar Street, the rich earthy smell of the wet grass, the flowers dipping under the weight of the water—sharpens, becoming ultravivid and alive.

The screen door hits the wall, and the porch quakes. I pull back, and Callen's hand drops to his side. His father strides out of the house, holding his leather medical bag. He pauses next to the swing, to my left. I straighten up.

"Hello, Nettie." He nods at me before addressing Callen. "Possible appendicitis," he says. "I should be back in an hour and a half. Let your mother know."

"Got it." Callen lifts his index finger in acknowledgment. We watch his father go down the four steps and stroll over to the gleaming silver Harrow in the driveway, the envy of all our neighbors. My hands are in my lap now, knotting around one another, restless. The car starts up, its engine purring. I can't look at Callen. I think I've done enough, so I should just leave.

I stand. "You're right, um, this paint in my hair—I better go wash it out."

For the first time in weeks, there's a Missive I'm happy to see.

Congratulations, Nettie Starling. You have fulfilled your suggestion for the Initiative.

You will soon receive your reward.

Chapter 10

I wake up at dawn, and can't go back to sleep, so I lie in bed and relive last night. Callen had touched my *face*. What would have happened if his father hadn't interrupted us? Should I have stayed?

I think I'll like being a math teacher. Eventually, Lia and I will live in that apartment downtown, and I'll walk to work every day, just like she said.

I float over to my desk to listen to the radio. I've checked it almost every day since I stumbled on the Media1 walkie-talkie channel, but all I've been able to pick up is static. I usually try at night, though, so maybe giving it a shot in the morning will help. I sit on my chair and pull my legs up, resting my chin on my knees. I pick up the receiver and tap one of the wires with the metal stick, tweaking the frequency. I think about how the same hand working on the radio touched Callen's.

I haven't kissed anyone since Witson. Callen must be a better kisser than Witson. Witson had thin lips; his upper lip was practically nonexistent.

Static roar. Nelly and George, again. I tap a new spot, then another and another. Static. I'm about to give up when I hear a more solid sound underneath the static. I press the receiver closer to my ear and hear Reals again. I strain, trying to understand them.

"They delayed my sabbatical, *again*," a man says.

A woman responds. "Well, they say this batch needs a lot more hours, but don't worry, after they move them"—*garble, garble*—"but—"

The radio cuts out, then comes back on with the man saying, "When are they moving Stork, Cademia"—*garble, garble*—"Cannery?"

A chill runs down my spine. Those are the last names of the recent Patriots.

"Saturday, April twentieth. Then out of the Sandcastle"—*garble*—"off to the caves in the"—*garble, garble*—"survive"—*garble, garble*—"Drowned Lands."

Static sears my ears. I set the receiver down with a clunk. The fairy-tale word again: *Sandcastle*. Loud and clear this time. Scoop was right. It's a place, and they're in there, but they don't stay there.

Out of the Sandcastle, off to the caves. Almost three weeks. April 20. The day of the Double A. I know the transmission was garbled, but it sounded like Media1 is moving the Patriots to the Drowned Lands, not to an office in Zenta. Specifically *caves* in the Drowned Lands. The place Luz said was getting more dangerous by the day.

• • •

As soon as I step inside the math classroom, Terra Chiven raises her head in triumph. She's taken my chair next to Scoop, who's bent over some papers. Actually, technically my place—the chair and desk are different. The square wooden desks and spindly chairs have been replaced with metal oblongish ones with glossy black chairs attached to them. *Voxless*. The new motif. I saw the Missive about it right before I left for school.

> The motif for the seventy-third season of *Blissful Days* is *voxless*! What is *voxless*? *Voxless* is the future. *Voxless* is fragile. *Voxless* is delicate yet strong. *Voxless* clothing is sleek and glimmering. *Voxless* music is electronic and soothing. *Voxless* art relies on straight lines and dark colors.

I tied up my hair with a black bow and left it at that. Other Characters have done more—Terra's all in black; she even dug up a necklace with a piece of obsidian at the end from somewhere. I pause in the doorway, contemplating her. Normally I wouldn't care that she stole my place, but I want to talk to Scoop.

While I deliberate, Scoop looks up and sees me. "Nettie, you're out of luck," he teases. Terra scowls. I take a deep breath and stride up to them. Terra pretends not to see me.

"Terra, actually, do you mind if I sit here today?" I keep my eyes trained on the top of her head.

She deigns to look up. "Sorry, Nettie," she says, tossing her pigtails over her shoulder. "Scoop and I need to talk about the senior class Flower Festival float."

"Terra, I need Nettie to help me finish last night's problem set. We'll catch up about the float after school." Scoop flashes her a winning smile. Terra's mouth moves like she's chewing a pound of gum, but eventually she gathers her books and returns to her regular seat next to Mollie.

"The last one, seven." He shows me his problem set, holding it up by one corner, like it's trash. "You can see I tried. I derive no pleasure from derivatives."

I snatch the paper from him, ignoring the wordplay. I only have a few more minutes before Mr. Black gets here. "Okay. I can take you from an F to a D."

"Whatever you can do," Scoop says affably. I write on his paper along the x-axis, tiny letters marching like ants. *We need to talk—I heard something about the Patriots.* I pass the paper back to him, pointing with my pencil tip at my writing. He peers down closely, then writes down the y-axis: *Janitor's closet before lunch?*

I read it and nod—the janitor's closet in the basement is a popular place to frall, since Media1 never fixed the sole broken camera there, and it's right next to the boiler room, excusing problems with mics.

"Plus ten," Scoop says on-mic as I pass the problem set back to him. Then Mr. Black comes, and I forget all about the Patriots as we're whisked into the world of logarithmic functions. Eventually I get bored and start writing NETTIE + CALLEN, in bigger letters than usual in my notebook margins, heat sweeping over me as I think about what happened on the porch. The bell rings, and I leap up, slamming my notebook closed, ready to talk to Scoop.

"Nettie, can you chat for a moment?" Mr. Black calls out from his desk.

"Yes, Mr. Black?" I didn't think it would happen so soon. I straighten my tank top and walk over. Glad I did the Skin Sequence today. Obviously this scene will be broadcast.

"Nettie, I want to encourage you to apply for the math teacher apprenticeship. As we've discussed, there's a slot available, and we'd like to consider you." He grimaces and pulls at his tie, checkered today, avoiding my eyes.

"Oh. Wow." I clasp my hands, overwhelmed with relief. I knew it was coming, but hearing the words brings me to a whole new level of joy.

He plays with an eraser and when he speaks, his tone is solemn. "Yes. Would you like to help with my freshman geometry class next week? They'll be working on a golden ratio project."

"Okay," I say. He's still not looking at me.

"Plus ten," Mr. Black says, wiping his sweaty brow with his sleeve. "Glad you'll apply, Nettie." He sounds tired, and his chair groans as he settles back into it and begins shuffling through problem sets.

Mr. Black seems less than enthusiastic. I back away from the desk, my heart sinking. I'm guessing Media1 sent him a Missive with instructions, and he's irked because he didn't have any say and prefers Revere. The thought of Revere being anyassigned still makes me uncomfortable, especially after he worked so hard for the apprenticeship.

Scoop hovers outside the classroom, waiting for me. He cocks an eyebrow. "Ready for some fun?" he says suggestively, and he starts walking before I can respond. I glare at his back. Sometimes Characters make out in the janitor's closet. Lia says it's a thrill to kiss without the cameras. I don't plan to find out. I follow Scoop down the hall to the stairwell that leads to the basement, keeping a distance between us.

Scoop turns a knob, and we step into the dark closet, carefully navigating obstacles from memory—a row of mops here; the depression where the floor drains there. The boiler room rumbles next door, helping to mash the audiotrack. I safely reach the clear space in the back, and Scoop is right behind me.

"I don't understand any of it," Scoop says on-mic. He continues with a cover story for Media1. It's better than making out, but not by much. "Next week, while you're taking the test, can you push your paper over a little?"

"Um, I can help you study, but I won't help you cheat," I grumble into my mic. How bad is it for a future teacher to cheat?

He bends down and whispers, "What'd you hear?"

I stand on my tiptoes to reach his ear and whisper everything that came from the two transmissions I caught on the radio. When I say *Sandcastle,* he inhales sharply, but I keep talking, concluding with, "So I'm not so sure about the Patriots doing publicity in Zenta anymore. What did your aunt tell you? Does it match either story?"

"Not really. One day Aunt Dana was in the Character Relations lobby and overheard a cricket name a woman who'd been cut. He said that 'this batch is weak' and that 'they won't survive long.' Then he said that 'one of them might not even make it out of the Sandcastle,' and another one asked about her 'fitness results.'"

"That could mean anything," I whisper.

"My aunt Dana was sick a lot. She said the show doctors went crazy trying to figure out what she had—they were so obsessed with health on the island, she thought maybe they were *experimenting* on the Patriots. Think about it. How else could Media1 figure out which weather chemicals are safe? Or which vaccinations work?"

"Wait, so she thought 'they won't survive long' meant they would *die*. Because of experiments." I shudder.

"And that 'fitness results' was about whether the Patriots were in good enough shape to be used as subjects."

Goose bumps rise on my arms. I'd never thought that Media1 could *hurt* us. Fine us. Make us pretend about the weather and promote products. Take us off the island. But not hurt us.

"No way. Aren't the Patriots guaranteed lodging and food provisions for their lifetimes? That's what the Contract says."

"And that's *all* it says. There are no rules, really. My parents trusted Media1, but Belle and I thought Aunt Dana might be right."

"Yeah, but you were kids. You probably believed in witches and ghosts too. Besides, why would they do experiments in Drowned Lands caves?"

"Maybe keeping Patriot experiments in the Drowned Lands lowers the risk of some kind of medical catastrophe if an experiment goes wrong."

"Or they could just have more offices there," I whisper. "I'll talk to my source again. We don't know enough yet."

Scoop mumbles something on-mic about how he'll fail the test if I don't help him, then whispers, "Forget your source. We need to find out what's going on in the Sandcastle ourselves. You said they're moving everyone on April twentieth?"

"Yes. But we don't even know where the Sandcastle *is*." I frown in the darkness. "I wish they would just tell us what's going on. I'm sure there are a lot of other Characters who'd like to know."

"We'll be the first ones to find out," Scoop whispers.

"You're going to sneak around the Center? You'll get cut if they catch you. Show Risk."

"I don't have a choice. I have to know what they're doing to Belle, to Revere, to all of them."

It takes me a second to realize what he just said.

"What do you mean what they're doing to Revere?" Numbness settles over me, like my body is icing over.

"You don't know? They *cut* Revere," he says slowly, almost apologetically. "I heard the Authority got him on the Tram last night."

Chapter 11

"I can't believe it," Selwyn says. I cough in alarm, picking up the napkin next to my glass to stifle the sound. *She's going to get a huge fine.* Talking about Revere on-mic. With crickets only a few feet away, focusing on Terra's table but still within earshot.

"How could they choose Conor over Lissa to write the Double A poem?"

I put my napkin down, feeling stupid. "It'll be fine."

"I hope so, but Conor's poems are such downers." Selwyn pouts. "I want to be happy during the Double A."

"If Conor does the poem, it'll probably be about all our *doomed* hopes and dreams," Lia says. "Honestly, I didn't want him, but Henna pushed hard because they're friends, and the committee folded. She's actually quite charming when she needs to be."

I steal a glance behind me at the misfit table before I sit. Henna, in zebra leggings again, is balancing toothpicks and forks on a saltshaker. "It won't matter. No one listens to the poem anyway."

The last part of my conversation with Scoop is running

through my head. I'd just told him all about how me and Selwyn and Lia are in the Initiative, what the suggestions and rewards have been so far, and how Mr. Black had just offered me the apprenticeship. Offered it to me only hours after the Missive about Revere. The Missive I'd missed because I'd woken up early, obsessing about Callen, and ended up heading to school before Media1 sent it.

He agreed that it couldn't be a coincidence.

"True," Lia agrees. She's holding her head higher than usual, showing off the silver necklace on her swan's neck. How do she and Terra make the motif switch so quickly? She fusses with her tight bun, then asserts, "I wish I had a say. I think the adults trust Henna more for this stuff because she's artsy. They asked me to make the schedule, which I did, and photocopy the programs, which I don't even have to do until the night before. I want to help with the design and content of the program too, but they don't want my input. I think I should get closer to Henna if I really want my opinion to matter. I didn't sign up for this position so I could be ignored."

No, she didn't. She was worried that there wasn't enough suspense around her apprenticeship, so she joined the committee to make sure the Audience kept watching her.

She edges over to me. "It's not your fault," she whispers. I nod, feeling queasy.

"Guess what? An orchestra member came to our practice, and I'm sure I did better than Thora." Selwyn smiles broadly. She sees me watching and folds her lip over her fixed tooth instinctively, then remembers the chip is gone and smiles again, brighter and broader than before, until abruptly, the smile vanishes.

Lincoln's here.

"Sit, Lincoln," Lia chirps. "What's up?"

His shirt is buttoned wrong. His curly hair is matted, like he didn't wash it. His eyes are dull. "The ceiling," he says, taking his seat, his movements laborious. Selwyn laughs and then becomes absorbed in cutting up her sandwich. Lincoln picks at a piece of bread. Something about his tray is different. It takes me a moment to place it. No cards. And one less seat at the table. Media1 removed it.

I stare at my plate, wondering how we're going to survive this lunch. Revere's gone, and so is the easygoing energy he brought with him. But Lia is unfazed. She gulps down Kofasip and murmurs something into her mic about how tasty it is—we got a Missive last night ordering us to do some propro for them. Selwyn follows Lia's lead, praising Kofasip like it's from heaven, but with less confidence, eyes flicking back and forth to Lincoln. I meant to ask Lia about Bek and the Sandcastle, but I feel immobilized in the face of his despair. Why are such young Characters being cut?

The situation is so tense that I'm actually relieved when Lia's ex-boyfriend, motormouth and senior class president Martin Fennel, comes over.

"Is there room for me?" he asks, sitting in Callen's old seat next to Lia without waiting for an answer. Martin is cherubic with his fat cheeks and bright eyes behind rimless spectacles. "Glad to have the chance to catch up with my favorite juniors. How's life?"

"Plus ten, Martin," Lia answers smoothly. "We're talking about the Double A. I'm on the planning committee."

"Ah, the good old days. I was on my year's planning committee, remember?" Martin intones. A born politician, he's careful to look at each of us in turn, but his gaze lingers on Lia. "When you're a junior, all you think about is the Double A. Now that I'm senior class president, I have to juggle a million responsibilities. I'm chairing the committee for the senior Flower Festival float, I'm on all the dance committees, and I meet with the principal once a week."

"Wow, that is a lot," Selwyn chimes in. "I think—"

Martin steamrolls over her. "And on top of all that, I have my apprenticeship in the mayor's office." Martin removes his glasses, blows on them, and wipes them off with the bottom of his shirt. "It's tough holding down an apprenticeship while you're in school, keeping up with your friends, and in my case, being president of the senior class—"

"Martin, we *know* you're the president of the senior class," Lincoln says flatly. He's expressionless, his usual sneer absent. There's a brief silence, which Martin fills with nervous giggles. Selwyn saws at her sandwich again, knife squeaking loudly against the plate. I glance at Lia, panicked. It's obvious something's off at the table, and we need to fix it before Media1 notices.

Lia jumps in and starts explaining her vision for the play. Lincoln, at least, has raised his head and seems to be listening.

I try, but my attention wanders. I count three crickets roaming the floor. I watch Characters line up to get Kofasip out of the soda machine. I look over at Callen's table and think about sitting with him on the porch yesterday.

Martin brings the conversation back to himself, so Lia turns to me while he talks to the others. "We didn't do the Diary this weekend because of the game," she says, popping a grape into her mouth. "Bummer."

"Yeah, too bad," I agree, though I didn't miss doing the Diary at all. I should. It's probably good for ratings.

"It's all about word choice," Martin proclaims. "They have to sound natural, like words Mayor Cardinal would say, but also strike the right chord with the crowd," he continues. Lincoln's returned to a catatonic state, his hand resting on his sandwich, like he's forgotten how to pick it up and eat it.

"So, you did it, you took the suggestion?" Lia whispers, leaning close to me.

I nod. "And Mr. Black basically said the apprenticeship is mine. You're wrong. It is my fault. I think they cut Revere so I could have it."

"The Missive said Revere was cut because of low ratings, like anyone else," she mouths. "Anyway, you got out of Fincher's, which is amazing," she adds, but there's a stiffness to her mouth as she speaks, and the words that come out next seem practiced. "So how was the flirting?"

I glance pointedly in the direction of the crickets, hoping Lia will take the hint and finish this conversation later. She doesn't budge, her eyes drilling into mine.

"We just talked on his porch, and I smiled a lot," I finally whisper.

"That's all? Did he seem into it?"

"I don't know," I mouth, uncomfortable. "I was so—so— focused on myself. It was really a nothing conversation. I was surprised it was enough." I bump her elbow so she's aware of the crickets edging closer to our table.

"Okay," Lia mouths. To my dismay, the crickets are now zooming in on Henna's impromptu sculpture, giving Lia another chance to frall in the clear. She slams down the rest of her Kofasip and turns back to me. "Don't talk to him anymore, okay?"

"Whoa, you're giving out suggestions now too?" I whisper, annoyed. Her lip curls back. I wasn't planning on talking to him, but her thinking she can just order me around bothers me. Our heads are right up against each other, side by side, both of us holding our hands flat against our mics. The picture of unity, but it doesn't feel that way. She stays in place, her eyes insistent. "The suggestion's over," I say, choosing my words carefully. I haven't said I won't talk to him again.

"Plus ten," she mouths. "Let me know when you find out what your next suggestion is. I'm sure after your scene bombs with the Audience, Media1 will change their mind about any loveplot between you and Callen. Bek actually doesn't have much faith in the Initiative."

Bek. "Lia, about Bek—" A camera hums right behind me. The crickets are here. Filming our Revereless table. I shut up.

Anger builds in me all day. Aimed at the audience. I blame them for not watching me in the first place, which led to this mess with Revere. I don't care what everyone says—there's no way the timing of his cut was a coincidence.

When I leave school, a light rain is falling, and the anger is still with me, so I pass the bike rack and march to the theater. I need to know exactly what Bek said to Lia.

I rush into the auditorium, hoist myself onto the empty stage, push behind the velvet curtains, and emerge into the dimly lit backstage where Characters are perching on stools, chairs, and costume and prop trunks. Lia is the ringmaster at the center of their circle.

"This play is totally about becoming a whole person and how—"

"Um, Lia, can I talk to you—alone?" I interrupt.

Embarrassed, Lia shifts from foot to foot. The muffled roar of the lawn mowers is the only sound in the place, which gives me an idea.

"Is this important, Nettie, I was right in the middle of the—"

"It'll only take a few minutes," I insist, ignoring the whispering and the disapproving huffs from Ms. Pepperidge, the Drama Club adviser.

"Okay, okay," she says, looking around and shrugging, like *What can I do?* I lead her downstairs and out the door, veering over to the lawn. She makes a show of putting her hands over her head, as if the sprinkling of rain is too much for her to handle.

"Where do you want to meet on Sunday, for the Diary?" I improvise, speaking loudly into my mic.

"Your house," she says, puzzled. "Is that *it*? I have a club to lead."

"No, that's not all," I say into my mic, mind scrambling for something better. "I was thinking of visiting your mom. Maybe having company around will help her." The nearest lawn mower is only a dozen or so feet away and coming closer, and I touch her hand. My eyes are pleading her to understand that I need her to stay in place until they're near enough for us to frall properly.

"A visit probably won't help, but that's sweet of you, Nettie," she says warily.

The mower comes close enough, and I whisper, "Do you think it's possible Bek lied about the Patriots doing publicity? What exactly did she tell you?"

Lia looks down. Lia, who faces everything straight-on, is cutting off the connection between us. My touch on her hand changes to an iron grip, like I can squeeze the truth out of her, but I don't need to, because I think I get it. Bek didn't lie.

Lia did.

"I'll come over around ten," she says for the mics and then closes the space between us, whispering into my ear. A cool cucumber scent drifts over the grassy one—a new perfume for *voxless*.

"Nettie—I knew you obsessed about your dad, and I thought

you'd be able to focus on being a good Character if you had an answer . . . I wanted you to be happy. Does it really matter what the Patriots are doing?"

I drop her wrist. "Yes, it matters," I mouth angrily. "You *lied* to me. About something really important."

"Lied to help you," she says, fingering the band around her neck. "Haven't you been happier? Why are you asking, anyway? Did Scoop put you up to this?" she mouths, glancing back to the theater. She moves her face back to the mic. "Listen, I have to go. But we'll catch up later."

I shake my head. "Whatever," I say, turning around.

"Nettie," she calls as I start to walk away. "Onward through the turmoil?" she calls out, our old in-joke.

The faint desperation in her voice makes me the guilty one suddenly, so I turn back around and yell back, "Tomorrow beckons." I'm still angry, but it seems like sacrilege to leave the line hanging.

Click-click-click-click. My shoulders tighten as I hear the cameras in the ceiling swivel toward me. They were installed while I was at school yesterday. It's lucky they can't see what I'm thinking. Before leaving school, I tracked down Scoop and told him about Lia's lie. The look on his face was sad but not surprised . . .

Even if the Patriots aren't doing publicity, I still don't believe that Media1 is *experimenting* on them.

Ugh, I don't want to think about it.

I finish washing my hands and go downstairs, looking for something sweet before bed. Mom is at the dining room table, steam spiraling above her evening tea. A stack of paper lies by her elbow, and a newly installed 'bile unfurls from under the table and points its lens at her.

"Up late," she mutters, reading a scrap, placing it at the bottom of the pile, then filling in a line on the grid. She's compiling requests from library customers. Books from the Sectors used to be banned, but island writers can't keep up with the demand, so Media1 decided to let in some books, though they make sure to keep out books that reveal too much about the Sectors.

"Yeah, I am." I keep thinking about Revere. How cheerful he was. I never would have guessed he was on the E.L. The house reeked of the lavender disinfectant when I got home, but Mom seems calm enough now.

I wonder how Mom would feel about the Patriots if I told her Dana Cannery's theory. Would she be worried about my father?

"How's Fincher's going?" she asks.

I hesitate, but she has to know. "Mom, about Fincher's," I say as I begin a clandestine search for cookies—she baked some for her upcoming book club. I'm not supposed to have any; she worries about cavities.

"About Fincher's?" she repeats sharply.

I take a deep breath. "Mom, I'm going to apply for the high school math teacher apprenticeship. Mr. Black says I'll probably get it."

Mom drops her pen, and her chair screeches as she leaps up and rushes to the kitchen entryway. "But you've been preparing for Fincher's for so long!"

I shut the cabinet door before she suspects I've been cookie hunting. "I know. But I think I'll like this more than being a repairman."

"Really?" She sighs, exasperated. "Nettie, what's gotten into you?"

"Mom, it's all right. Everything's going to work out," I mumble, grabbing a pear instead. Thanks to her unspoken rules about fralling, I can't even begin to explain what really happened.

"Nettie, you've been so secretive lately," she says, following me into the living room. "And no food outside of the kitchen, you know that."

"I haven't been secretive," I snap. I sit on the couch and put the pear on the coffee table, wishing she'd go away.

"Well, why didn't you tell me about the apprenticeship earlier?" she asks, standing above me with her arms crossed. "You know you can talk to me if you're having problems. I'm here for you."

"Did you read that in *Perfect Your Parenting*?" I joke, sort of. Mom loves self-help books. Other notable titles I've seen over the seasons have been *Friends after Forty* and *Attention, Belief, Clarity: The ABC's of Adulthood*.

"No, I'm serious, Nettie. I'm worried." She takes off her glasses and puts them on the mantel above the fireplace, rubbing her eyes. "You've seemed different lately."

"I just feel like things are changing," I say, resting my head back on the couch and staring up at the ceiling. I can't tell her what's actually on my mind—we don't frall.

"What do you mean?" She sits down next to me. A lamp shines directly on her hair, and I can see a few new gray strands alongside the brown ones. Without her glasses, she seems softer, a little more approachable.

"With me and my friends." I try to think of something I can say on-camera. "Lia and Callen broke up."

"Oh." Mom purses her lips. "Tough for Lia. She must be relying on you a lot now."

"Yup, tough." I spin a letter opener on the table behind the couch—Mom collects them. She doesn't have much of an eye for aesthetics, unlike Violet or Eleanora Burnish, Lia's mom. I feel like a more normal mother would collect, I don't know, animal figurines or something.

"How about you?" she says abruptly. "How's your love life? Are you dating anyone?"

Eek. She's trying so hard to be the textbook mother now. At least I can use her interest to my advantage and add more to the plotline Luz says will definitely be broadcast.

"There's someone I like," I say slowly. A part of me still feels guilty about Lia, but, really, should I? She doesn't feel guilty about lying to me about the Patriots. "I think *I* actually, um, like Callen."

Mom makes a startled noise, but quickly composes herself. "That seems complicated." Mom hasn't had a boyfriend since my dad and always seemed more bemused than moved by the men who've asked her out.

"It is. I don't want to hurt Lia, and I'm not sure how he feels, anyway."

"Oh, these situations are hard," Mom says, gaze drifting toward the window behind me as she gets lost in memories. I wonder if they're about my dad. "Just be honest, and it'll work out."

Work out for who? Me, maybe, but not for Lia. "I hope so," I say, keeping it short and vague. "Anything new happen in the library today?"

Her face lights up. "Mr. Gardene brought in his poodle, Jingle. Cute dog, but he chews up dictionaries. I had to lay down the law . . ."

Hearing about Mom's job is a nice escape. I giggle as she recounts the showdown between her, Mr. Gardene, and the neurotic poodle, Jingle, and how the new cushioned reading space has been used more for napping than reading. Munching on my pear and listening to her work travails, I can almost fool myself into thinking everything's okay.

Chapter 12

Luz barks into the mic attached to the end of his headset. I can only make out bits and pieces like "better for everyone" and "I'll get them another." He throws the headset onto his cluttered desk when he's done, disgusted, and gestures me over to the couch, but I remain in front of his desk, clenching my hands, working up the courage to ask the questions that have been hounding me since Monday.

He's oblivious. "These bureaucrats," he grumbles, caressing the fallen headset like a kitten. He has the beginnings of a beard, a feeble attempt that only accentuates his youth. "Despite its obvious successes, the Initiative has met with some resistance." His voice becomes high-pitched as he mimics his Media1 bosses, wagging his finger at me like a disapproving teacher. "What if Characters hate their suggestions? What if the rewards don't entice them? What if they start complaining about the mobile cameras?" He sighs. "Why can't they be content to watch viewership climb?"

"Did you cut Revere so I could have the math apprenticeship? Because there wasn't any apprenticeship slot for him if

I took it?" I keep my voice level, but take a step closer to the desk.

Luz waves me over to the couch as he answers. "As reported in the Missive, Revere's ratings fell 10 percent below his target. He was on the E.L., and the producers' circle selected him to be cut. Besides, he hardly needed to be cut for you to get the apprenticeship—he could have just been anyassigned."

"It just seems like a strange coincidence." I remain standing. My shoulders are heavy, my book bag still on. "Even if he was on the E.L., what were the chances that *he'd* get cut at the most convenient time for me?"

Luz opens his mouth, ready with a response, but his eyes catch mine, and there's silence. He recovers in an instant. "Because of the Contract, I can't discuss Revere with you." Luz starts searching through the sea of objects on his desk. "Nettie, I'd much rather talk about you and your ratings. Sit down."

I ignore his order and plant my hands on his desk, leaning forward. I may not have the bulk of an Authority, but I'm hoping that I still can cut an intimidating figure in the small, narrow office. "Were you in the producers' circle? Did you say, *Let's cut Revere so we can give Nettie the teacher apprenticeship*? Did you do it because you knew Mr. Black would argue against me getting the slot with Revere still around?"

"Hypothetically, say that I had," Luz says tartly. "Would it really be so much worse than how any other cut is made?" He sifts through a paper clip spill. "Characters are added to the Eligibility List because they're not popular with the Audience.

The ultimate decision comes down to the vote of the producers' circle. There are no rules about how the decision's made there."

"If you won't tell me the truth about the cut, can you at least let me know where he's going? What happens to the Patriots?" I try to say it casually.

"You know I can't say. Besides, Nettie, what's it to you? You're so far from being a Patriot," he says, withdrawing the familiar green envelope from under a pile of rubber bands. He holds it up in the air. "Found it. Take a look. Nettie, please *sit down*."

"Okay." I remove my hands and retreat to the couch. He passes me the ratings envelope. I'm frightened by what it contains, the memory of last quarter's disappointing card still fresh, making my hands shake as I rip into the envelope.

I gasp when I see my mark. "Really?"

"The porch scene with Callen was a major hit with girls ages nine to eighteen," Luz says, triumphant. He rubs his hands together. "I knew you could do it."

I'm holding the contents of the envelope in my hand like they're sacred offerings. So many bills: 300 ceteks. A 200 cetek bonus for exceeding my target by way over the minimum 10 percent. The mark on the flat white card: 342. My predicted mark was 250. I can't stop the smile creeping onto my face. "I'm safe this week?"

"Yes, you're off the E.L. You should also know that I saved you from a fine. Your teachers might care about cheating on the math test, but you don't have to hide it from the Audience. You should have been more aware of staying on-mic while in the janitor's closet, especially since there is no camera coverage there—a situation that will be rectified."

"Right," I murmur, counting the bills again. "I'll be more aware."

"And of course, you're firmly on the path to getting the math apprenticeship. Clearly, your first week as part of the Initiative was an unqualified success. Are you ready to hear your next suggestion?"

"What is it?" I slide the money and card back into the envelope and put it in my jeans pocket. Selwyn wanted to go downtown and shop for *voxless* clothes tomorrow. Now I'll be able to buy some too.

"Three more conversations with Callen. I'll send you a Missive with more specific instructions for each. *Hi* doesn't count."

"More flirting, you mean?"

Luz jots notes on his yellow notepad and comments without raising his eyes. "If it comes naturally, sure. Only make sure you talk to him. I think you'll like the reward—I noticed how upset you were when your grandmother was fined for fralling. How would you like it if I ensured that she was never fined again?"

Getting Violet out of trouble permanently *and* getting to hang out with Callen again. "Yes, let's do it," I say right away, but I get quiet when I think about dealing with Lia.

"Fantastic. If you do as good a job as you did last week, your ratings are going to go through the roof," Luz says, getting up and stepping on a purple jumpsuit. He kicks it unceremoniously into the pile in the corner. "Do you have any more questions about the suggestion?"

"No," I say. "Just—Lia is so mad at Callen. I know she doesn't want me talking to him again."

"Listen, Nettie—there's more to life than being Lia Burnish's best friend. Lose the old idea of yourself. And help your grandmother." He comes around in front of the desk, stretching his arms like it's the first time he's moved around in ages. "Do you think the stars on *Blissful Days* put anyone before themselves? Start thinking like a star. What do *you* want?"

"I want to talk to him," I say without thinking. I could sit on the porch all day with him. Corner him in art class and ask him how he likes our new self-portrait project. Saunter up to him in the hallway after lunch and walk with him to his next class.

"That's what the Audience wants too." Luz turns around and shuffles through some papers, pulling out another envelope. "Here's the proof. I got permission from Media1 to share a fan letter with you. I thought it might be inspirational." He passes me the envelope. "You can read it on the set, if you want," he tells me. "Media1 won't broadcast it, but they won't fine you either."

"Oh, wow, crazy," I say, grabbing the envelope. I've never heard of anyone getting letters from fans. I never realized they'd *want* to write to us. Pretty plus ten. I put the envelope in my back pocket, next to my ratings card. Eager to get to it, I stand up, ready to leave, but the buzzing sound of a fighter jet catches my attention. Reflexively, I look out the window behind Luz, trying to get a glimpse, but the stone building behind Character Relations blocks the sky.

"Seems like things are pretty nasty in the Drowned Lands," I throw out, one last try for a clue about what they're doing with the Patriots there.

"Yeah," Luz says, sitting behind his desk again. "You should be happy your ancestors got out."

"They were from the Drowned Lands?" I frown. "*All* my ancestors? None from the mainland?"

"Almost all the Originals came from the Drowned Lands; they're the ones who needed the securities of the island the most."

Of course, it makes perfect sense. The poorest. Lia was wrong. We would have never been Zenta guttersnipes. Without the Originals, we would have been Drowned Lands peasants. Descendants of drownclowns, all of us.

Luz is bent over his yellow pad, writing something, leaving me with a full view of the stone building. My heart speeds up as I realize something: it's the perfect candidate, at the outskirts of the Center, far from Characters and the sets, and right near the beach—where the ships that take the Patriots away dock.

The Sandcastle.

A sharp electronic wail, and I tear my eyes away from the window. "Oh, God." Luz leaps up in the air, right arm thrust out, trying to reach the smoke alarm that's piercing our eardrums. He fails. "I keep telling them to stop smoking in the halls, but no one listens . . . God, the alarms on Bliss Island." Four seasons ago there was a massive fire in the Heights, and Media1 replaced all the old smoke alarms with supersensitive ones that candles and even cigarettes can set off.

"All right, see you next time," I yell. I clap my hands over my ears and rush out of the office, my exit slowed by other Reals. I can read their lips as they complain about having to leave the building, even though it's not an emergency. I glance over my shoulder—sure enough, Luz isn't exempt. He's pulling on a jacket as he sprints out of his office. Yet another alarm joins in the chorus, and I start running, eager to escape the noise.

Lia sprawls out on my bed, paging through the Diary, her long legs encased in tight dark jeans. I'm straddling my desk chair, half listening, half dwelling on my Character Report. She writes in flowing cursive, saying aloud, "Good Things. Well—" She stops and reaches behind her ear, our signal for the suggestion. "I've decided I'm going to visit the hospital and ask about counseling for Mom." She practically sings the words out. She's gotten better at pretending she wants to talk about this.

A fake self. I think. That's what the Initiative makes. But isn't it better than what I had before? The fan letter might shed some light on that. I glance over my shoulder at the letter, still in its envelope, lying next to the radio. Lia was already here when I got home, so I had to put off reading it.

"I think the counseling's a plus-ten idea." I rise slightly so I can see over her and check my hair in the mirror hanging on my closet door on the other side of the bed. I've been trying to keep it under control, to fit in better with *voxless*.

"Your turn," she says, pointing her pen at me. "Good Things?"

Good Things. I sit down again. I can't talk about my spectacular ratings. I can't talk about the moment I had with Callen on Monday. Given the situation with Revere, it feels like a mistake to call the apprenticeship a Good Thing. "I got a hundred on my math test," I say instead. The test Revere had graded. I can tell his handwriting from Mr. Black's. I see it peeking out of my folder on my nightstand, a missed reminder.

Lia laughs. "All right, human calculator." Her gaze shifts to the desk behind me. "You finished the radio, right? Does it work?"

I nod, still not sure if I should tell her about overhearing the Reals. "It works. You have to keep your ear glued to the receiver to hear it, though."

"Still counts," she says briskly, writing in the notebook. It's getting warm in here, and I open the window behind my desk, discreetly checking the porch for Callen. "All right, Bad Things." She bites the top of her lucky pen as she thinks. I can't mention those either. Learning that the Patriots are in the Drowned Lands. Revere. I struggle to think of camera-appropriate information.

"Nothing." I shrug.

"Gosh, living in Nettieworld must be nice. Very, very peaceful," she says with a tinge of sarcasm, scrutinizing me. I crack a weak smile.

"Well, moving on to me. This week," she says, turning on her side, "Mom kept us up with her crying last night." She records the event in the Diary.

I get up off the chair and lie down next to her, running my fingers through my hair to hide my face from the cameras.

"So, the counseling is a suggestion?" I mouth.

"Yeah. I'll survive, and they'll get Mom a cat. She's wanted one since she was a kid, but all her requests have been denied." New pets are as tightly regulated as pregnancy on the island, for the same reason—population control. "What's yours?"

I swallow hard and look away, staring at the shelves across from us. I can't get the words out. Then I notice that my books are out of order. Someone was in here. Sure enough, on the underside of the top shelf, I see a new 'bile, its red light beaming. Great.

Lia jabs me. "Just tell me," she mouths.

"Luz wants me to keep talking to Callen. If I do, the crickets won't bother Violet anymore."

Lia's eyes flutter, like someone who's been knocked unconscious coming back to life. "I knew it. They think you two are going to fall in love," she mouths slowly. "Or have you already?"

"In *love*?" I mouth. "Relax. You said yourself that Callen doesn't want anything to do with me. So how much farther can they go with it? Oh, guess what, I'm off the E.L." I hope she'll drop the Callen stuff now.

"About time," Lia mouths matter-of-factly. "Nettie. You should talk to him, but don't lead him on either. Hopefully, Media1 will pick up that you have no chemistry and let it go. Okay?" Her eyes drill into mine.

Part of me wants to be honest, like Mom said, but I don't want to upset Lia either. In the end, I just mouth, "Got it," and sit up, ending the discussion.

"Okay, Vows." She sits up straight, pushing her flame hair back and poising her pen. "Anything apprenticeship related?"

I slide back down into fralling position. This is when I appreciate my thick, dark, wavy hair the most, when it so effectively shields my face from the cameras. Lia follows suit. "Revere *was* cut so I could get the apprenticeship."

"Wait, that Initiative idea guy told you he cut Revere *for* you?" she mouths.

"No, but he didn't say he hadn't, so—"

"So you're jumping to conclusions." She begins to draw herself up again, and I reach out to stop her.

"Aren't you worried?" I whisper into her ear while pulling her back toward me. "About what they're going to do with him? We have a right to know."

"That's not what the Originals agreed to. God, Nettie, calm down. I thought you were over all that," she whispers. "Listen. I'm sorry I lied to you about Bek." She puts down her pen and gives my hand a squeeze. "That was wrong."

I'm grateful for the apology. We haven't spoken about it all week, and even though I'm not angry anymore, it's still been nibbling at the back of my mind.

"I understand why you did it," I mouth. "I know you just want me to be happy."

"Exactly," Lia replies, clasping my hand in both of hers now, and for a moment, things feel right between us again. We both laugh, a nice tension-releasing laugh.

I feel brave enough to continue. "I probably would have kept believing if I hadn't heard on my radio that—"

And with that, the moment's gone. Lia yanks away her hands away and shakes her head adamantly. "*No.* Nettie, knowing the publicity thing isn't true just means that you and Scoop have to live like everyone else on this island—trusting the company to keep them safe. It's in the Contract. It's what we promised."

I didn't promise anything.

Before we walk through the revolving doors into Delton's, Selwyn pauses to look at me. "Nettie, are you *sure* this is okay? Do you have enough money?"

"I have enough," I say. I scratch behind my ear, and she smiles knowingly.

"Plus ten," she murmurs, pushing on the glass door, and we walk onto Delton's marble floors, dodging perfume sprayers in the cosmetics section as we make our way to the escalators, headed toward the juniors section, third floor of five. I raise my head and gaze at the immense glass dome that caps the building, making it one of the highest buildings on the island. This is the first time I've felt like I belong at Delton's.

It's fun to shop with enough money to buy what I actually want. Selwyn takes charge, selecting outfits for me, giving me a thumbs-up or thumbs-down when I model her selections.

I take a break in the shoe department while she promenades, showing off sparkly stilettos. "What do you think? Imagine these with jeans at the Flower Festival. Like, casual sexy."

"Awesome," I say absently, running my hand along the bench, which is upholstered in velvet. The *voxless* music is soothing, a single guitar strumming a melody that Selwyn occasionally hums along to. It's been much easier lately to spend time with Selwyn than with Lia. No weird boy tension.

She stops in front of a three-sided mirror in an ornate gold frame, turning her foot to study the shoe from every angle. "Yeah, they're high, but I think I'll survive the parade. Looking camper—hot is worth it."

"I might skip this year." I've never really liked the Festival, and with my ratings climbing, I feel less compelled to attend the Special Events.

She turns from the mirror, distraught. "You don't want to go to the Festival?" she says. "But you'll miss the sing-along! *The coming of spring, the joy that it brings.*"

"I haven't decided yet," I hedge. "I've never had much fun at those things, but Lia makes me go . . . You know how she needs to be involved in *everything.*"

"That's just Lia," she says, bending down to pull off the shoes.

"Yeah." I stretch over the carpet and pick up the discarded stilettos, putting them back into the box next to the bench. "Lia's been getting sort of controlling. She's on the verge of forbidding me from *looking* at Callen."

"Well, have you been looking at him a lot lately?" she asks coyly. "Are you two . . . hanging out?"

"He seemed to like hanging out with me on the porch," I say. "I *would* like to talk to him more." I rub behind my ear.

"Plus ten. It's a tricky situation, but you two are so cute together. At least you don't tower over him, like Lia does," she says, doing a pirouette. "Whoa, check this out." She skips over to a rack and pulls out a clingy magenta dress with a low neckline and black belt. "Try this on. April twentieth, you in this dress, a total knockout."

I walk over and take the dress from her, holding it out dubiously.

"It will go so well with your earrings," she says. Way back in seventh grade, Lia, Selwyn, and I had gotten earrings and vowed to wear them for our Double A—identical imitation pearl drops, but in different colors.

"My earrings are more purple than magenta," I inform her. The dress is way too sexy for the ceremony. "Selwyn, do you want me to be the slut of the Double A?"

"No, no, no. Sexy, not slutty," she laughs. "Okay, maybe it's not for the Double A, but just try it on. You have to lose the old idea of yourself. Stop being so dowdy."

Lose the old idea of yourself. Luz's words. Does she realize that she's parroting Media1? Luz must write out what the other producers should tell their Characters. I examine the dress again, wondering if it really is that simple. Change my dress. Flirt with Callen. Be new, be fresh, be someone the Audience loves. Most of my life I've been seen but not really noticed. With a few suggestions, I'm changing—becoming better than I ever thought was possible.

I take the dress into the changing room and peel off my jeans and tank top. Dowdy, she called them, and suddenly my old look does seem plain. Is that how the Audience sees me? I shimmy into the dress and burst out into laughter when I see how different I look.

The dress hugs my curves, making me look at least three years older. I pull my hair back, and my eyes become bigger. I look like someone to watch.

Selwyn pops her head in. "See? *Sexy,*" she croons. "Beautiful, even. The hottest math teacher around."

I wince, the Revere guilt coming back. I gesture her inside the fitting room and pull her into a corner, out of the camera's range. "I talked to Luz about the math apprenticeship. He wouldn't say outright that Revere was cut for me, but he didn't deny it either."

Her mouth makes an O of shock.

"Do you have any ideas about what Media1 does with the Patriots? I've been thinking about them a lot lately." I haven't brought up the Patriots with Selwyn in a long time—like most Characters, she thinks all questions end with the Contract.

"I guess one of the rumors is true," she mouths. "But I don't really know which one."

"My radio tapped into walkie-talkie transmissions—Reals talking about sending the Patriots to caves in the Drowned Lands." I'm mouthing a lot more than I intended. Selwyn leans on the wall for support and shakes her head over and over. "Scoop thinks they might do medical experiments on them. There's a building behind Character Relations—it's called the Sandcastle, and that's where they keep them before sending them to the Sectors."

There's a long, long pause. Selwyn's lower lip is quivering now. "Nettie," she whispers, "I don't know why you're trying to dig this up or what you think you're going to find, but I need you to leave me out of it. I just want to stay on the island, get my cello apprenticeship, and help my family."

She's steps back, firmly on-camera. "You should buy that dress."

I glance down at the dress, suddenly unmoved by its sexiness, the whole exciting transformation seeming a million miles away. Scoop is the only one I can talk to about this stuff. I start changing, feeling unsteady. Scoop is nice, but it's Lia and Selwyn I depend on the most on the island, and it's like they've abandoned me.

"The dress might not be right for the Double A, but you'll find a good time to wear it." Selwyn puts the dress on the hanger slowly, her hand trembling, while I change. "You really do look fabulous in it, Nettie."

It's a pity compliment. She feels guilty because she's not supporting me.

"I'll take it." The dress is definitely not for the Double A, but I have the cash, so why not?

"Yay," Selwyn says, picking up the shoebox. "I'll get these."

As we make our way to the cash register, she finds a dark blue pencil skirt, sleeveless silk top, and sparkly silver socks for me, and a pair of tight pants for herself. By the time we exit Delton's, she's back to her cheerful self. Trundling along with bags in both hands, she stops at every store window, cooing over rings and lamps and toys. She yanks me past the yarn store and the Game Palace, stopping in front of a window with sticker sheets on display. I'm puzzled until I notice the ceramic arm next to one of the sheets, an eagle etched on its biceps. Aha: they're not stickers, they're sample tattoos. The sign above the door confirms it: INKED UP.

"Isn't that one pretty?" She points to a rose.

"Yes . . . but I thought you decided *not* to get one." I wait to see if she scratches behind her ear.

No. Arms stay at her sides. "I haven't changed my mind. Too permanent." She shudders. "But I thought I'd say hi to Garrick," she says, grasping the door handle tentatively.

I hesitate. I don't want to tell her what to do, exactly. That's a Lia move. "Just remember, he's not really boyfriend material, okay, Selwyn?"

"Don't worry. I know that. Besides, it's not ab—" She pauses and shakes her head. "Actually, Nettie, I think I might be a while. You can go on without me."

"Okay," I agree. "But be careful." She enters, and I stay long enough to see Garrick saunter over and shake her hand, the old devilish smile on his face. I hope she stays smart.

As soon as I get home, I grab the fan letter and sit on my bed. The handwriting is labored and big. A young girl's writing.

Dear Nettie,

I turned eleven last month, and I've watched Blissful Days my whole life. I am so excited about you and Callen being together! You were so cute on the porch swing. My mother, brother, and I started looking at archived episodes featuring you, too, and I guess I never realized how cool you were before. Mom says that you're just like your parents: funny, tough, and smart.

Sincerely,
Kat Deva

I fold the letter back into the envelope and put it on the night table. Callen and me *being together*. She sees things the way I've always wanted them to be. I feel like I'm so close to making what seemed like ridiculous fantasies a reality, thanks to the Initiative. So close . . . but I don't know if it'll happen without Lia detonating.

I get up and start putting my new purchases away. But the

letter keeps running through my head. Especially the last line. *You're just like your parents.* She must have meant *parent,* because she's too young to have seen my father. But she'd written *funny, tough, and smart.* Mom is obviously smart. Mom maybe is tough, if you count hushing up Characters in the library. But I don't think Mom is very funny.

Chapter 13

I linger outside the history classroom, waiting for class to let out. Callen's inside, and Lia is too—it's the site of the great battle over the seats. I'm going to try to bump into Callen as he leaves. I have a plan. I recite it to myself. *Is your mom stressed out about the Flower Festival?* Ms. Herron is in charge of the Arbor neighborhood float. *Does she need help? I could come by after school this week.* If I volunteer for the Arbor float, I'm bound to run into Callen. Three conversations should be easy.

Hopefully my asking now counts as one. I'm jittery, and seeing Lia makes it worse. *Forget her.* I take a step closer to the classroom. I have to do this. For Violet's security and even for little Kat Deva. But most of all for me.

I painted my nails for *voxless* last night, with the Temptress Tin nail polish Lia had left me when she came over to do the Diary, and this morning I put on the new socks I bought with Selwyn yesterday. I did the Skin Sequence, and I dug up some makeup Selwyn bequeathed to me for a birthday party.

I'm as ready as I'll ever be.

The bell rings, but Mr. Primer's determined to make them stay until he's done with his lecture. While I wait, I wander over to Henna Shelter's poster for the Drama Club play auditions. The play's title is *The Big Steal,* the words encircled by cetek bills.

"Enjoying the view?" Scoop joins me in front of the poster. I'm glad to see him.

"Yeah, it's a nice poster. I have something to give you." I'd wanted to pass him a note about the Sandcastle in math earlier, but Terra had taken my seat again and Mr. Black was on time for once.

"A surprise gift. Lucky me," Scoop says. In a light blue button-down shirt and nice khaki slacks, he hasn't changed much for *voxless.*

"Don't get too excited—it's just notes for the test." I scrounge in my book bag for the note. Buried in the string of math tips is my idea that the stone building behind Character Relations is the Sandcastle.

"Thanks. Every little bit helps," he says, casually tucking the papers into the book on whales he was reading during math.

I peer into the history room again, and Scoop chuckles.

"Callen?" he guesses, tossing the book from hand to hand playfully.

"Shhh." I whip my head around and scratch behind my ear fiercely.

"Oh, okay." He nods. "Sometimes I think Callen might kind of like you too."

"Really?" Now he has my attention. "Why? Has he . . . said anything?"

Finally, the history room door swings open, and the students pour out. Scoop takes off, saying something about needing to get to physics on time.

Callen is nearly the last to leave the classroom, but he sees me and smiles. For a second, everything seems simple.

Then a familiar voice makes me look away.

"Nettie, were you waiting for me?" Lia strides out of the classroom. "Nice nails," she says, holding up her hand to show off her identical ones.

"Um." Callen's still standing in the hall. He has to be waiting for me. I reach behind my ear, hoping that Lia will see the gesture and step aside, but her gaze just drifts behind me to the poster.

"The poster looks amazing," she sighs, positioning herself beside it so a nearby camera can get a good shot of her. "Doesn't it?"

"Yeah, plus ten," I agree, but she needs more and waves to a passing Pastel, one who I think is a stagehand for Drama Club. Skinny, skittish Geraldine Spicer, who seems surprised that Lia noticed her.

"What do you think of the poster, Gerry?" Lia calls. I take a furtive step away from them, but Lia shoots me a glance, eyebrows raised, and I stop and turn back to gaze at the poster with her and Geraldine. Out of the corner of my eye, I can see that Callen's still waiting for me. He didn't see Lia's *stay* signal.

"*The Big Steal* is such a great title, and the cetek bills fit perfectly. It makes you want to know more." Geraldine bobs her head enthusiastically.

The second bell rings, and I catch Callen's eye, but he shrugs and starts walking down the hall in the opposite direction.

"Literature, Nettie," Lia says, abandoning Geraldine with a smile and dragging me down the hall. "Mom's going to go to that counseling appointment I made for her at the hospital."

"That's great, Lia," I respond, using all my strength to resist the urge to turn around and run after Callen. You'd think she'd help me with my suggestion, since she's so diligent about her own. Did she get me away from Callen on purpose?

"Selwyn says you bought a sexy dress yesterday," she says, walking fast. "I'm sure it looks nice, but probably not the right fit for the Double A."

"*Understood,*" I snap. She seems oblivious to my irritation, holding up her arms and fluttering her fingers about, examining the nail polish.

I return home that afternoon, defeated. I wanted to try to talk to Callen at lunch, but he and Rawls ate in two minutes flat and took off. Art was a failure too, after Ms. Shade's instructions to "paint with silence as your inspiration."

I have five more days.

After dinner, I curl up on my bed and halfheartedly page through *The Player in the Attic* before tossing it aside. "Boring," I mutter into my mic. I put down *Player* and pick up *Blissful*

Nature, the book Violet gave me. I flip to the back, where there's a map of the island ringed in blue. My eyes drift southwest, to where the Drowned Lands should be. Where Luz said the Originals came from. How long did it take them to get to Bliss Island? I wonder how long it will take Belle and Revere to make the reverse journey.

I pinpoint where they are now, the approximate space where the Sandcastle is, behind Character Relations, though there's nothing that marks the Center on the map, so that the Audience remains ignorant of its existence.

Avalon Beach is marked and the neighborhoods are all there: the Granary, the Heights, Treasure Woods, Four Corners. I'm drawn into a long section about the Brambles. *As the largest green space on the island, the Brambles attract thousands of migrating birds every spring, many moving from the chillier climate of the northeast.* The mainland Sectors. *The diversity of birds found on the island is the greatest in the world. Come spring, the birds will leave the Brambles and fly off the island, headed southwest.* To the Drowned Lands.

An idea occurs to me: Callen talked about missing the Brambles—maybe he'd be interested in the book. I could give it to him now.

I go over to my window and see that his car—a hand-me-down junker with a lopsided antenna—is there. I grab *Blissful Nature* and dash outside, conscious of the cameras embedded in the trees and of a neighbor mowing the lawn across the street. I ring the doorbell, practicing what I'll say. To Callen's parents: *Is*

Callen here? To Callen: *Here's a book.* I frown. Not good enough. *Here's a book I thought you'd like.*

After what feels like a month, his mother answers the door, her hands and arms encased in long yellow gloves with traces of dirt on them, like nature's embroidery.

"Didn't mean to keep you waiting, Nettie. I was out in the garden," she says, standing in the door frame. She has the same blue eyes as Callen, but hers are icier.

I fumble with my words. "Yes, um, Callen's not expecting—I brought this book over for him."

She steps back, which I take as an invitation. "Callen," she calls upstairs as I sidle inside, her voice reverberating in the spacious front hall. The interior of his house is solemn as a cathedral. The walls are covered in dark blue wallpaper with golden vines, and plants in exquisitely patterned ceramic pots provide most of the decoration.

A few seconds pass, then we hear steps overhead. Should I ask her about the float?

"I think he was napping," she confides. She sees the book's cover and her eyes light up. "What's that? A nature guide?"

"Sort of. My grandmother gave it to me." I pass *Blissful Nature* over and watch as she peels off a glove and pages through it, clicking her tongue admiringly at the pictures.

Callen appears at the head of the stairs, hair rumpled, tufts sticking up like hay. His voice is thick with sleepiness. "Hey, Nettie," he says, blinking a couple of times as he descends the stairs. "What's up?"

"Nothing much," I say hastily. "I was just reading this book that my grandmother gave me, and there's this section about the Brambles that made me think of you. So, here, I'm lending it." I am talking superfast, almost like a Real. It's awkward coming over here, not as natural as it was just running into him on his porch.

His mother yawns as she hands the book to him.

"Callen, honey, can you finish watering the garden for me?" she asks apologetically. "I'm just so tired after today's back-to-back Festival meetings." It's my chance to ask about helping out with the float, but my mouth is dry, my whole body suffused with shyness and fear.

"Not a problem," Callen says, patting her back.

"Nice to see you, Nettie," she says, and heads upstairs. I'm too nervous to even get out a good-bye. Callen sets the book down and finds his sneakers. I watch as he bends to lace them up, but I can't think of anything to say.

Maybe those few words sufficed? My Missivor will tell me.

"I think I'll go home," I croak.

He stands up in the blink of an eye, body unfurling with the same graceful movements that define him on the baseball field. "Wait, do you want to come outside?"

"Yeah, okay," I say quickly, not giving myself any time to chicken out. I can't tell whether he actually wants me here or is just being polite, but I'm encouraged by his smile.

"This way—it's faster." He leads me downstairs, through the basement, piled high with gardening tools and seeds and fertilizer, and out into the blooming backyard. A rabbit sees us, freezes, then races into the bushes.

Bees and butterflies tangle among the flowers and plants, their vivid colors swirling together like a finger painting. Callen unravels the hose curled up at the back of the house while I watch the lilies bobbing in the breeze at the outer edge of the garden.

"I see your mom out here every morning," I say, jumping back as he turns on the faucet. Droplets fly in the air, making a rainbow.

"She's dedicated," he says, squinting as he aims the hose toward the hollyhocks against the fence. "She lucked out—she was anyassigned to the Botany Society."

"You're kidding. That is lucky." I follow him down a woodchip trail to the back of the garden, where waves of flowers break against a row of pine trees.

"It's a nice surprise—you stopping by. We've been next-door neighbors for years, but you never visited before," he says, watching the water fall over a patch of violets. "But I guess you surprise me a lot. I just can't tell what you're thinking, Nettie. Like, why did you ditch me in the hall today? I thought you wanted to see me."

"Ditch you in the hall?" I ponder the statement for a few seconds. "Do you mean after history, when Lia—I didn't think I was ditching you, she—"

"It's okay," he interrupts. "That's not the only time I've been curious about what you were thinking. I used to wonder about you during lunch, when you were always so . . . watchful. You've always been sort of mysterious."

"Me?" I say. "Thanks. Or . . . sorry? I don't know—is that a compliment?"

He smiles. "You decide."

"Well, I don't mean to be mysterious," I say, thinking about the last few weeks and dealing with Luz and the apprenticeship. I do feel like I've been hiding a lot. Lia said Callen would freak out if I told him about the suggestions, but I could just tell him a little. Dispel the mystery. "It might be because of the Initiative," I whisper.

Callen moves a few feet over, putting us out of the range of the cameras in the pine trees. "I'm not in it," he mouths. "What are they making you do?"

Straight to the point, of course.

"Random stuff, like about getting my apprenticeship," I mouth. He raises a sandy eyebrow.

I pretend I don't get that he wants to know the actual suggestions. "I came up with a signal, to tell people when something's a suggestion." I demonstrate for him.

He stares at me pointedly for a second, as if he's waiting for me to say more, but I don't, and he does a sort of half shrug. "Smart," he says, easing us back on-camera.

And that's it. He hauls the garden hose toward the sunflowers. The greenery is thick here, and I have to swat away leaves.

"Yeah, sometimes she goes overboard with the plants," he

says, even though I haven't said anything. "Anything new at the lunch table?"

"Not really," I say, gliding over Revere's absence. "Martin's around a lot now. Henna Shelter too."

"Still Lia's show, then?" he says, shaking his head. "I don't miss it." *Or her* goes unsaid, but I hear it. He turns the water off, and side by side, we walk to the front of the house. My hand drags along the rosebushes as we round the corner.

"I miss you at lunch," I blurt out when we reach the bottom of the porch steps. The fading light blurs his features, but he's so close, I can feel his breath on my skin.

"I miss having lunch with you too," he says quietly.

Panic seizes me. Followed by guilt slamming down. I almost feel like Lia is here, watching everything and hating me, realizing that I actually do like Callen . . . and that maybe he likes me too. "I should go catch up on *Player in the Attic*." I step back.

Flustered, he looks away, and I see his disappointment in the way his eyes fall and his jaw twinges, like he wants to say something, but can't.

My bike ride to school feels like flight. I barely have to push the pedals. The sky is cloudless. Must be natural, not scripted, since I didn't hear the helicopters last night, and I was up past midnight, thoughts racing. I had received the Missive confirming my conversation with Callen in the garden counted toward fulfilling the suggestion, then I got a second Missive inviting me to a Makeup Session at the Center on Thursday.

I'm unstoppable, I think as I breeze into Bliss High, grinning all through my morning chat with Lia and Selwyn at our lockers.

"What's gotten into you?" Lia asks. She's brushing her hair in front of her locker mirror. Selwyn starts humming again.

"Nothing," I sing. I squeeze my face next to hers, trying to get a closer look at my own hair, which I'd braided this morning.

"There's not really room for two," she says, closing the locker.

"Okay," I reply, not wanting to start an argument. I do a quick scan of the hall, searching for Callen. I walked away out of guilt yesterday, but I'm ready to continue our conversation now. I want to tell him that I'm shy, not mysterious. The bell rings, though, before I find him.

The day zooms by, and soon it's nearly lunchtime and I'm back at the lockers with Selwyn, who's been in a bad mood all day.

"I wish I had a crush. That's so sweet, Callen helping his mother with her garden and you joining in," she says, pulling at the collar of her black turtleneck. It's too hot for it, but I guess she wanted to stick with *voxless,* and it was the only black she had. "I'll never have anything like that."

I guess she and Garrick didn't rekindle anything. "It was nice," I allow, not wanting to encourage her self-pity. Over her shoulder, a cricket with a camera approaches us. I recognize her from the aquarium.

"We'd like a reenactment," she says. This time I understand her right away. "Starting with 'I wish I had a crush.'"

Selwyn nods, repeating the line to me. We do the scene over

and over again, and I'm happy to do it, sunnily delivering my lines.

When it's over and the crickets have left, Selwyn and I finish putting our book bags in our locker, and I notice a note, folded into a triangle, at the bottom of my locker. Someone must have slipped it through the grate.

"Just a minute," I say, kneeling. I unfold the note and squint in the locker's darkness. My body shelters it from the cameras behind me and the one inside the locker can't crane down. Scoop's handwriting. *I think you're right. Come to the Sandcastle with me?*

I do want to know what's in that stone building, but getting in is a whole other level of dangerous. I stare at the note for a second, all the shock of his aunt Dana's theory returning, pummeled by images of Revere and Belle, and even the father I don't remember, chained to hospital beds. *But Ms. Cannery did have an active imagination.* I crumple up the note and put it in my pocket. I've already done a lot for Scoop.

"Okay, let's go." I stand, and we head to the cafeteria.

Selwyn stares listlessly at the food, not even noticing the pileup of Characters behind her as she stops the line. I grab her plate and put a hamburger on it.

"Selwyn, it'll work out," I assure her, looking over at our table in the distance. Scoop is there. Ordinarily I'd think he was a better addition than Martin, but I sigh, knowing he's going to ask me about the note.

I straighten my shoulders as I approach the table, determined to appear unfazed by his presence. Scoop flashes me an easy grin as I sit, and continues his debate on the pros and cons of the newest model Harrow, the fancy car the Herrons recently bought, with Lincoln. Martin keeps trying to insert himself, but they deftly divert the conversation away from him.

"Henna and I are finalizing the Double A program this week," Lia informs me. Henna sits on her other side, a silk purple scarf wrapped around her head, nodding along. "We're thinking a star by each name in the listings and then on the cover, like, a starscape, with planets and meteors. What do you think, Nettie?"

"That's like when we had to draw the solar system in third grade," I say without thinking.

"You think it's childish." Henna's lip curls upward.

"Yeah, thanks, Nettie," Lia says sarcastically. "Can always trust you to speak your mind."

"I think it's perfect for the Double A. It's important. Of cosmic significance," Scoop says from across the table.

Lia laughs and kicks me under the table. "Talk to him," she whispers when I look over.

I shake my head. "We're math friends," I say to her, lowering my voice. "That's *it*."

"Math friends. I need one of those. Oh, Nettie, guess what?" Lia says. "Lincoln's having a party Thursday night, since we have Friday off for the Flower Festival. He's calling it the Antithesis," she explains, eyes sparkling. "So we're all going to dress the opposite of how we normally would."

"Nettie, that dress we got on Sunday would be perfect," Selwyn pipes up, speaking for the first time since we got to the cafeteria. I'd almost forgotten she was here.

"True," I agree. I notice she's cut her hamburger up, but hasn't had a bite. Her hands are in her lap. "Are you okay?" I ask. "Is this about the cello?" Her eyes are shimmering—is she crying?—and she just looks at me, her lower lip quivering again. She moves her hand to her collar. "Is something wrong with your neck?" I guess. "Do you need to see a doctor?"

She starts to speak, but Scoop interrupts us. "Nettie, did you have time to take a look at that problem set I left in your locker?"

Caught. "So, Scoop," I say, turning to him. "I can't help you with that stuff anymore. I have too much of my own homework."

He doesn't miss a beat, just nods and bites into an apple.

Lia latches on to the conversation. "It's true. Nettie doesn't have time for private tutoring anymore now that she'll be assisting Mr. Black."

"I understand," Scoop says, picking up his tray and angling his head toward Terra's table. "I'm going to finish up over there. See you."

Part of me wants to call him back and apologize.

Lia watches him, smirking. "Nettie, poor Scoop is hurt because you don't want to talk to him. I can think of some ways to make him feel better. Why don't you—"

"He'll be fine." I pick up my burger again, but now I've lost my appetite.

The conversation takes off again as Lia discusses paper stock with Henna, and Martin and Lincoln trade Antithesis ideas. I sneak a glance at Scoop's table, long enough to see he's already immersed in conversation there. I'm not sure he can pull off getting into the Center alone. What if he gets caught? I'll feel responsible.

"Since it's the Antithesis, how about fruit juice instead of alcohol?" Martin suggests.

"Don't go overboard," Lincoln scoffs. "It's still gotta live up to the standards of past Grayson parties, and that means booze."

Lia chuckles, and Henna smirks. Only Selwyn doesn't react, and the food on her plate is still untouched.

"Are you upset about Garrick? What happened when you saw him?" I hiss, furious. He's done it again. This is exactly how it used to be: she'd see him, then be depressed for days.

"Not him—it's nothing," she says, casting her eyes down to her tray.

I don't believe her. "I can't stand him," I declare, amped up. "He's such a loser. He thinks he's so cool, that's what *makes* him such a loser. I can't believe Callen was ever friends with him."

Lia turns from her conversation with Henna. "What about Callen? Have you been talking to him?" she interjects. Selwyn picks up her fork and stabs into her hamburger, relieved the attention's off her.

"I saw him last night while I was helping out in his mom's garden," I say. I need to get out of this. "By the way, I think you should go with the high-quality paper. The programs are meant to be saved."

"I agree." Henna tucks an errant lock of hair back underneath her turban in one swift motion. "It's just a matter of persuading the rest of the committee."

"Of course." Lia nods, but her eyes wander back to me, and I know she's dying to ask me more about my conversation with Callen.

I stand abruptly, nearly knocking my chair down, and mumble something about needing fruit.

At the counter, I grab an orange and roll it in my hands, watching the cafeteria. I'm not ready to go back to the table and face Lia. Does she even have to be involved? *She's* not dating him anymore.

"Nettie, hey." Callen comes up to me. Only a few inches separate us, and I can smell that soap he uses, with woodsy undertones. "I took a look at that book you gave me."

"*Blissful Nature*? What'd you think?" The words come out smoothly enough. I feel less nervous here than at his house.

"I liked it," he says. His hands are empty, I realize. He doesn't seem to be here to do anything but talk to me. I'm not going to run away from him like I did last night. I can't stay worried about Lia forever. "It inspired me. I'm going to skip the Flower Festival and spend the day in the Brambles instead. Some nature might be nice after the party."

"You mean the Antithesis? You're going?" I say, glancing back at my table. Lia locks eyes with me. I hesitate, the guilt rising again. My hand rises, about to scratch behind my ear, but I resist the urge. Callen knows about the signal now.

"For sure. You are too, right?"

"Definitely." I toss the orange from hand to hand, and he steals it in a flash, smiling. I try to snatch the orange back, but he steps out of my reach, smile growing wider. Rawls's voice calls him back from across the cafeteria.

"Here," he says, handing me the orange before he goes. I watch him walk back, waiting to calm down before going to my own table.

I sit down and dig my Temptress Tin nails into the tough orange skin. Selwyn's knee bumps into mine under the table. "I saw you two up there," she whispers, the most lively she's been all lunch. "He likes you." I put my fingers to my lips warningly.

Lia watches me peel the orange. "What were you guys talking about?"

"Nothing, just, um, I lent him this book."

"That so?" Her eyes are hard and flinty.

"He's coming to the Antithesis," I add. I can't tell if she's digging because she's suspicious or because she thinks it's what the Audience wants. She chose Callen to be her boyfriend for ratings, and she'll make the most of him being her ex-boyfriend for the same reason.

"Of course he is," she says, rolling her eyes. "Callen pretends he's above it all, but he loves being surrounded by trac groupies at parties." My heart falls. Like all of Lia's bitchy comments, the sting comes in there being an iota of truth. But I let it go. I'll let him show me what he's there for instead of having her tell me.

Chapter 14

I've never been at the Center this late. In the darkness, I keep stepping right into the litter that I'm always so careful to avoid during my daytime trips for Character Reports. Dozens of the Authority pass by for what I guess must be a shift change, marching into a concrete barracks. I duck across the road and out of their way.

I pass the apartment buildings on my way to the Character Relations offices and smell roasting meat. Smoke eddies up into night sky, and out by the pool I see a grill glowing and the dark forms of Reals doubled over with laughter. Bottles clink amid carefree howls and exuberant conversation. A splash as a flabby Real cannonballs into the pool.

Their frivolity sounds menacing to me, as if they're just minutes from rioting. I cross the road and climb the stairs to the fourth floor of the Character Relations Building. Dr. Kanavan is at the head of the stairs, her blond curls drawn in her usual loose bun.

"Welcome, Nettie. I won't be leading this Session, but I design the curriculum, and it will take place in my office." She guides me down the dimly lit hall, white lab coat swishing as she leads me into her office and has me sit on a stainless-steel table.

"Your skin has improved," she observes, her finger at her chin.

"Thanks, I've been better about the Skin Sequence," I say proudly.

"Yes, yes, it's about time. I'll let Til know you're here." She leaves, and, alone, I examine my surroundings. The shining scale. The calendar and the X's counting down to her next furlough. Zenta. Where the Patriots aren't.

A white shade lifts in the breeze at the far corner of the room.

I can't pass up the opportunity. I know I'll get a better view of the Sandcastle from up here than from the second-floor producers' offices. I dash over to the window and poke my head around the shade, heart beating fast.

Since the Sandcastle is set farther down the hill leading to the beach, I can see directly into what appears to be a well-lit courtyard.

Swirling shadows punctuated by beams of high-intensity spotlights reveal sweaty, bedraggled faces. Faces I recognize.

Patriots.

They're running laps around the courtyard. It's some kind of obstacle course laid out around the central square of grass. A few Authority are in the middle of the square, watching. What had Scoop's aunt said? *Fitness results.* Vaulting over hurdles, crawling through a mud pit, swinging on monkey bars. They pass directly under a glaring light, and one by one, I recognize them.

First I pick out a nurse who worked with Selwyn's mother, cut a season ago. But I forget about her when I see a familiar face, now thin and hollowed. Hazel eyes stare out dully from behind her crooked tortoiseshell glasses. Her hair is short, in a buzz cut. Belle. She moves by, shrouded in darkness. In the center, a cricket's drilling them, though I can't hear what he's saying.

One Patriot separates from the rest, stumbling forward and grasping a lamp pole. I gasp—it's Revere, retching. His ponytail is shorn, and he has bristly porcupine hair now, just like Belle. His hands are on his knees as vomit spatters his fatigues. He looks up and squints, his gray eyes widening with surprise. *Does he see me? No, he can't.* But he lifts his hand in a saluting sort of motion that I think is a wave hello, and I lift mine in response. He smiles feebly.

I hear heels coming down the corridor, so I release the shade and hoist myself onto the examination table with shaky hands. The Real who walks in bumps into a cabinet and apologizes profusely in a helium-high voice. She reminds me of the way Witson acted at Fincher's, when he'd skulk around, trying to see me.

"I'm Til," she says. She's short, her elfin face swallowed by voluminous chestnut hair. She has smooth, cinnamon-colored skin.

"Hi, Til," I respond, my voice robotic. Why would they get them in shape before medical experiments? That doesn't make sense. What I saw would weaken them, not make them better subjects. Unless being put through those maneuvers is part of the test.

"I'm here to show you how to apply makeup in a way that will make the cameras love you even more," she warbles.

I picture the Patriots in their camouflage—like they're in the army and they're being trained. How does the Contract put it? *Enlisted in the service of Media1.* Just like you would enlist into an army . . . but why would Media1 have an army? They're a television company.

Til goes over to the corner, regulation purple jumpsuit scratching. She walks back to me, pushing a rolling mirror. She positions the mirror in front of me, then presents me with a white-and-pink cotton bag. "These will be your instruments. The tools to make you beautiful!" She has trouble meeting my gaze straight on. *Is she starstruck?* Lia always complains about the Reals being nervous around her. Is this what it's like?

"I can't wait," I say, forcing myself to smile. What was the word Scoop's aunt had used? *Batch.* They send them out in batches. The latest batch is outside now? I catch myself looking over at the blocked window again, and I take a deep breath and try to focus on the makeup.

Til pulls out a tube from her teaching kit. "This is your lipstick. Take out the identical one in your bag."

I've used makeup before, but under Til's tutelage, I learn how to maximize its effectiveness. For instance, I should also be using lip liner and powder when I put on lipstick, to make the color last longer.

Til leads me through tips and tricks with mascara, foundation, blush, and eyeliner. By the end, I can see that my face does look more camperf.

"Love it," Til squeaks. "Do you like your new face?"

"It looks really nice," I say. Not a lie. I have more defined cheekbones and my oft-lamented muddy brown eyes have a new depth to them, framed by eyeliner and eye shadow. Wiser. Older. I draw back, wondering if it's the makeup or if what I saw aged me. Is this who the Audience always wanted?

"You're going to wow them at the party tonight." Til smiles.

The party. Scoop will be there—I can tell him what I saw.

"Are you finished?" Dr. Kanavan asks primly from the doorway. "I need to get out of here," she says with a yawn, bringing the back of her hand to her mouth demurely. She doesn't wait for us to answer, just walks in and pulls the mirror back into place. Til gathers up her supplies and bounds out of the room. I linger, packing up my new makeup bag slowly.

I watch Dr. Kanavan tidy up errant files on her desk and think about our relationship. I've listened to her brag about her vacations. Tried to please her with my weight and my skin, like an obedient puppy. I've always been eager to prove how stoic I could be with the vaccination sequence. I've spent a lot of time trying to make everyone at Media1 happy.

She reaches for the television, then remembers I'm still here.

She turns and faces me, finger poised over the on button. "Don't you have a party to get to?"

"That's right," I say, jumping off the table and grabbing my book bag off the floor. "Thanks for *everything*," I mutter as I leave, but the noise from the television masks my sarcastic comment.

Chapter 15

I shiver as I knock on the door of the Graysons' beach house. I'd changed into the Delton's dress in the bathroom of the Tram stop near the beach, and now I'm wondering if I should have worn something with sleeves instead. After seeing the Patriots running around in their camouflage, I feel foolish in the sexy dress and new makeup.

I smush my face against the front window, trying to see through the thick curtains, wanting to find Scoop as soon as possible.

"Nettie, why are you out here all alone? Did you knock?" Selwyn scampers up the steps. "Oooh, you look nice. Is that mascara?" She seems to be shaking off the blues that have dogged her all week.

"Yeah, a little," I mumble, knocking again. I wish I could tell her what I'd seen at the Center, but she'd freak out again, like she did at Delton's. Freak out big time. She might even faint or something. I feel resentment prickling in me. I want her to be stronger.

"You look a little like Lia," she observes. "With your makeup like that. Sharper cheekbones."

"Really?" Til must show everyone the same techniques.

"It looks good, though, don't worry. Lia won't mind," she assures me. She's wearing heels, and we can see eye to eye. Her wide smile is a flash of white in the darkness. "And this looks as plus ten as it did on Sunday." She reaches over and plucks at the fabric of my dress, and I realize she's in a sweater and jeans. The sweater isn't even *voxless*; it's a soft pink cashmere, probably from *blueblood*. And there's another turtleneck underneath it.

"You're kind of dressed down, aren't you?"

She giggles and tosses her head. "The antithesis, silly! I'm wearing the *opposite* of what I'd normally wear."

"Yeah, you sure are." I knock on the door again, harder. Nothing.

Selwyn reaches around me, turns the knob, and pushes it open. She walks in, grinning at me over her shoulder. "You're out of it, huh?"

"I can't believe I didn't try that earlier." I follow her inside. She has a skip in her step . . . it's almost too much, like her last suggestion was to *be incredibly peppy and upbeat.*

Hypnotic *voxless* music, at the highest volume allowed by Media1, pulses through the house, and we go to the den, which is teeming with drunk teenagers. Their faces are glistening with sweat, and the room stinks of beer.

"Yikes." Selwyn presses closer to me as we dump our bags in the pileup at the entrance and make our way through the crowd, aiming for the table at the back where beverages are usually laid out.

"Nettie! Selwyn!" Martin booms, looking foolish in convict stripes—the opposite of a politician, I guess? They hug his middle-aged-man belly, and his glasses are steamed from all the heat in the room. He's pressed against a cabinet containing nautical-themed china. I smile tightly, deliberately staying on the move. Caren Trosser tosses handfuls of confetti in the air as she leaps across the room like a deer. Beryl Shiner, a freshman, and Shar Corone, the guy from my art class who used to sit next to Belle, are twined together in a corner.

The host himself, Lincoln, is wearing torn-up jeans and a T-shirt with an obscene word in large bold letters. He's directing a drinking game that involves pebbles on a cleared-off coffee table. Witson drinks, then slams a shot glass down after he . . . loses a pebble? He clamps his hand over his face, worried he's going to throw up. I make the mistake of gawking—I've never seen Witson so much as sip a beer—which he takes as an invitation and comes wobbling over.

"Nettie, you're here! So plus ten," he gushes. "I was waiting for you." His thin brown hair has been teased up with massive amounts of gel.

"Hi, Witson." I grimace, moving firmly ahead, Selwyn still at my side. He follows us all the way to the drinks table at the back of the room, right in front of a window.

Moonlight falls over his face, illuminating it in a ghastly way. I remember the way Belle's face was lit up in the courtyard, and I shudder.

"Are you all right?" Witson asks, lurching forward and touching my elbow.

"Yeah, I'm fine." I pull away, and he's clearly crestfallen. Annoyance twinges me. Why can't he just move on?

"I wish you still came to the store," he says, in this way where I can tell he's been waiting to say the words forever. He takes a breath. *Oh, no, there's more.* "Nettie, I—"

"Witson, can you help me find a cider?" Selwyn tugs his sleeve and steers him toward the table. I know he won't stop until he finds it. *Thank goodness for Selwyn.*

I don't usually drink at parties. Mostly because Lia's mom's antics turned her into a teetotaler. I grab a Kofasip and turn to watch the crowd, recalling for the first time all evening that I need to talk to Callen a third time to accomplish the suggestion. I'm looking for Scoop instead. Before I lay eyes on either Callen or Scoop, however, I see a slash of red.

Lia, her flame hair down, matching her long, flowing, gossamer dress of pinks and reds. She's nodding, her long arms crossed in front of her, clutching a Kofasip and listening to Henna Shelter. Her eyes don't leave Henna's face, and an intense yearning grips me. I know what it's like to have Lia's attention.

I should tell her. She needs to know that we can't trust Media1. Our lives might be in danger.

I set my Kofasip down on the crammed tabletop and move toward them. "Lia, can you come to the bathroom with me?" I smile winningly, pretending I don't see Henna. "I need to borrow your lipstick."

"You need lipstick? Since when?" She laughs, but then she peers closely at my face. "Whoa, you don't just need lipstick— you need *more* lipstick, hmm?"

"Yeah."

I pull her out of the den, and she shouts, "Be right back," to Henna over her shoulder.

I usher Lia into the bathroom in the hall, and the lenses swivel toward us. We stare at them together and avert our eyes at the same time.

"So, I heard that Lincoln tried to slip Mollie some tranquilizer-pill-thing at the last party," Lia says.

"Oh, come on, even Lincoln wouldn't—"

Lia shoots me a silencing glare, and I obediently shut up, catching on as she swings open the cabinets, pokes her head in, and clucks. "Nothing here but some aspirin, but maybe . . ." She kneels and opens up the cabinet underneath the sink. "Help me look for the magic pills, Nettie." I sit next to her, checking the cabinet for cameras behind the jumble of disinfectants and toilet paper rolls. We're concealed.

I take a deep breath. "I was in my Session—"

"You had a Session?" Lia interrupts, then, quickly switching to on-mic: "Geez, who buys this many toothbrushes at a time?" She picks up a stack of unwrapped toothbrush boxes and waves them above her head, giving the cameras something to see.

"Rich people," I respond on-mic, before whispering into her

ear, "To teach me how to do makeup. But that's not important. I'm close to finding out what happens to the Patriots." I'm too caught up in my story to spend time thinking of how to go back on-mic to fool Media1. I mouth everything I saw in the courtyard, then tell her Dana Cannery's theory. Her eyes wander over my face while I speak, like she's more interested in my makeup than what I'm saying. When I'm done, she takes her time responding, fiddling with the toothbrush boxes.

"I'm not sure what to say, Nettie," she mouths finally.

"Don't you think it looks bad?" I prompt her. "Like they're sending them into battle or something? They didn't want to be there."

"I don't know, Nettie. To me it sounds like the Patriots need exercise. We have gym."

"That wasn't *exercise,* Lia. They were wearing uniforms. Revere was vomiting. And why would they get sent to the Drowned Lands?" My own words sink in. "Oh, God, are they sending them to fight *Drowned Landers?*" The Reals we're most closely related to.

"Your imagination is out of control. Besides, Scoop's aunt was always kind of weird, so I wouldn't believe anything she said. It doesn't make sense—they're doing experiments on them *and* making them exercise too hard?" She places the toothbrushes back into the cabinet and sighs. "I told you Revere wasn't your fault. You need to stop worrying."

"Are you serious?" I say, pushing her hand aside. "We *should* be worried. We could be next."

"That's *always* been true. Nothing's changed, except you saw something you shouldn't have been looking for." She grabs me by the shoulders. "Unsee it," she hisses, loud enough for the mic to pick up on it.

There's a sound of shattering glass in the den, and she scoots back from the cabinet, a dazed look on her face, taken aback by her audiotrack slip. She gets to her feet, flicking her mic firmly up. "Let's go back. Seems like it's getting crazy in there."

I stand and readjust my battery pack. "Yeah, hope no one's getting hurt. That would be the worst." I push past Lia and head out into the hall. I should have known she wouldn't care.

"Nettie," she calls, but I ignore her, entering the den and trying to locate my Kofasip.

Thora, Selwyn's cello competitor, is next to me, shouldering her way to the beer. She uncaps a bottle and hands it to me. "Here, Nettie," she says. "You look like you need one." I take a sip and look for Scoop again.

But he's not here.

I find Callen, though. He's sitting with Rawls in front of the smoldering fireplace. For the Antithesis, Rawls has changed teams—he borrowed a red cap and jersey from an Ant. Callen has forgone the required switch entirely. He's wearing a dark blue jacket, zipped all the way up.

Usually the sight of Callen can obliterate all my angst, but seeing him doesn't make me better tonight.

Terra comes up to the table wearing a low-cut dress. Her chestnut hair is loose, instead of in pigtails, and she looks great.

"Do you know if Scoop's coming?" I force my voice to sound lighthearted, relaxed. I brace myself for a snide remark.

Terra gapes, taken aback that I dared address her. She opens and closes her mouth, wavering before finally deciding just to answer plainly. "He's at home. He said he didn't want to be hungover at the Flower Festival."

"Thanks," I say. Depressed, I slump against the drinks table.

Selwyn sidles over to me. "Beer?" she exclaims. "Don't let Lia see you." Her face is red, and I guess that the cider in her hand isn't her first.

"I don't care, Selwyn. She's not in charge of me."

"Have you talked to Callen yet?" she asks, smiling mischievously and scratching her ear.

"Nope." I take a long swig.

"This place is packed." Henna Shelter comes up to us. Her hair is out, unleashed from her makeshift turban, and it turns out she has bangs. She's wearing a demure solid black dress. She seems uncomfortable in it, sort of hunching down, like she wishes the dress were a shell she could fold into.

"Yeah, one of Lincoln's best parties yet," Selwyn agrees.

I wonder if Lincoln is having such an excessive bash to prove that nothing has really changed since Revere was cut.

"Lia's coming," Henna says, her eyes shifting to focus behind me. She runs a hand down the skirt of her dress, and the sight of the pleats triggers my memory.

"Wait. Is that Lia's dress?" I ask. Lia wore it to some dance last season, I realize now.

"Yeah, fits like a glove, doesn't it?" Henna says, taking a sip from her wineglass. Standing behind her, Selwyn raises her eyebrows, and I shrug.

"It's nice," I say. Despite the friction between Lia and me, I feel a stab of jealousy. It doesn't feel good to be replaced.

Lia saunters over to us, balancing her elbow on my shoulder. She looks down at my hand and purses her lips. "Nettie, are you drinking?"

"Yes," I say unapologetically. I see Rawls get up from the couch, leaving the space next to Callen free.

"You don't need that," Lia says lightly, reaching over and giving the bottle a tug.

"Stop it," I mutter, tightening my grip.

"Oh, come on, you never drink beer," she insists, smiling tightly. Her cat eyes search my face. She's scared she lost me.

"That's not true." I wrench the bottle out of her grasp.

She holds her palms up in a surrender gesture. "Whatever. It's probably time you start making your own decisions."

"To the basement! The antithesis of the first floor!" Lincoln shouts, flicking the light switch for a strobe effect to capture everyone's attention.

"All right, let's go," Lia says, and starts moving out of the room, Selwyn and Henna at her heels. I look back at the couch, but Callen's gone too. I catch up with my friends, and when we reach the hall, I see him again, gliding out the front door.

"I want to grab some Caddy Gum from my bag," I say. Lia stops in her tracks.

"Gum?" She raises her eyebrows quizzically.

"Yeah, go on downstairs. I'll be back in a few." I smile and return to the empty den, where I grab another beer, hesitate a few seconds more, then head outside. To find Callen.

Chapter 16

The porch is empty. The wind coming off the surf is just as cold as it was earlier, but after the suffocating heat of the Antithesis, I welcome it. I stand beneath bamboo wind chimes, just me and my beer, surrounded by darkness.

If I left the beach now, I could reach Treasure Woods in twenty minutes. Knock on Scoop's door. Make up something about homework or a school project if his parents answer.

"Nettie?" Someone says my name from the path to the shore.

I squint and see a glint in the darkness, moving closer. "Callen? Is that you?"

"Yeah," he confirms, stepping into the circle of dim light spilling out from the house. "You had to get out of there too?" He brushes the sand off his bare feet, and now I see his abandoned sneakers on the top of the porch steps.

"Too noisy," I agree. I set the mostly full beer down next to his discarded sneakers. I slip off my heels, place them next to his sneakers, and trot down the steps. "Definitely saner out here than inside. Everyone's so rowdy."

"Yeah," he says, looking past me at the house. "I'm not sure where I belong at those parties."

"It's another world in there," I say. In wordless agreement, we walk back toward the beach together.

"Totally." Callen puts his hand out flat, fingers separated slightly, feeling the wind, then stops abruptly when he realizes I'm watching, plunging both hands into his jacket pockets. He looks away, then back at me, and then away again.

We're nearing the jetty. It curls out like a fallen ribbon onto the ocean, and I pause, memories returning as the cool tide tickles my feet.

"Do you remember coming here in sixth grade?" I say while tiptoeing onto the rocks. The camerapoles on the beach loom far above us. I know this scene will be broadcast.

"Sort of," Callen says, keeping up with me across the rocks.

"Aieeeeeeeeeeeeee!" A scream that sounds almost operatic, coming from the beach house, reaches us as a whistle, flying over the crashing waves.

"The party of the century," Callen observes, the glimmer of his eyes bright in the darkness.

"Shame that we're missing it," I say absently. "Wait, stop," I say suddenly, crouching down to where three rocks rise up like a fortress, creating a space where water collects into a natural well. I've hiked my sexy Delton's dress up over my thighs, but it doesn't matter out here, in the darkness. This is the crevice where Belle found the bottle. I peek inside, half expecting to see it nestled against the rocks.

"Are you looking for something?" Callen asks.

I can't mention Belle. "No, just—I remember being here, in sixth grade. Things were so simple back then," I say. I sit on the rocks, stretching out my legs so my toes skim the water, and he settles down next to me. We're as close as we were on the porch swing. I want to be closer.

"Not always so easy," he says. His leg is alongside mine, and every once in a while, our feet touch.

"Well, that's true. I remember being lonely, even back then," I admit. I wasn't friends with Lia—in those days, to me, she was just the Popular Tall Girl.

"I was lonely, too, and also . . ." He trails off.

"Also?" I prompt, noticing that now our toes are touching and not moving.

"I don't know. Trapped?" he says tentatively. He moves his hand over mine, just like I wanted him to on the porch. Sensation shoots through me, and I find it hard to listen. "That's when everything began to feel like a trap—classes, homework, my parents." He's even closer to me now, his breath feather light against my ear. "It felt like the island was one big trap."

I know he just shared something important, but all my attention is focused on our hands. And on his mouth, so close to my ear. The sound of the ocean is overwhelming, but I swear I can hear his heartbeat. I turn to him to signal that I need him to fill the silence, but when I do, the urge to be closer overwhelms me. I don't say anything, but I shift until our shoulders are touching. I feel like I can't breathe.

He kisses me, and energy spikes out and burns through any need to fulfill suggestions or think about Patriots or worry about Lia or anything at all. Kissing Callen is utterly natural and explains in an instant why talking always felt too complicated. This is familiar and new. His lips, the ones I've daydreamed of so many times, are eager and tender, and all I want to do is keep kissing him forever.

Another scream. Then more like a squeal that ends in a burst of laughter. At first, my only response is to draw Callen closer, but then I hear a higher-pitched scream, definitely a girl, and think it might be Lia. Reluctantly, I pull away, glancing behind me. Shadows are racing around in front of the Grayson's beach house, and I start thinking about the Patriots.

Callen touches my cheek, and I turn back to him. His hand drops and traces the line of my collarbone. "Ignore them," he says, leaning forward to kiss me again.

I decide to follow his lead, closing my eyes and melting into the kiss. But I'm tense and aware of the growing noise coming from the shore—the Graysons' screen door screeching open and shut, Characters carousing.

I break off the kiss, but keep my hands in Callen's, our foreheads touching, our eyes drinking each other in. I'm caught between wanting to stay with him and needing to be on guard—Lia might come out. I was thinking she'd just have to accept Callen and me being together if it ever happened—but *not now*. This feels too soon.

"We need the Antithesis of a bonfire." Lincoln's voice. That ultraflat calm way he speaks whenever he's very drunk and wants to pretend he's not. "A smoke pit?"

"A smoke pit, no!" someone yelps.

"I think these are Nettie's shoes." It's Selwyn. Lia might be close behind.

I tear away from Callen. "I have to go, it's just—"

"You don't want Lia to see us," he says, running his hand through his hair, rumpling it more than ever, as I stand up, brushing off grit.

"Sorry." I turn around, trying to make out her silhouette among the others in the yard. No sign of her. I glimpse the cameras on the beach again and feel a glimmer of excitement, thinking about the Audience getting to see us. For them, it's the fulfillment of unrequited love.

We're separated now, and I feel the magic fading and worry creeping in. Like if I'm not literally holding him to me, I can't trust anything. *I can't lose Callen.*

"I'm getting out of here. But I want to see you soon," I say, glad now that I can't really see his face.

"Me too." He speaks with an urgency I've never heard from him before. "I wanted to ask you in the cafeteria this afternoon— come to the Brambles with me tomorrow. Skip the Festival."

The Festival. I was already wavering, and now I picture girls sashaying around downtown with their garlands and Lia judging them all. As she said, whatever. I'd much rather be alone with Callen for a few hours.

"Well . . . okay. I mean, yes. Yes, I'd love to. When?"

"Eleven? Let's meet at the statue at the gates."

"All right." I grin, feeling ridiculously, stupidly lucky. I just kissed Callen Herron.

"Let's just do a bonfire," Lincoln declares from the beach. "Bring out the logs from the basement." Someone howls.

"We should go back, before they notice." I smooth my hair down and try to rub away what I imagine is smudged eye shadow and mascara. Callen kisses my cheek one last time, and we leave the jetty, walking down the shore side by side but keeping a carefully platonic distance between us. There are twenty or so Characters outside. Some are setting up the wood for the bonfire; others are stretched out on the porch, tipsy. Lia isn't there.

"Callen, give us a hand," Lincoln says briskly, like he's directing a servant, barely noticing me. He can trade in his fancy clothes for beaten-up ones, but he can't trade in that aristocratic hauteur.

Callen flashes me a rueful grin as Lincoln drags him away. A shiver of pleasure runs through me. I feel weightless.

Selwyn jogs over from the porch, meeting me on the sand, huffing and puffing, clasping Callen's sneakers and my heels.

"Here are yours." She shoves mine into my hands. "Now, where is he, and *what happened?*"

She's loud, and I look around, worried someone will hear her.

"Come over here." I hustle her behind the house for privacy, stopping behind some shrubbery.

"You did it," she says, with a mix of awe and pleasure. "You did . . . something."

"We kissed," I confess. Now it's out there. I bury my face in my hands, embarrassed and giddy. "I can't believe it. We kissed."

"Finally!" Selwyn squeals, dropping the sneakers and hugging me.

"Selwyn, I really like him."

"I *know,*" she says.

"We're going to the Brambles together tomorrow," I add. The wind intensifies, and I wrap my arms around myself, freezing. My eyes drift up to the cameras pinned to the side of the house. What would Kat Deva want to hear? "I think we're going to be together."

The Tram ride home seems to take forever. Without the party or Callen around to distract me, all I can think about is the courtyard. A very Bad Thing.

Lia didn't want to hear it. She might even have thought I was making it up. We needed to get proof from the Sandcastle, something to give Characters the same visceral shock I got. Something that will force them to confront Media1.

I glance at the window reflection and fix my messed-up hair. Tall brick buildings slide by. The outskirts of the Heights.

I won't get to see Scoop tomorrow if I'm with Callen in the Brambles, so I bolt off the Tram at Treasure Woods and head toward the Cannery house. Treasure Woods is noiseless, utterly still, but I feel uneasy. Exposed. The mansions and trees are set farther back from the road than in the Arbor, and there are lights and cameras lining the telephone wires instead of perched discreetly in the trees.

I walk fast, skipping my usual turn onto Lia's block and making a left onto Pearl Lane, or Luxury Lane as it's sometimes called. But Scoop's house is unassuming for Treasure Woods: no columns, no fountain. Chalkboard white with blue trim. Flower boxes full of geraniums.

I cross the lawn. There's no light on in Scoop's room on the second floor, so I slow down to pick up a few pieces of gravel from the driveway and aim carefully, praying I don't wake anyone else up. The stones ping against the windowpane and shower down into the grass.

I hear the window slide open. "Nettie?" Scoop whispers, a note of disbelief in his voice. "Be right there." I scurry backward, into the shadow of a tree, reclipping my microphone that got knocked off my collar when I bent down. Seeing it reminds me that I have to come up with some sort of reason for being here.

When he comes around, he's carrying a cable-knit wool sweater. "I thought you might be cold," he says, passing it to me. "It looks like you got in a fight or something." He gestures toward my hair, messy from the wind on the beach and probably from Callen running his hands through it.

I put on the sweater. "No fight," I say, sheepishly gazing up at all the cameras pinned to the back of the house. I'm at a loss for what to say. No one's going to buy that we need to talk about math. If I were running into his arms after kissing Callen on the beach, it'd be the kind of ratings gold Lia spends late nights dreaming up, but I can't pull it off, and it seems stupid to care about ratings now, with the memory of the courtyard hovering over me. "But—I want to tell you something, um, about the party. Walk to the playground with me?"

"Okay," he says, steering me around the house and back to the road. As we trek toward the Arbor, I ramble on about the party.

"Lincoln's parents would kill him if they saw him in that shirt. Shar and Beryl were, like, in maximum exhibitionist mode, and it was awkward—you know Shar's hands are like flippers." I do a credible imitation of Shar's hands, flopping around Beryl. "Then Lincoln ordered us down to the basement, but I went outside with Callen."

"Oh, Callen was there?" he teases.

"We, you know, anyway, I guess you were right, about him liking me, because we kissed."

"Cute. For everyone but Lia, I guess." He looks at me sideways as I undo the latch on the gate to the waist-high playground fence.

"She doesn't know yet." I fumble with redoing the latch.

"You wanted to do it, right?" He's digging to find out if it was because of the Initiative. I finally get the gate shut and face him.

"No . . . ?" He scratches behind his ear.

"Yes," I say hotly, tugging him toward the swings. "I wanted to."

"Well, maybe Lia's over it," he says. "Although she did kind of have crazy eyes for a week after he dumped her."

"Sit there," I say, ignoring him and gesturing at a swing. I sit on the one next to him and start swinging. He probably used this trick when he was a kid too.

"Yeah, and the nearest camera is broken too," I mouth, jerking my head over to where the dead red eye droops.

"Crisped," he mouths. "That's what the Reals say when the cameras break. That they crisped. Just like—"

"Like when someone's cut as a Show Risk, people say they crisp?" He nods. Charming. Puppets, equipment—anything but people.

"I saw something tonight." I tell Scoop about the courtyard, and it's such a relief to be with someone who cares.

The more I say, the more he frowns, all traces of his customary good nature vanishing. "If Aunt Dana's right, they could be getting them into shape before they start the experiments."

"That was my first thought," I mouth grimly. "But it seems unlikely, especially with the camouflage. I had an idea. What if they're fighting against Drowned Landers, as some sort of Media1 legion?"

Scoop listens intently, nodding with each idea, but when I'm done, his response is simple. "We won't know until I get into the Sandcastle," he says, jaw clenched. "I'm going next week."

It's just what I wanted to hear. "You need to bring something back, something to make Characters believe you. Proof."

"Yeah," he mouths. "Will you come now? I could use your help."

I hesitate for a couple of swings. I'd thought about it, but it was before I kissed Callen, and now I feel the old anxieties creeping in—I have so much to lose if we get caught. "I can't," I say softly—Scoop doesn't press me. "But I want to help. Do you have a plan?"

"I sometimes take out the aquarium's boat, and I found a cove on Eden Beach. I can take out the boat again, ditch it in the cove, cut through a fence, and sneak into the Center. I stole a cricket's code—just stuck close behind one entering Character Relations—to get into the Sandcastle."

A memory surfaces, Mik reprimanding me for trying my code out at a nearby apartment complex before one of my first Character Reports. "Because ours don't work on the other buildings."

"Right. But I still need to pass as a Real. I'm getting a wig from the scene shop, and I'm going to wear sunglasses, but what I really need is a jumpsuit."

The jumpsuit pile in Luz's office. "I might be ab—" I freeze. A rustling in the dark, and suddenly I see three crickets at the gate. In an instant, they're inside, gathering at the foot of the swings like circling sharks.

I hold my breath, wondering what they've heard. Fear grabs me as I imagine myself being dragged away by the Authority. I force myself to keep swinging, and for a minute, the only sound is the squeak of the hinges. "I might be able to help you with that problem," I say on-mic. I try to speak clearly, but my voice is small. "We can talk about it later."

"Thanks," Scoop says. In silent agreement, we stop swinging and rest in place, the cameras humming around us. I slip my feet back into my heels, heart accelerating, staring at the ground.

"Are you going to see Callen again?" he asks, giving them what they want.

"Yeah, tomorrow," I confess.

"Lia doesn't know?" he says. The cameras come closer and closer.

"I'm not sure. She might—Selwyn said she noticed we'd disappeared at the party." One of the crickets coughs, and I feel myself tense.

Scoop whistles low. "Tough. Well, you'll do the right thing. I know it." He reaches over and tousles my hair. Exactly what he used to do to Belle. "Just remember, the truth always comes out." He raises his voice so the clueless crickets hear every word.

Chapter 17

"Nettie Starling." Eleanora Burnish, Lia's charming, gorgeous—and today, clearly buzzed—mother, swings the front door open, and suddenly there are scents: perfume, alcohol, and another, more pungent, acidic odor that I can't place.

"Haven't seen you in a while." Every element of Mrs. Burnish's all-*voxless* look is askew: Her plum lipstick is smudged. She has a diamond stud in her left ear but not in her right. Tendrils of strawberry blond hair have escaped her bun.

"I know. I've been busy, with the Double A coming up." *Is that urine?* I cover my nose with the back of my hand while I look behind her, horrified. *What is going on?*

"What an adorable pursh." She means purse but it came out slurred. I gulp. Uh-oh. She straightens up, trying to convince me she's sober. "You look so beautiful. Are you doing something new?"

"It's my mom's," I pat the leather purse under my arm. "Nothing new." A lie. This morning, I put all the Makeup Session lessons to use, wanting to look good for Callen. I braided my hair, then spent almost an hour figuring out what to wear.

In the end, I paired the sleeveless top Selwyn chose for me at Delton's with checkered shorts—I didn't want to look like I was trying *too* hard.

"Well, whatever it is, it's working. Come in, come in." She ushers me inside, flinging out her arm dramatically, like a matador facing a bull. "What's up?"

"Is Lia here?" I step into the dark front hall. A massive chandelier drops from the ceiling, hunks of glass shimmering in the pale morning light, making a daytime constellation on the polished wooden floor. The odor grows stronger.

"Yes, she's getting ready for the Festival," she trills. "Are you going downtown with her?"

"Actually, I'm skipping it this year." I inch farther down the hall, toward the staircase. My hip grazes the sharp edge of a tarp-covered bulk. It must be furniture she ordered for the motif change. More draped pieces are scattered down the hall.

"Be careful. That's my new armoire," Eleanora confirms, her voice wavering unsteadily. "Haven't had time to uncover the new furni . . . shur." She slurs the last word.

"You'll find the time," I murmur, taking a few more quick steps until I'm right at the foot of the stairs.

Eleanora arches her back coquettishly, bumping into a silver-rimmed clock hanging on the wall. "Ow." She rubs her head, a cracked smile emerging on her face. "You're in such a rush," she croons, a light admonishment.

Nine according to the clock. I can't stay long. "Yeah, I'm meeting someone after. I'll talk to you later, Eleanora." I gallop up the stairs, away from the nasty smell and her desperation. I idolized Eleanora when I was younger, but it's difficult to be around her now. I thought the suggestions Lia got for the Initiative might help her, but she actually seems worse than ever. Is that what the Audience wants?

I knock on Lia's bedroom door, but walk in without waiting for a response.

"Nettie?" Lia whirls around from her full-length mirror. She's wearing jeans and a sleeveless blouse with a bib collar, and a garland of violets and bluebells around her head. My carefully chosen outfit looks plain by comparison. "Why are you here? Selwyn said you were sick. Staying home from the Festival."

"I'm not sick," I say, studying her face. I need to tell her now, before more lies get spun around this situation.

"There's something I want—" A crash downstairs interrupts me, followed by a squeal. Lia rushes to her door and closes it, blushing. She begins running around the room, pitching clothes into her closet, throwing out wrappers, and returning hair ties and fallen jewelry and lipsticks to drawers.

"I didn't know you were coming. It's a mess in here," she says, biting her lower lip. She pauses, hand on her hip. "Was my mom really bad?"

"No." I walk over to her bed, push aside her beloved colony of stuffed animals, and sit cross-legged. "But what's up with that smell?"

"The cat," Lia says, scratching behind her ear. Lia's reward, I remember now. "We got her two weeks ago, and my mom isn't changing the litter box in the kitchen. I refuse to, and I don't think my dad even noticed. Oh, the cat's right there." She gestures toward the stuffed animals, and now I see that one of them is moving. A sleek white cat stretches out her paw and purrs flirtatiously.

"She's cute," I say, shifting over to avoid the paw. I'm not much of an animal person.

"Oh, Nettie. That's how you looked when Witson used to kiss you." Lia laughs. I freeze at "kiss," but Lia's oblivious. "Luna, you adorable little thing." Lia comes over and strokes the cat's head. "You vanished last night. What happened?"

I trace the pattern on her comforter, at a loss for words.

"I thought my black dress looked pretty plus ten on Henna," Lia says, bumping heads with the cat and giggling. "I really like her. I want her to be artsy and stuff, but not, like, an outcast. She's my latest project."

I think about Henna stuffed into that dress and glance down at the remnants of Lia's Temptress Tin polish on my nails. Have I been a project too? "She seems nice."

"Like Luna?"

"Hmm?"

"You called Luna nice too," she says, sitting on the bed. She lets her hair fall in front of her face and ducks so her chin is right above the comforter, on the left side of her bed, in a place we know is difficult for the cameras. "Did you leave the party because you were upset about the courtyard?"

She didn't seem to care about that before, and that's not what

I'm here to talk about. I straighten up and say on-mic, "Lia, about last night. Last night, Callen and I—we—we—" I breathe in, steadying myself. She inches backward, snatching up Luna and petting her roughly.

I grind the toe of my sneaker into her carpet, creating a flat space in the shag. Without looking up, I say, "Lia, we kissed."

For a long moment, silence envelops the room until finally, she speaks, lifting her head, a familiar, imperious tilt to her chin. "You and Callen?" she says. "Wow." Luna springs off her lap and prowls the floor. Lia falls back into the fralling position, and I copy her, a mirror image, safe from the cameras.

"Luz didn't suggest *that*," she mouths, bringing her hand casually to her lips to be extra safe. "Did he?"

"No, he didn't," I mouth back. "It just happened, but—"

"But you like him, don't you?" she finishes. "I knew that's why Media1 gave you those suggestions." She switches back to on-mic. "You lied to me. Nettie, you *lied* to me. You said you didn't like Callen, and I believed you. I thought you were, like, congenitally honest."

Congenitally. What does that mean? It sounds dirty.

"Lia, I've been scared to tell you, and it was already awkward, with the two of you going out—"

"Does everyone know?" she asks, sitting up, righting the garland. I follow suit. "Does Selwyn know? How long have you felt this way? Since before we were dating?"

"Yeah, but I didn't want to—I didn't think he did, and

besides, you were dating, and I didn't want to ruin things for you."

"Nettie, you couldn't *ruin* things for me." She laughs, her voice skidding up and down, reminding me uncomfortably of her mother. "I mean, whatever. I don't want to be with him. I *don't* want to be with him," she repeats. "But I can't believe you lied to me."

"You know, you've lied to me, too," I say pointedly.

She rolls her eyes. "Nettie, I asked you not to talk to him, and now you're sticking your tongue down his throat. Who else knows?"

"Selwyn and Scoop."

"So everyone will know soon." She sighs, looking down and twisting a ring on her finger while she thinks. "Callen's so . . . Sometimes, Nettie, you put people on a pedestal, and you don't really see them. Callen's complicated. Nettie, are you sure you want to be with him?"

"I don't know," I say, which is sort of another lie. "But I want us—you and me—to be honest with one another. I don't want to have to hide my feelings around you."

Lia sighs again and raises her eyes to the ceiling. For a long moment, she's silent, a range of emotions crossing her face: frustration, sadness, and right before she grabs my hand and turns to me, one I've rarely seen on her: resignation. "Nettie, I know—things haven't been so easy lately, between us, Double A pressures, my play, my mother—and you know, other stuff," she tacks on vaguely. "We're friends, okay? Whatever happens with you and Callen. Our friendship is more important than boys."

"Okay," I say, just wanting to make peace, fast. "Yes, more important than boys."

She gestures me back down into the fralling position again. "Callen doesn't know about the suggestions, does he?"

I shake my head.

"Don't tell him. He'll freak out," she mouths emphatically. She gets back on-mic. "You're seeing him today, aren't you? That's why you're not coming to the Festival."

I nod. "We're going to the Brambles."

"Oh, God, like that's so much better than the Festival," she says, rolling her eyes. "Okay, never mind. If that's what you want to do, go ahead. I have to finish getting ready." She stands. "Onward . . ."

It's not until I'm downstairs, heading out the door, that I realize that Lia was quoting from our play and that I didn't return the gesture.

I recognize the Pigeons cap right away. Callen is smoking in front of the statue of the first mayor, an Original. She stands with one stiff index finger raised, and it looks like she's rebuking the teenage smoker below her. I lock my bike by the gates.

"I'm here," I announce as I walk over to him. "Sorry I'm late."

"I thought you might have gone to the Festival after all," he says, stubbing out his cigarette and tossing it into a nearby trash can.

"Nope." I stop a foot or so away from him, unsure how we're supposed to greet each other, excruciatingly conscious of the sweat trickling all over me—I biked hard in my attempt to get here on time.

"You got home safe last night?" Callen asks. The cap shadows his eyes, so I can't read his expression, but he shifts from foot to foot. Nervous.

"Yeah." With bleary eyes and a stomach tight from being trailed by crickets all the way from the playground to my front door.

"You're being mysterious again," he says, his lips curving up in a slight smile.

I tense. "Oh, oops."

"No, it's okay," he says. "I like it. Come on." He takes my hand. I relax and let him lead me down a path through a thicket of scabby birch trees. "Watch out," he says as we turn onto another, narrower trail, ducking to avoid low-hanging branches. Thankfully, a soft breeze dries the bike ride sweat, and the farther we walk, the more comfortable I feel. The path gets steeper and shadier, smothered in ferns and shrubs, crowded with saplings shooting to the sky, and covered by ancient gnarly oaks. Holding hands makes navigating clumsier, but neither of us lets go.

I don't mind not talking. The deeper we delve into the forest, the more comfortable the silence becomes. Callen glances at me once, then a second time, a shy smile on his lips, as we trample over twigs and matted leaves. The third time he does it, I tug his hand before he can look away.

"Is everything okay?" I ask.

He leans over, and we kiss again, my forehead bumping into the brim of his hat.

This time is different, slower—I didn't think I was timid before, but now, as I put my arms around his neck, and his hands press into the small of my back, I know we both were. I pull away, to breathe, and his smile appears. I smile back, this tension I didn't even know was there melting away. Our faces are inches apart.

"How long?" My fingers play with the soft hair at the nape of his neck. "How long have you liked me?"

"How long have you liked *me*?" he counters.

"I asked first," I protest. The sun beams down between the branches, and above us the sky is completely clear. No weather chemicals, either, just one glorious day.

"I know you did," he says.

I think back. "I remember the first time I knew. You gave me a ride to school, and the car broke down when we were only two blocks away. Do you remember?"

"Yeah." He holds my hand and guides me down the winding path made out of mulch and twigs. "I missed my first two classes, waiting for the tow truck."

"And you told me to go ahead, so I walked and just made

the bell. But it was before all that, when the car cranked out, and you—" I feel silly for a second, but I go ahead and say it. "When the engine stopped, you just smiled and looked outside, and said, 'We were so close,' and you weren't swerved off at all. That's when I knew."

"So way before Lia," he says, climbing over a fallen branch. "Good to know."

"Your turn." I give him a playful shove. He wobbles but stays on the log.

"Six months ago," he says. "I was behind you in the lunch line, and you were telling Selwyn how excited you were about this telescope you'd built. Your eyes were all lit up, and suddenly I knew I needed to know you better. But you were with Witson."

"And then I wasn't." I can't keep the reproach out of my voice.

He looks into the distance, and I remember Lia's perfect imitation of his evasive stare. "Nettie, you were kind of ignoring me," he says finally. "I actually started thinking you might *dislike* me . . . until that day it rained on the porch, when . . ."

When I had flirted with him because of the suggestion.

"It's okay," I say quickly. "Guess what? I told Lia about last night."

He hops off the log. "Really?" He takes my hand in his again, and we start walking downhill along the trail toward the Brambles lake, a perfect circle with a camera-horror spigot coughing up water in the center. Not a shining moment for the crickets— it makes it obvious the lake is fake. "How'd she take it?"

"Like you'd expect. Angry, but then she calmed down, and I think she might end up, just, okay with it," I say.

"I hope so," Callen says, tugging me off the path and onto the grass. "Let's get closer to the water."

We walk up to the water's edge, where pondweed and cattails burst out from under the surface. Callen points out tiny frogs hopping around, then starts to identify scores of flowers and plants.

"Wow, you know this stuff pretty well."

"I picked it up from Mom," he says, sitting on the grass and tugging me down next to him. "Those are called popcorn flowers." He points to the tiny white and yellow flowers crowding around a tree trunk.

"Plus ten," I say, and the flowers are nice, but I'm more interested in how much he likes them. "Can't you apply for an apprenticeship that's environment related? Like your mom? Hey, wait"—I get excited—"isn't there a park ranger slot?"

He shrugs. "Dad wants me to do baseball."

I picture Mr. Herron in the brand-new Harrow that they must have gotten off of the baseball ratings boost.

Callen takes off his Pigeons cap and lies on his back. Feeling bold, I straddle him, bracing my hands on the grass on either side of his head and dropping down to kiss him greedily. His breaths are shallow and fast; his arms around me grow tight.

"This is so much better than the Flower Festival," I whisper. He laughs, and I move off him, flopping onto my back, letting the sun dazzle my eyes.

He reaches into his back pocket and takes out his cigarettes. "Do you mind if I smoke?"

"Noooooo." I stretch languorously, then turn on my side and watch him light up. His lips pucker when he inhales, then part. The smoke floats up into the air, and I remember how he said he used to set off the alarms in their house. *Smoke.* The smoke from the burning toaster that sent all the Reals racing out of Character Relations.

I know how I can get the jumpsuit for Scoop.

"Could I try a cigarette?"

"Really?" he says, but he's already fishing one out. I put it in my mouth, lean forward, and he lights it for me. I puff delicately and manage not to cough.

"Not bad," I force out.

It does make me feel light-headed and giggly. Between the nicotine and the natural high of being with Callen, I feel charged, and all I can think about is getting closer. And not just physical closeness. When the cigarette's finished, we're lying facing each other, and I fling my arm over him, pulling his head toward mine, concealing both our faces from the cameras. "Do you ever think about the Patriots?" I mouth.

"Sometimes. More since Belle and Revere. But not a lot." His eyes soften. "I know you must, because of your dad."

"And because I've been on the E.L.," I add. Some shame steals in, but I want to share everything with him—including our ratings. "Have you ever been on?"

He shakes his head. "Not with baseball."

It's so silly, but something about how he says it makes me want to leap on top of him again. Short. Simple. Direct. I trace his cheekbone, then his nose, then his jaw, marveling that I'm here, we're here. That there *is* a we. I slide closer.

"I saw them yesterday, Callen. I saw the Patriots." I tell him what I saw in the courtyard and what I overheard on the radio about the caves in the Drowned Lands. "And—" I hesitate, uncertain about whether I should bring Scoop into this. I decide not to. "Someone told me that they use them for medical experiments. Then I thought—what if they're in the army?"

Callen listens intently, stroking my arm the whole time. He nods and asks what they were wearing, which names I heard on the radio, and so on. But when I'm done relaying the facts, the questions stop. I like how cautious he is with words, and how steady and comforting he can remain when hearing all this. His calm balances everything inside me.

"I've never trusted Media1," he mouths finally. I'm tempted to tell him all of it, my mind running through wild scenarios where he helps Scoop and me, but a cloud moves, unveiling the sun, and light fills his blue eyes again. Mesmerized, I realize the last thing I want to do is risk him in any way.

"Let's not talk about it anymore," I mouth. He raises his eyebrows, surprised, so I go in for another kiss to distract him. In between lip-locks, I catch sight of the cigarette pack lying on the rocks near us.

"Hey." I quickly switch to on-mic, before he can mouth

anything else about the Patriots. "Is it okay if I take a few more cigarettes? I kind of liked it."

"First the graffiti, now the smoking? You're really going wild." He smiles and passes me three. I tuck them into my mom's purse, then lay my head on his chest, listening to his heartbeat, trying to sink back into the moment, but I can't. In my head, I'm working out how I'll secure the jumpsuit. First, I have to remember to grab the lighter at the bottom of the kitchen junk drawer on my way to the Report tomorrow.

Callen seems to sense my distraction. "Up here," he coaxes, pulling me up to kiss him, and as I do, for a second, I think, *This is all I need.* And it should be enough. If I could make it be enough, if I could banish all the worries I have about the Patriots, I would.

But I can't, and it's not.

Chapter 18

Ratings mark: 392. My target was 321. The Audience is on my side this week. Media1 is compensating me accordingly. I keep my eyes trained on the contents of the envelope, an infinitely less distressing view than the human being in front of me, whom I should never have trusted. The money is even more impressive than the mark—800 ceteks. Enough to do another *voxless* wardrobe spruce-up. I never did buy a dress for the Double A. I finally look up, and Luz is watching me, waiting for me to thank him or crow over my victory or at least smile. That last I can manage. I smile mechanically.

"Excellent job. Violet Starling will never receive a fine for fralling again." Luz takes a long swig of coffee. His beard has grown unkempt, and his hair is in need of a trim. Totally disheveled.

I pat my back pocket for the hundredth time, making sure the cigarettes are still there. The window behind him is open, and I listen carefully, but all I can hear is the foghorn of an arriving ship and the shrieks of hungry seagulls.

"You deserve it," Luz continues as I slide the ratings card and the money back into the envelope. "The Audience is eating this loveplot up. We haven't broadcast the Brambles scene yet, but they've already nicknamed you two. Callettie."

Callettie. It's very . . . long. Sounds like a pastry. I shove the envelope into my back pocket, next to the three cigarettes, and check the wall behind him as discreetly as I can. I have to distract him.

"Is this what you wanted all along? For me and Callen to be together? Why didn't you just suggest that we date?"

I finally locate the smoke alarm: it's almost directly above me, a metal splotch on the bright white ceiling.

"No, I couldn't suggest outright romance." Luz's hands form a steeple on the desk, and I can tell he's pleased to have the chance to explain his work. "I didn't want the scene to lose its authenticity."

I roll my eyes. With all the manipulation the Initiative has done, I can't believe he's bringing up *authenticity.* "Can I have a cigarette?"

"Ah, the Callen influence. Go ahead." Luz pulls a lighter out of his drawer. I fumble at first but succeed soon enough and concentrate on keeping my fingers steady.

Luz watches, pushing an empty mug forward on his desk for me to ash in. "You don't seem happy, Nettie. Don't you have what you want now?"

"Does what I want really matter?" I retort, brushing my hair out of my face. I know it's safer to play along, but I can't stop myself from frowning. Luz said the Initiative was supposed to make my big, unsaid dreams come true, but that's only as long as they coincide with ratings. I'm lucky they have. Selwyn didn't really want to do the graffiti. Lia didn't really want to make her mom's issues a plotline. And then there are the things the Initiative will never get for me: the chance to know my father and protect the Patriots.

"Of course it does," he sighs.

"No, *you* tell me what I want." I mean to sound sarcastic and rude like Lincoln, but instead my voice is raw and plaintive. "What do I want today?" Weak. My voice is weak.

Luz opens and shuts his mouth a few times, then drops his eyes to his desk.

"Are you okay?" I ask warily, the smoke creating a thin haze between us.

He fidgets with papers on his desk. "You should know we're tweaking the system. No more rewards. You'll still get higher ratings, of course, and bonuses."

"No more rewards?" I repeat. My eyes float up to the alarm, exasperated by its enduring silence.

"No rewards. The Initiative's success green-lights us to go ahead and integrate it more fully into Characters' lives. Following it is not a favor to us; it's compulsory. To hammer this home, we've amended the Contract. If a Character doesn't comply with the Initiative, they'll qualify as a Show Risk, to be cut at our discretion."

The cigarette falls from my fingers and into the mug. "You would cut someone for not taking the suggestions? I don't believe it." I fish a second cigarette out of my pocket and light it with shaking fingers. But I *do* believe it. After seeing the Patriots in the courtyard, I know Media1 is capable of anything.

"The legal department cleared it," Luz says, straightening his collar, unable to meet my eyes.

I inhale deeply, smoke scratching my throat. Tears come to my eyes as I struggle not to cough. "The Originals wouldn't have agreed to that."

"The Originals are gone. The show has changed because the world has changed, and you have to change too," he says quietly, voice tight. "On to today's suggestion. Media1 would like you to close up with Callen."

I'm horrified and embarrassed at once. How could he even say this to me?

"Is this a joke?" I cry, pounding my fist on the desk. "He's not even my boyfriend. Is this some kind of perverted producer fantasy? Last week, all I had to do was talk to him."

"It wasn't my idea." Luz jots down notes, avoiding my glare. At least he's blushing. "But that's not important. I stand behind it as being firmly in the spirit of the Initiative. Also, before I forget, we're moving your Report to Sunday, just for this week, since the ceremony is on Saturday. This week is a big one for you, Nettie. You close up, and you attend the Double A. You'll capture the whole teen Audience."

"You're disgusting. How can you live with yourself?" The cigarette is almost done. I might have to do the third. Luz is still too scared to look at me, and I press the stub of the cigarette into the underside of his nice new desk, drop it in the mug, and light up a new one. My lungs are scorched and it's so gross, but I have to.

He stares into his own coffee mug. "Nettie, it's not your place to decide what's best for the Audience. Media1 *knows* a close-up with Callen will be a ratings bonanza. Further, I must tell you that the company is well aware of all the breaking of the fourth wall, or fralling, that goes on, and in this case, it will absolutely not be permitted. If you share the content of your suggestion with anyone, you will both be cut, as Show Risks. We're serious about protecting the Initiative."

"That's not—" The smoke alarm shatters the air, cutting me off. I wince as the sound pierces my eardrums.

"Oh, no, not again." Luz scrambles to his feet. Outside I can hear doors swinging open up and down and the corridor.

"Oops, I didn't mean to!" I squeal, stubbing out the cigarette hastily on the desk again.

"Last time it took forever for them to turn it off," he shouts, moving out from behind his desk. I hear employees filing out into the hall. "Let's go." We rush out of the office, eager to escape the noise, and merge into the green and purple sea of Reals filing out of the building. I stick close to Luz, palms sweaty, trying to drum up the courage to execute the plan.

"Oh! I forgot my book bag in your office," I say, sighing.

"Well, hurry," Luz says, but he doesn't wait for me. I dash back down the now-empty hall toward his office, where I pull Scoop's sweater out of my bag. I pick up a handful of jumpsuits from the pile in the corner, stuff them inside the sweater, then rush back out, joining the last of the Reals exiting the building in the lobby.

A heavy hand clamps down on my shoulder as I step outside. Luz. He steers me off to the side of the building, away from the other Reals, near the Contract display.

"Nettie," he says, looking around him and lowering his head, trying to make sure we're not overheard. "You don't want to be cut. Trust me. Take the suggestion."

Just beyond the Center gates, I see Scoop pacing in a small circle, book bag on his shoulders. I called him last night after the Festival and asked him to meet me here so I could return his sweater.

The sweater conceals the jumpsuits well, and I chose this place because of the spotty camera coverage, so we're doubly protected. "Here." I balance my bike on my leg and take the ball of material out of my bag. "Success, and I got backups too," I mouth, adding on-mic, "Here's your sweater."

"Thanks," he says, putting it in his book bag. When he's finished, he mouths, "Are you okay? You look upset."

I don't reply right away. Scoop's got the backpack hoisted over both shoulders, tugging the straps, and he's wearing a concerned frown. Even so, he exudes charisma and cool sexiness, his hazel eyes dancing, his tall, lean frame. Scoop doesn't have a girlfriend, but there are always girls around him. He's probably closed up before.

But I can't say anything to him. A fine is one thing; being responsible for someone getting cut is something else.

"I'm fine," I assure him.

"All right," he says, skeptical. He mouths, "Last night, I thought up a way to let everyone know about what I find in the Sandcastle, but I need your help. It involves someone else."

"Really?" At least one good thing has happened today. "Tell me." He jerks his thumb behind us, toward the Center, and we move a few steps back, only a foot away from the entrance booth where a helmeted Authority sits.

"Okay, here goes," Scoop mouths and bends down to whisper his plan in my ear.

I dump my empty book bag on the floor and fling myself into the chair across from Violet. Thoughts about the close-up dogged me all the way here. It's not only the close-up—although it's definitely too soon for that—it's that Media1 thinks it's okay to invade my life like this. Besides, would Callen even want to? I recall the awkwardness of Lia trying to lure Callen into bed.

"Ugh," I groan, burying my head in my hands.

"Nettie, you sound like a dying animal," Violet clucks. "Would a walk raise your spirits?"

"Okay," I say, standing again. "You want to go to the gazebo?"

"Yes, that sounds nice," she says.

I help her slip into a light coat. "No one has, um, been bothering you lately, have they?"

"Hmm? There is a new aide who hums a lot." She bangs on the window with the end of her cane. "And these squirrels who have discovered the feeder. Go away. *Scat.*"

"Good. I mean, not good, but good that everything is basically okay." We walk out to the hall together and through the door that leads to the manicured grounds between the Brambles and Hidehall, following the tulip-lined path to the wooden gazebo next to the lake.

"But *you* seem bothered," she says, sitting on the bench and propping the cane up next to her.

"Do you remember Callen Herron?" I nibble at my nails, trying to figure out how to put this.

"Your next-door neighbor? I knew Dahlia Herron quite well."

"His grandmother?" I pace the gazebo.

"Yes. She did a funny thing with numbers—if she didn't concentrate, she'd write them mirror-image by mistake." Her eyes crinkle at the memory. "And what hair she had!"

"Very blond," I guess, finally sitting down next to her.

"Yes! Like snow. What about this grandson?"

"Well, he and I sort of started seeing each other last week. But—there's a problem."

Violet snorts. "A problem already?"

"Yeah, but it's not him—or me. It's not either of us," I say, scanning the lawn for crickets, then taking in all the cameras pointing at us from the rafters, and I know what I'm doing is risky, but I can't keep it inside anymore. "Violet, do you ever feel as if—like, say, someone is trying to help you? But maybe they start *interfering* with your life too much?"

Of course she doesn't get it. "You'll have to be more specific," she says.

"I—I can't be," I stammer.

Violet picks up her cane and bangs it on the floor. "Snap out of it," she says. "Goodness, no one should be so glum at the start of a romance."

I turn and face her. "I just don't think it's fair that some people on Bliss Island control other people." I meant Media1, but when I hear the words spoken aloud, I realize I'm thinking about Lia too.

"Oh, Nettie," Violet says, smiling sadly. Then she sighs, a typical, extravagant Violet sigh. Her emotions are so oversized. "Rebellion's in your *heart,* dearest." She pauses significantly.

Rebellion's in your heart.

Her face is blank, only the faintest hint of a smile. Am I crazy to think she's telling me about my father? Heart. Hart. This is the first time she's mentioned my father while lucid.

She speaks again. "The desire to reject authority," she continues, a mischievous glint in her eyes. "You're tough, sweetie."

Funny, tough, and smart.

"I don't feel that tough." I walk over to her, kneel, and say into my mic, "I like your earrings," and they are nice, large wire hoops with red coral beads. I touch the earrings and whisper into her ear, "Are you talking about my father?"

Her eyes seem crystal clear, but she doesn't move a muscle, and it's as if she doesn't hear me. I wait, the only sound our breathing, and a few seconds later her hand tightens around mine, and she pulls me back to whisper in my ear, "Yes. He was tough, and he got in trouble. Be careful."

Chapter 19

"Here." Lia slaps a paper onto my lunch tray. "Double A application."

"Thanks," I say, but I'm barely paying attention. I've had trouble falling asleep every night since my Character Report. I hid out in my room all weekend. A Missive came—something about promoting a new brand of bread. I barely read it, just turned it off and sat on my bed, contemplating how good it would feel to smash the Missivor to pieces.

I've spent every second since I left Hidehall thinking about how I can get out of the suggestion without getting cut.

"Nettie, you're not even looking at it," Lia chides.

I examine the paper. "The Apprenticeship Announcement Application" in bold at the top. Stars on the borders. Two lines dead center: "Name" and "Apprenticeship Selection." I flip the paper over. A listing of all the apprenticeships, each with the number of slots available in parentheses. There's mine: *High School Math Teacher (1)*.

"Hot off the press," Lia trumpets. "We're handing them out tomorrow. But, for my friends, a head start."

"A head start on a lifetime of drudgery," Lincoln drawls across from me. "Thanks." He's wearing sunglasses inside; it's an affectation he likes to take up after parties—even if the party was more than seventy-two hours ago. He should give the sunglasses to Martin, who could use them. His face looks dim and dull, and he has a hacking cough that he keeps trying to stifle with the plaid handkerchief Lincoln lent him. Too much partying.

Lia rolls her eyes. "I'm excited about being a Blisslet, Lincoln. Too bad whatever you're doing sucks so much." Lincoln's refused to share his pick. She turns to Henna. "The stars look so plus ten. Great job."

Henna's wearing a turban again; this time it's pink. "It was your idea," she replies, the faintest trace of a smug smile on her face.

Lincoln fills his application out and pushes Lia's lucky red pen across the table to Selwyn, who picks up the pen, scribbles her name and then quickly, *Cellist.* "There, done," she says briskly, putting the pen on my tray. "Your turn."

I look at her composed face, her serene black eyes. She must have been promised the apprenticeship as her last reward. There's no other way her attitude would change so fast. What did she have to do for it?

I eye the pen on my tray warily. "I'll do it later," I mutter, passing it back to Lia.

"What's wrong, StressNett?" she sighs, putting the cap back on.

"Nothing." I fiddle with the hemp bracelet I put on this morning. I'd been so out of it, I forgot about the motif change, and now I'm back in the stupid tunic too.

"I heard things are going very right for Nettie," Lincoln says, his almond-shaped eyes slitting slyly. I brace myself, knowing what's coming. "Don't you have a new boyfriend?"

"Stop it." I glare at him.

"Who's the lucky guy?" Martin asks.

No one speaks. I can't look up.

Lia breaks the silence. "Oh, it's Callen." She laughs, short and sharp. But at least she's trying. "Nettie and Callen are dating. Kind of strange, but life moves on."

"Oh." Martin fiddles with a fork, speechless. "Oh."

"Impressive, Nettie," Lincoln says, punching me lightly in the arm, like tracs after a good play. "Watch out, though. You might end in Mollie's gossip column with a scandal like this."

"Hanging out with Mollie a lot these days, Linc?" Lia asks innocently, at last revealing she knows the girl he had us guessing about so fervently three weeks ago.

"Who told you that?" he demands, eyes blazing. Selwyn's eyes are glued to her plate, but he doesn't notice. He and Lia argue, and I'm glad to have escaped further scrutiny about Callen.

"He's looking at you," Selwyn whispers to me.

"Yeah?" I glance across the room, and our eyes meet. He gives me a half wave, and I smile back weakly. I hadn't wanted to see him this weekend, debating what I should do about the suggestion.

"You two are so cute," Selwyn pronounces. Her gaze falls on the application again. "You're really not going to fill it out?"

I fold the application and put it in my pocket. "Later, I guess." My plate is clear, and there are still fifteen minutes before class starts. Over the weekend, I'd had a flood of ideas about how to get out of the suggestion, but most were desperate and crazy, like stow away on a freighter. Only one seemed feasible, though still a long shot. I decide it's now or never.

"You're almost done eating, right?" I say to Selwyn. "Wanna come with me to the bathroom before class? I need to fix my makeup."

"Okay," Selwyn agrees, finishing the last of her fries.

"I'll come with you," Lia cuts in.

I hesitate, but can't think of a good excuse to leave her behind. "Yeah, come on." I lead them to the first-floor bathroom, which hasn't been outfitted with new cameras since a pipe burst there a week or so ago. In addition to flooding, the lights cut out. They cleared up the mess, but I think it has to dry out before they can install any new electric wiring.

As soon as we enter, I heave open the window that faces the road, then flatten myself against the door so no one can interrupt us. Lia turns on some faucets and leans against the wall opposite me, crossing her arms. Selwyn stands in the middle of the floor, tapping her cello case.

"They've gone crazy with the Initiative," I mouth. "Ending the rewards. Cutting people who don't do what they want. I want to stop them."

Selwyn gasps on-mic, and Lia shushes her, but her eyes are wide—she didn't know either.

"They didn't tell you at your Reports?" I ask.

Selwyn shakes her head and clutches her cello case more closely to her body.

"No, same old, same old with the reward for me," Lia mouths.

"But you started earlier than me." I'm swerved off. "Why would they tell only me?"

"Well, maybe it comes with being the special favorite of the Initiative. What's the suggestion?" Lia leaves the wall and strolls over to me. "I bet it's something they think you won't do without such a harsh threat."

"The suggestion itself isn't important," I mouth, Luz's threats about cutting anyone I tell ringing in my ears. "What's important is that I don't want to do it. I think if we all refuse to take the suggestions, they might listen and let us out of the Initiative."

"What would we say?" Selwyn lets go of her cello case and joins us by the door. "They haven't threatened me with being cut yet, but I—I didn't like my last suggestion very much. I don't want to be in the Initiative either."

"Well, I haven't liked *any* of mine," Lia mouths emphatically. She put her hands on her hips. "But I did them. What is it, Nettie?" she presses.

"Forget what it was," I mouth, avoiding her eyes.

"Nettie," Lia mouths, eyes narrowed, "how bad could it be? Don't you always pretend like you don't want to do them? Remember the flirting one? You told me, 'I don't even want to have to *see* him after what he did to you.' Just stop." She says this last word on-mic, her voice dripping with disgust.

Selwyn touches her arm. "Lia, I think Nettie's right. Threatening to cut her is *horrible*. I'm sick of the Initiative too. It's not worth the ratings. Look what they made me do." She pushes her blouse down over her shoulder, and there on her skin is a huge collage of musical notation: bars, notes, and clefs, starting at her collarbone. She turns, and I see the rounded curves of an instrument, what must be a cello, on her shoulder, continuing down her back under her blouse.

Lia stays quiet but backs away, stunned. The tattoo looks awful. I remember our shopping trip and how Selwyn had ducked into Inked Up and sent me home. I thought she just wanted to flirt with Garrick. She'd been getting a tattoo.

"They promised me the cello apprenticeship," Selwyn mouths. "But now I have to see this every day of my life."

"I don't know, Selwyn—a lot of Characters would kill for their first choice apprenticeship," Lia mouths. She's recovered from her shock at the tattoo. Her hands are back on her hips. "You two are so sensitive. Bek has given me suggestions my whole life. She didn't call them that, and there weren't any rewards, but she's always given me tips on how to raise my ratings." She shrugs. "And it worked. Just listen to Media1."

"But—" I break off as the bathroom door jolts against me. Someone wants to get in, and I push back with all my strength, praying it's not a cricket. The pressure subsides—must have been a student.

"But I *have* listened," I finish. "I listened, and it got Revere cut, and now they think they can do whatever they want."

Selwyn's eyes get teary. "Revere."

Lia throws an accusatory look in my direction. *See what you've done.* She puts her arm around Selwyn, consoling her, and when she next looks at me, her eyes are flashing with rage.

"Nettie, God, all you think about is yourself lately. Your apprenticeship, your love life, your suggestions. Other people have problems too. Now you want help getting *out* of the Initiative? Haven't I done enough for you? I gave you the idea for the math apprenticeship in the first place, and I obviously helped you pick your boyfriend."

"*I'm* the one who only thinks about herself?" I demand, anger rising so quickly in me that I don't have time to think. Words come flying out, things I've buried for a long time. "I bend over backward for you *constantly*. I swear, if I let you, you'd tell me a better way to breathe. And if I have to hear about the stupid Double A program one more time—"

"Oh, I'm sorry for caring about my future." She throws up her hands. "It's so terrible that I care about creating a memorable day for other Characters. I guess you and Callen think I should just shun the world and find a rock to sit on all day," she mouths, her face red with fury. "You two are perfect together. I am sick of your superior attitudes."

"What about 'friendship is more important than boys'?"

"I *am* being your friend," she mouths. "I'm being honest. It's not about your being with Callen. It's about how you act about *everything*. The company had to push you into this romance because you refuse to ever take changes. You're always worried you'll end up like your mother, but it's too late. You *are* like her. Scared."

"I'm right to be scared," I mouth back. "You should be too, after what I saw in the courtyard."

Selwyn breaks away from Lia and turns to me. "Wait, what'd you see?"

I hesitate; the sight of her wan face and terrified dark eyes makes me want to protect her from the truth. But if I'm going to help Scoop tell the whole island, I should be able to tell Selwyn.

"Remember I told you about the building behind Character Relations, where they keep Patriots before transferring them to the Drowned Lands? I saw them there, and . . ." I move closer to her ear, whispering everything while Lia paces the floor. Selwyn brings her hand to her mouth, biting down on her knuckles. When I'm done, I take a step back, and she looks worse than ever, her eyes now vacant.

"Selwyn?" Lia says on-mic, darting back over to her.

Selwyn begins to mouth something, but all that comes out is a huge wail. Lia looks over her shoulder at me, alarmed.

"How could they?" Selwyn says on-mic, tears running down her face. "To Revere? To your dad?"

"Shhh." Lia brings her fingers to her lips. "My dad is fine," she says hastily on-mic, even though that's not the father Selwyn meant.

"Media1 hates us," Selwyn says, her voice loud. *Still on-mic.* "I'm sick of the Initiative too. I never wanted to—"

Lia quickly claps her hand over Selwyn's mouth.

"We have to get to class," I say, my voice trembling. I step away from the door, but then none of us move. We're frozen in place until Ayana Lemon comes in, her high ponytail bouncing behind her. Lia drops her hand from Selwyn's mouth.

"Is everything okay in here?" Ayana asks, hugging herself as if she needs to be shielded from the frostiness between us.

"Yeah," Lia says quickly. "But we should get going."

We file out of the bathroom, Ayana watching us leave, plum lips slightly parted, on the brink of asking us what's going on again. She doesn't get the chance. I stick close to Selwyn, scanning the mostly empty hall, tense, waiting for a cricket to emerge and reprimand her. Selwyn's walk is listless, and the squeaks of the rolling cello case seem to mock her somber mood.

Lia's ahead of us, and she's just about to turn the corner to our lockers when I call out, "I'm going to walk Selwyn to her lesson."

"Fine," she calls back without turning around.

Selwyn and I trudge together in silence, wordlessly turning right into the hallway lined with the soundproofed music practice rooms. Selwyn clings to me. I squeeze her hand. We pause outside her practice room. Inside, her teacher is doing her own warm-up exercises.

"I don't want to go in," Selwyn says, nails digging into my arm. I understand this feeling between us now, a bond of fear.

It yanks me back to the day they took Belle. I remember Selwyn twisting her long necklace and her wobbly voice and my own split-second certainty that they were coming for me.

"You don't have to. I'll skip history, and we can go somewhere else."

"To the zoo," she whispers, a smile breaking out across her tearstained face.

"Or the beach." I gently start to pry her hand from my arm.

"Or the Granary depot tunnel." She giggles, releasing me.

"Yeah, let's tag," I joke. We dissolve into laughter, and the cello playing stops. Mrs. Taro appears at the door.

"Selwyn, you're late. Please come in now."

"Sorry. Just a sec." Selwyn takes a deep breath. "Thanks, Nettie. I appreciate it—everything."

"No problem. See you later." As I walk away, the only sounds in the hall are the dolorous notes of the cello and the brief, crystal silences in between them. Appropriate.

And then I hear the thud of heavy boots. Several pairs, and they're coming closer. I know what's about to happen. I turn the corner and flatten myself against the wall. I see working cameras everywhere, looking at me. I know I should run, but I stay put, closing my eyes.

A door swings open roughly, hitting the wall behind it, and the music stops. Selwyn's scream is bloodcurdling. I hear Mrs. Taro murmuring and thuds and jostles. A *clunk* as something topples over and then a crack, the crush of wood bending and breaking. I open my eyes—I have to know. I lean around the corner, and I see a burly Authority yanking Selwyn out of the music room. Selwyn pulls back. She keeps screaming, but no one comes. Gone is the subdued, worn-out girl I left in the music room. She looks desperate, her black hair flying wildly, teeth clenched as she struggles. One of the Authority takes out a metal instrument and aims it at her neck. A high-pitched zapping sound rings out, and Selwyn goes limp.

I sit through history without any books or writing materials until Clemma Gosling takes pity, tears a page out of her notebook, and hands it to me, along with a dull pencil. Somehow I make it through.

When I finally make it to my locker between classes, I can feel the heat of stares on me. They know; everyone knows. I avoid looking at Selwyn's locker as I shove my books into my bag. Where is she? What do they do in the Sandcastle, when they're not running obstacle courses? I only have three more classes. I want to be home in my room. I want to be alone.

The reminders. I'm going to have so many reminders.

I see Callen farther down the hall, talking to Rawls at his locker. He's blurry because my eyes are full of unshed tears. I blink them back furiously and hurry past. I don't want to see him. Because I won't be able to actually talk to him, not in the hallway, with tons of cameras watching.

Lia's already in the classroom. She's wearing her most confident pose—head high, hands primly out on the desk—but she's pale. I look away from her as I sit. There's a rushing in my ears, as if I've just been dunked underwater, and it's a struggle to pay attention as Ms. Pepperidge draws a diagram on the whiteboard, showing all the characters in *The Player in the Attic.*

I shouldn't have brought them to the bathroom. But how could I have known she would crisp? Lia glances at me, but I stare straight ahead. I'm not mad at her anymore. Compared to Selwyn getting cut, Lia's bitchiness in the bathroom is trivial.

"Lia, what do you think?" Ms. Pepperidge asks, coming up to her desk.

"About what?" Lia snaps to attention. "I didn't hear you."

"Why did Bruno choose to stay in the attic when the other children went to the carnival?"

"Um . . ." Lia's forehead wrinkles. "I think the idea of the carnival scared him. Meanwhile, the attic—even though it was just a shabby little room, it was *his.* He felt powerful there."

Ms. Pepperidge beams. "Great answer. Power comes in many forms . . ."

Power. I think about the word as Ms. Pepperidge drones on. I felt powerful when I first started taking the suggestions. With Callen, when I began to suspect he liked me. Spending my bonus money at Delton's, doing the reenactment with Selwyn by our lockers. Power gave my life a jolt, a thrust it had lacked before. But no matter how powerful I felt, I'd always been a puppet. With Media1 pulling the strings.

I'm heading for the door at the end of class when I feel a hand on my arm. Lia. "Wait, Nettie—" She hesitates. "Do you want to do the Diary of Destiny after school?"

Anger bites at me again. Selwyn's *gone*.

I imagine Lia sitting on my bed, explaining that Selwyn will be better off, like Belle, or that it's her own fault for breaking the Contract. That she deserves it. "No, thanks. Um, I gotta go to calculus, but I'll call you tonight," I say, skirting around her and out of the classroom.

For once Mr. Black is on time. I sit at my usual desk, not looking at Scoop but wishing I could talk to him. His trip to the Sandcastle is my last chance to save Selwyn from the army or slave labor or whatever miserable fate is in store for the Patriots when they leave the island on the twentieth, five days away. We need to expose what's going on before then, or I might lose her forever.

I write a note at the corner of the page and nudge it to the edge of my desk. Scoop looks down briefly and nods, the smallest trace of a smile on his face.

I'm coming with you.

Chapter 20

Selwyn Baker became a Patriot today under Clause 53, Item B, Risk to the Show. As per the Contract, please refrain from mentioning Selwyn. As per the Contract, rid your personal sets of any reminders of Selwyn.

It's official: Selwyn crisped. Seasons ago, it might have been a fine. Now she's cut. It's like they're choking the life out of the island. I turn the Missivor off and go downstairs to get a garbage bag, aware that my room needs more than the five-minute scans I gave it after Revere and Belle.

I pass Mom, who is vacuuming the couch with a fabric hose. Her face is screwed up in concentration, her hair tied back tightly, like some sort of home facelift. The sound of the vacuum rasping over the fabric makes me cringe.

I escape upstairs and start filling my trash bag. There are silly ballpoint cartoons from when she used to draw in her spare time, birthday gifts—a checker set, a jelly bean dispenser, a hot pink wig, a book on watch repairs. All into the bag. In the midst of my hunt, I come across the fan letter Luz gave me, and I stuff it in my pocket, taking it with me as I haul the trash bag downstairs.

I dump the trash in the basement and come upstairs, letter still in hand. I pause in the kitchen, reading it one last time. *You're just like your parents: funny, tough, and smart.* I used to feel sorry for the Audience, but now I feel too sorry for myself to care about their drab Sectors lives. I click the gas on, hold out the paper, and watch the flames eat Kat Deva's letter.

The smoke is faint, but predictably, the alarm goes off. I'm scrambling on top of a stool to disable it when Mom comes in, frazzled, arms swooping about, like she can catch the noise in the air and quell it. My fingers are clumsy. I can't figure it out, and I resort to banging the alarm on the counter until the batteries pop out.

"Oh, my goodness," Mom says, her hand over her heart. "What was that about, Nettie?"

"Burning some junk mail," I say, washing my hands.

She pushes her glasses up her nose and fixes me with a stare.

I wipe my hands on the dishrag and cross my arms over my chest, daring her to ask more. Her eyes flit to the cameras in the ceiling. "Would you come with me to my office?" Her voice has that don't-mess-with-the-librarian air, and I follow her, too surprised by the invitation to refuse. Mom's office is her sanctuary, and though I used to come in here when I was younger to play with blocks on the blue carpet, I hardly ever go inside it these days.

"I want you to see my plus-ten view of Ginevra Herron's snowdrops." She steers me to a corner by the windows. All I see, however, is a blur of white as she jostles me tightly into the corner, then, to my astonishment, begins fralling with me for the first time in ages.

"Nettie, I don't know what got into Selwyn, but I'm worried about *you*. You're old enough to know now: your father was a Show Risk."

I blink. *A Show Risk? That's* what Violet meant when she said he was rebellious. I didn't realize she meant he acted out toward Media1. I thought she meant he got into trouble with Characters, not Reals.

"Toward the end, he was completely careless about fralling. He'd wave to the crickets. He even deliberately broke a few cameras, and one day—" She closes her eyes, like she can't bear to remember, then opens them and forces herself to go on. "He took his mic off. I saw him do it, before he went to work, and I tried to stop him, but he wouldn't listen. All he would say was that his life wasn't a performance. Who hasn't felt that way? But he didn't have to— I got home, and there was the Missive."

"Wow." I know Mom wants to scare me, but the only thing I feel is a weird sort of pride.

"Nettie, there's no *wow*," she mouths. "I'm worried you're going down the same road. You're not yourself—you've abandoned your building hobby, you didn't go to the Flower Festival, and now one of your closest friends was a Show Risk cut."

I take pity on her. "Mom, I've been acting differently because of the Initiative. Have you heard of it?" On-mic, I add sweetly, "Those flowers are gorgeous."

"I know. Ginevra told me they were hybrids—a cross be-tween lilies and roses?" she says on-mic. She switches back off. "The Initiative? I hear it can do wonders for your ratings. Is that why you're buying all those new clothes? I'm so proud of you, sweetie. This is wonderful."

Her reaction baffles me, but then I realize what's behind it— she thinks I'm a success now. She doesn't see beyond the Au-dience. "Mom," I mouth gently, "the Initiative is an excuse for Media1 to interfere with our lives."

"But your ratings are going up, right?" she mouths.

I'm conscious of how I can't see behind her. Her tall form blocks me off from the rest of the house. Her brown eyes im-plore me to say what she wants. Be who she wants me to be. I imagine telling her my latest suggestion. She'd probably ask what night I was planning for and offer to stay out so Callen and I could have the house to ourselves.

But instead I ask something that's been on my mind forever.

"Mom, do you miss him?" I mouth.

She stiffens. I wait, hoping she'll answer, and she does, but she's speaking on-mic, something about the Flower Festival and a display Mrs. Herron put together outside town hall. I nod, ask a few questions, and don't push her any further. I am who she wants me to be.

Safe in my room, I lie on my bed and think about our plan to get into the Center, imagining each detail as vividly as I can, scru-tinizing each step for potential errors. My brain gets exhausted, and I can't even drag myself to my feet to check the radio for Reals chatter.

I just want to sleep and forget about what happened to Selwyn. I turn on my side and stare at the empty space. Where Callen is supposed to be this week. But I can't do that.

I'm over wanting to be a Media1 pet like Lia is, but there's one thing she has that I still want. I can't quite come up with the perfect word for it. Resolve? Certainty?

Callen would probably just say she's bossy.

I sit up straight. I have an idea. I look at myself in the mirror and tilt my head in my Lia pose, the one that I use to give me confidence. I need to act like Lia used to with Callen. Right before he broke up with her, she came on too strong about the close-up. What I'd always thought of as confidence, he viewed as manipulation. If I do that, he'll refuse me for sure. He might even break up with me.

That's what I need, I realize. A breakup. The one thing that could get me out of the suggestion.

I rummage through the fridge late Wednesday afternoon, searching for whatever requires the least preparation. I settle on strawberries and bread, but perching on the kitchen stool, I find I'm too nervous to eat them. Instead, I fidget with the wire cutters I dug up in the garage. They're for Scoop and me to bring with us on Thursday, to cut through the fence that surrounds the Center. Oddly, breaking into the Center is causing me less anxiety than this close-up. Or is it a setup? A setup close-up.

All day, anxiety has swirled inside me. As I handed my over-due Double A application in to the principal. As I met with Scoop behind the loud fridge in the cafeteria to make sure he'd stolen the wigs from the scene shop. As I sat between Lia and Martin during lunch, pretending Selwyn never existed.

I give up trying to eat after a few strawberries. They taste more sour than sweet. I dump the rest of them back into the big bowl in the fridge, wash and dry my plate, and return the un-eaten bread to the bread bag. I go into the living room and lie down the couch for a second before straightening up Lia-style, checking myself in the mirror above the fireplace to make sure I nail it.

The doorbell chimes. I jump up off the couch and run to the door. I fling it open, smiling. Too exuberant? *I'm already doing things wrong.*

"You made it. I'm glad," I say, struggling to come up with what Lia would say. "I haven't been able to stop thinking about tonight."

Callen's wearing his usual, a T-shirt—but this one's pump-kin orange and isn't faded at all—and jeans. He puts his arms around me, and I breathe him in. He feels so real and solid as I hold him, like he can withstand anything, and for the first time all day, the worry starts to fade.

"Whoa, tight grip." He laughs above me, the skin around his eyes crinkling in that way I like.

"Sorry." But I'm not. I finally let him go when I hear a cam-era swiveling. For a few seconds, I forgot about the suggestion. I take his hand and lead him up to my room, wishing I felt sexy. I hope my hand isn't sweating.

We enter my room. It's tidier than it's been in months: I'd done a lot the night of Selwyn's cut to make it spotless and even more when I got home today. Past projects are tucked away into drawers, books lined up on the shelves, mirror nice and clear. Soft evening light spills in from the open curtains.

"Plus ten," he says, stopping at the desk and picking up Belle's bottle. He flicks it, and a high-pitched note undulates in the air. I catch my breath, worried a Real behind the cameras might notice that the bottle is a reminder.

He puts the bottle down gently, and I relax. He surveys the rest of the room. "Everything's so organized," he says, smiling at me. "Not that I'm surprised. It's very you." He sits on the bed and plants his hands on either side of him. Now. Now. Now. I sit next to him. We have about two hours before Mom comes back. Our knees are touching. The seventeen cameras in my room flare at me.

"I can think of more fun things to do," I say, pushing him down so he's on his back. The words seem to stumble out of my mouth, but at least I get them said. I straddle him, but I don't feel at ease like I did in the Brambles. My whole body feels heavy, like it's working against me. I close my eyes, bend down, and kiss him.

He's underneath me and pushes my tank top straps down, the microphone going with it. I think there's actually a clause in the Contract about intimate situations. *Microphones can be moved* . . . I shouldn't be thinking about the Contract. Even if it's the whole reason I'm here. Kissing. I should be thinking about kissing. Thinking kissing. Frustrated, I open my eyes so that I can see his, but of course, they're closed. I check the clock on my night table. Got to stay on track. Callen notices my distraction, and his eyes follow the path of mine and latch on to what's next to the clock.

"Are those . . . ?" He sits up on his elbows and picks up the condoms.

"Um, yeah," I say. "I mean, yes, of course. For us. Tonight." My tank top straps are halfway down my arms, and I don't know what to do with them. What would Lia say? "I'm *so* ready. Aren't you? Don't you want to?"

"Well . . ." I tense again. What if it doesn't work? He starts to kiss me again, and I panic—is he going to go through with it? *I can't.* My first close-up *can't* be because of the Initiative.

He breaks off the kiss and mutters something, his eyes half shut so I can't read them.

"What? What's wrong?" My voice is too—so much more hesitant than Lia's. "Don't tell me you haven't before," I say, lacing the words with a hint of scorn. I pull my mic up so it's lying on the pillow next to my head.

He reaches down and cups my cheek in his hand.

"I want to . . . one day," he says. "I haven't either."

I'm both surprised and not by this. It's odd for trac Callen, but not for the shy Callen I've known most of my life.

Callen drops his hand and finds mine and holds it. He turns, and our foreheads touch, like they did on the beach. *I wish this were all the Audience wanted.* Because it's all I want now.

"Let's do it," I force out, pushing up his shirt again.

He looks over his shoulder at the clock. "Isn't your mom coming home in an hour? This is so sudden and so rushed. You're acting like . . ."

"Like what?"

"Lia," he says reluctantly. Yes. It's working. "She was always after me to close up, like it was some kind of competition."

My mind scrambles, trying to come up with whatever will turn him off the most. "Well, isn't it? We need to win."

Callen raises his eyebrows, incredulous. It's all I can do not to tell him everything—but I can't risk his getting cut. I couldn't live with myself.

"Come on," I reach for his shirt again. "We don't have much time."

"Stop." He pushes my hands away. "Nettie, this is crazy. Can we wait? Just until it's a little more, I don't know, just natural?"

"Why wait?" I pout. I get an idea. I get close to his ear. "We'll get such great ratings."

He recoils. "Are you kidding?" he says, switching to on-mic. Good. "Now you're exactly like Lia." He grabs his microphone from the bed and clips it back to his collar. I watch, hating his anger, but knowing that it's exactly what I need to keep both of us safe.

He sits on the edge of the bed and ties his shoelaces in brisk, fast motions. I decide to leave my tank top straps hanging off my arms—I don't want Media1 to suspect I didn't try. I have to fight down every instinct I have to leave him alone when I reach over and put my arms around him, murmuring, "Why don't you want to? You're being weird."

He throws my arms off and gets up. His face looks cold, his eyes icy. I lose my confident Lia pose, and I'm unable to speak.

But he can. "I think we need a break—maybe we shouldn't see each other for a while."

I raise my head, facing the icy eyes straight on. "Okay," I answer, making my voice small. He hesitates, lingering at the door. Like he expects me to protest. Snap back at him like I'm sure Lia did. But I just get up and start neatening the bed, turning my back to him. I hear him go down the stairs and out the door.

Chapter 21

The waterfall comes down in undulating blue-white ribbons. "I'm taking us under. You'll like it—it's an adventure," Scoop yells into his mic, nearly swallowing it in his effort to make sure Media1 hears. I squeal with feigned terror as we approach the waterfall, bending down to check that the plastic tarp is firmly in place, covering the book bag and radio at the bottom of the boat. Done, I straighten up and brace myself for the onslaught of water, pulling my jacket above my head.

It makes a seemingly infinite hollow echo in my ears, like when I wear a shower cap in the shower. I laugh and pretend I'm having the time of my life, and Scoop seems chipper too, grinning while steering the rudder. Focusing on my performance makes it easier to ignore the water seeping into my jacket and the butterflies in my stomach. Scoop maneuvers sharply, turning the boat so each of the four cameras takes a turn underneath a heavy stream of water. I hold my breath until I see the red lights on two blink out, just as we planned. The other two, pinned on the bow behind me, stubbornly stay on.

Shivering, I shout, "Enough!" and jerk my head toward the jagged rocks behind me. Scoop follows my glance and changes the boat's course.

"Oops," he says as the bow bumps against the moss-covered rocks. Both working cameras get battered, but not enough to extinguish those stubborn lights. Scoop grows frustrated, long face tightening as he rams the boat again and again into rocks.

"Be careful!" I yell. At this rate, we'll destroy the boat before we get to the cove by the Center. The cameras are still on. Time for the backup plan to the backup plan.

"I'm feeling seasick," I call out, our signal, and Scoop steers the boat away from the rocks, while I covertly work the turquoise ring off my finger and fling my hand downward, sending it flying into the water. It bobbles in the water.

"My ring!" I cry, dropping to my knees and leaning over the side of the boat, my torso covering a camera lens, while I plunge my hand in the water, trying to rescue the ring in the view of the other camera. I fish the wire cutters out of my back pocket with my other hand. The ring sinks out of view—I had a feeling I might really lose it, and was ready.

I reach behind the camera, pop off the casing and use the cutter to slice open the wires clumped inside. Unnatural crisping. I'm hoping that Media1 will assume the rocks are responsible. I scoot over to the remaining working camera, mumbling on-mic about seeing the ring being carried away by a current and needing to stretch out one last time. Now that I have practice, I disable the camera in a couple of seconds.

"I can't catch it." I turn back around. "The ring's gone, forget it."

"Too bad." Scoop pulls us away, aiming north, taking us along this last stretch of Avalon Beach below the Brambles. No red eyes, all the cameras dead. We round the tip of the island and sail south, parallel to Eden Beach. Tall, trimmed trees in the Brambles still loom above us for a minute and then we see the fence that separates the Brambles from the out-and-out wilderness at the outskirts of the Center.

"I took your advice," I say, to fill up the audiotrack. "I ignored Callen." I had told Scoop that Callen and I had broken up and that it hadn't been my choice. I'd begged him for advice on how to get him back—all my dialogue designed to convince Media1 that the breakup was completely against my will. "He didn't seem to mind," I add.

"He will. By the end of the week, he'll be eating out of your hand," Scoop reassures me, sprawled on the bench at the prow, hand on the rudder.

"I hope so," I say. I'm opposite Scoop, perched on the bench in the stern, toying with the nets the aquarium uses to dredge up specimens. Our front for being here. Officially he's out on the water today to catch some mackerel for a finicky dolphin who refuses the aquarium's stock chum.

"Are you ready for the Double A?" Scoop asks. "Conor showed me the poem he wrote to open the ceremony. It's . . ."

"Totally depressing?" I twist around, haunted by the idea that Media1 might send a boat after us. There's nothing but water.

Scoop cocks his head to the side. "No . . . just short. About childhood's end. He's right, you'll never be as innocent as you were before the Double A."

"So you feel less innocent?" My stomach twists as we drift closer and closer to land. Farther down the coast, I can see a docked freighter from the Sectors. I wonder if it's the one that's intended to transport the Patriots on Saturday.

"Not really, because I don't think I ever felt innocent to begin with," he says. "B—my family says I'm cynical."

The boat swerves sharply as he directs it toward the shore, to an inlet covered in a thick tangle of shrubbery, near the chain-link fence. He nods at me: we planned out what we'd say next.

"Let's put on some music." I dig under the tarp and take out the portable radio, turning to a raucous teenaddict music station. I turn the dial past the contractually prescribed volume. Scoop says Media1 is used to technical difficulties with the boat, but I'm prepared to get fined. At least twice: for the volume and for the cameras.

"I'm turning the motor off—the vibrations keep the fish away," Scoop says.

"It's so relaxing out here." I yawn into my mic. "I might even nap."

The idea is to prevent Media1 from sending cricket teams. We want them to think we're hanging out, but not talking.

"Go ahead," Scoop says. "I can handle the nets by myself."

He cuts off the motor and steers, tying the boat to a thick sapling bending over the water. He deliberately ties it loosely so that the boat jostles with currents, giving the audiotrack the impression that it's still sailing. I inspect the foliage around us for cameras. None.

Scoop stands up gingerly, slithering off his microphone and battery pack and setting them next to the blaring radio. I sling the book bag with our supplies over one shoulder, and we scramble over the side of the boat and up the rocky bank.

Once we're safely under cover of the trees, we stop to change. I unzip the book bag and pass him a purple jumpsuit, one of the wigs he stole from the scene shop, and wire-rimmed sunglasses that he brought from his house. Luz is taller and bulkier than I am, so the jumpsuit fits easily over my jeans and T-shirt. I pick up the straight blond wig Scoop got for me and pull it over my head, wiggling it until it's snug. Scoop hands me a pair of black boots with thick soles, akin to the workman boots the Reals favor. The final touch is a pair of sunglasses I'd found in our kitchen junk drawer.

I watch Scoop move down the steep banks to the boat, going to stash the book bag in the bracken. The combination of the gray wig and the sunglasses makes him seem like a middle-aged man trying to look hip.

I walk over to the fence, grip a link in the wire-cutter's jaws, and begin snipping through, wincing at the noise. Beyond the fence is a stretch of seemingly deserted land, but who knows? It might be on some Authority's patrol route. Scoop clambers back up from the boat, and as I clip the hole, he yanks out the metal impatiently.

"Let's go," he says when I'm halfway done, forcing the cut section of metal links down and urging me through. I climb through, the space smaller than I'd like, the metal clawing my jumpsuit, and Scoop follows clumsily, cursing to himself as the metal snaps back at him, catching his ankle.

"Are you all right?" I ask.

"Yeah," he says, dusting off his hands. He checks his watch. "Four thirty. We have half an hour." Media1 only allows island boats to be in the water for an hour. If a boat misses its check-in time, they'll send crickets to the scene.

"Got it." We walk straight out, toward the gravel road that leads up from the docks to the Sandcastle. I glance at the massive black freighter below. Authority are on the deck, small as ants from this distance. When I look up, my breath catches: three very human-sized Authority are stomping toward us, not thirty feet away, apparently headed for the ship themselves. I draw closer to Scoop.

"I heard they're lifting some of the flight restrictions next week," one says as they pass.

"I'd still avoid all the islands, even the so-called safe areas. Last year my cousin got pickpocketed by drownclown kids."

"Figures," the other says. He puts his hand on his forehead to block the sun. "Ship's here. I hope this batch is ready for departure."

Scoop and I exchange quick looks but move on without saying anything. The Center air is its usual collection of smells: salty cooking odors from the residential towers beyond Character

Relations, gas fumes spewing out of the trucks climbing the hill from the dock on the beach, and the fresh, sweet smell of new spring flowers on the hill.

A long walkway extends from the road to the entrance of the Sandcastle. A short line of Reals waits there, all in purple jump-suits. Scoop walks faster, about to get in line behind them, but I place a hand on his wrist.

"Look—there's some sort of ID too," I whisper. The code won't be enough. Two Authority are standing by the doors, guns gleaming in the sun. As the Reals pass through, they hold up badges that an Authority inspects before presenting them with a keypad to type their codes into.

We pass the turn and continue straight uphill, to the back of Character Relations. To our left, the ground slopes down, form-ing a valley that the Sandcastle rises out of. The courtyard is concealed from this angle. I study the building.

"There." I point toward a rectangular basement window. I can't see everything from here, but the glass looks cracked. "We can break the window and get in through the basement—you can cover me from the Reals while I do it." We walk down the hill, keeping our pace slow and casual to avoid drawing attention to ourselves. I gesture for him to stand between me and the road and put the toe of my sneaker against the window, giving it a nudge. Nothing.

I time my barrage of kicks to coincide with a truck rumbling up the hill. Its loud engine drowns out the sound of shattering glass. Scoop glances behind him and gives me a quick smile as I kneel and sling my leg over the sill, wincing as shards of glass at the edges of the frame prick my jumpsuit. I have to go quickly. I put my other leg through, close my eyes, and drop into the darkness. For a second, I lie there, my head aching from the force of the fall. *Get up.* I rise to my feet and shake off shards of glass. The boiler beats *pom pom pom.* There's only one patch of light, streaming in through the broken window I just came through. I hear Scoop struggling through. Loudly.

"Come on," I say under my breath. A few seconds, and he tumbles down, even clumsier than I was. I flinch.

There's a brief silence, followed by an "ow!"

"I don't know how we're going to get out," I mumble, feeling my way among the ducts, passing the boiler, and finally grasping a doorknob. I open the door and step out into the hall with Scoop. Fluorescent lights buzz. I examine the ceiling for cameras and find none. We're in a long and deserted hall.

He tugs at the first door we find, but it doesn't open. I see the keypad to the left and gesture for him to punch in his show doctor's code. It works, and we enter a stairwell, wordlessly heading up. There's a window on the first landing, and I pause, pulling Scoop over. It overlooks the courtyard with its obstacle course, less scary in daylight without Authority or Patriots on it, but the sight is enough to make Scoop wince. He doubles his pace, stopping at the first door we come across and typing in the code with nervous rat-a-tat fingers.

We enter a cauldron of activity. Reals stroll back and forth, talking, holding clipboards, laughing, scrawling notes. They seem more relaxed here than they are in the Character Relations Building. They don't look as ugly as I always imagine them to be, either. They seem . . . normal. Have they always been? I look down quickly, before I get caught staring, and merge into bustling Reals, Scoop alongside me.

The halls are lined with floor-to-ceiling windows, some shuttered by blinds. Scoop touches my arm. A crowd of Reals huddles outside one window, enthralled. He pulls me over to them.

"They're getting better," a bearded one next to me says.

A row of targets lines the far end of a shooting gallery, and the shooters are right below us. I count fifteen gunmen in all, each in a separate stall, their backs to us, arms thrust out, and hands locked around revolvers. Earmuffs cover their ears. They're in camouflage—just like I saw in the courtyard.

Patriots.

Their shots are muted by the thick pane of glass between us, but we can see their bodies jolt when they fire. Once a target is riddled with holes, it gets sucked up into the ceiling by silver claws and a fresh one replaces it.

"It's like the police academy," Scoop whispers.

One Patriot puts her arms down in between shots. A female Real in a purple jumpsuit approaches the shooter and molds her arms and hands back into position. Then the Real moves along to the next stall and the shooter glances over, watching her departure nervously. My stomach drops: Selwyn. Her eyes flit past me, and I realize the windows are one-way. We are an unseen audience.

They *are* being trained for combat.

I lower my sunglasses to see better. Is my father here? Would I even recognize him? No, all of these faces are familiar. Timon, the receptionist from Mom's optician's office, with the nose piercing. Haynes Mallerd, who lived on our block. Some Characters were cut months ago, but no one here has been gone longer than a season.

I nudge Scoop, but his eyes are glued to Belle's slim figure, her roughly shorn hair. She clasps the gun casually with one hand while waiting for a fresh target, as if the gun were no more than a purse.

"I can't just leave her here," he whispers, his voice hoarse, like he's holding back tears.

"Shhhh," I say. "Listen, we came here for proof, okay? You might have a chance of helping her once everyone knows, but not on your own."

I pull at Scoop's sleeve, and he backs up obediently, but his gaze is unwavering. He's mesmerized by the sight of his sister. I have to get him away from here.

"This way." I tug his jumpsuit again. "We don't have much time. Let's see what else is here." Scoop follows me down the hall like a zombie. We need to find something we can steal easily, and fast, something that will make it obvious to the Characters what's going on in here.

Too bad I can't pry off the metal plates adjacent to each door. *Munitions & Explosives*. I watch a man inside the room studying some sort of cube bursting with wires curling into one another, like a metallic bale of hay. It's Coran Thyme, who used to work in my dentist's office. Four other Patriots are with him, but I don't know their names. Scoop wants to linger at each room, but I keep pulling him along, worried we won't find anything to take back. The blinds are closed on the doors of *Biological Weapons,* *Wilderness Survival,* and *Communications Operations.* The next open window is for a room labeled *Undercover Techniques.*

Another person I know, a Real, stands in that room with a group of Patriots. It's Til. She's holding a compact mirror and applying fake eyelashes. She puts the mirror down onto a table and blinks a couple of times until her lashes are righted, then says—I can't hear her, but I can read her lips—"You try! You can't get caught, or the drownclowns will . . . Let's just say the ones who live often wish they hadn't." Behind her is Eveline Chromere, who was cut last summer, a nurse at Hidehall. Her hand trembles as she clumsily sticks the lashes onto her eyelid.

Scoop stirs to life beside me. "There," he whispers, gesturing to an open door at the end of the hall. Reals wander in and out, their demeanors more subdued. Lights flash against the door; I hear laughter and conversation and, running under it all, the noise of a television.

We walk into the room with casual strides, trying to blend in. Couches lie in rows, a makeshift theater, with a massive television at the front of the room instead of a stage. Reals idle on the couches, snacking and sipping coffee. Stale air pervades the room. Some of the Reals are talking, and some are gawking at the television. A suntanned older man with shark eyes intones on-screen, "For the month of May, we are rationing meat due to antigovernment activities in the Drowned Lands. Collect your ration coupons at your nearest government office. Counterfeiters will be punished." The screen fades to black, and the *Blissful Days* theme music comes on.

I usually seize any chance I can to watch the broadcast, but this time I only look long enough to see a farmer on a tractor in the Granary. Scoop and I search the room for something we can take that will make the Characters see what's going on here. I want to know more about the nature of this army—is it the Sectors army? Are they part of the attempt to stomp out the Drowned Lands rebellion? Table with coffee machine and napkins. Poster for the show with an aerial shot of the island. The file cabinet in the corner is tempting, but I can't imagine opening it without calling too much attention to myself. Everyone erupts in laughter as the farmer, stuck in a muddy ditch, pounds on his gas pedal.

"I'll be right back," Scoop says to me suddenly. "I have to see her again."

He's already slipping out the door before I can respond. I should go with him, make sure he doesn't do anything crazy. He's as rattled as Selwyn was in the bathroom. As I move toward the door, a colorful flyer on the floor catches my eye. Six people stare up from the page. The person nearest the middle is a woman holding up a pistol, a camouflage scarf around her head and flames behind her. I duck under a table and snatch it up.

Flora. The Health Haven cashier. We got a Missive about her

being cut three seasons ago. She's one of many small headshots on the page, which is made up of columns and rows like our yearbooks. At the top, in big bold letters: Patriot Adventures, *Thursday at 8.* I keep reading, my stomach sinking.

This Season on Patriot Adventures. *Who Will Survive? Who Will Make the Ultimate Sacrifice?* Then underneath the picture in small print: *Season Highlight Episode 1, The Electric Plant. Flora, one of our veteran Patriots, leads the destruction of an electric plant known to harbor fugitive Drowned Lands terrorists. Tally: Three Enemy Kills, One Patriot Makes the Ultimate Sacrifice.*

Enlisted in the service of Media1. It wasn't a lie, after all. There's another show.

Chapter 22

"Do you want a cup?" a Real asks from the nearby coffee machine. I look up, startled. The Real waits, staring right at me, and I drop my head again, pretending to be engrossed in the paper.

"No, thanks," I say, as fast as I can. I fold the paper up, tuck it into my shirt underneath the jumpsuit, and hurry away. I need to find Scoop, and we have to get out here. I'm almost out when I stop for a second, pulled in by the television. What's on-screen now isn't *Blissful Days*. It appears to be people giving commentary on the show. Three Reals sit on stools on a stage, two women and a man with pearly teeth. All three are in better condition than the Reals I'm used to seeing on the island—they could pass for Characters.

"*Blissful Days* was a doozy yesterday!" the man says. His pearly teeth wink and flash under studio lights. The camera pans over the audience, clapping in agreement.

The plump older woman says. "Yes, let's talk teens. Finally, apprenticeship application time."

"I saw a lot of second-guessing," the second woman trills.

"Lincoln Grayson changed his mind at the last minute and went for the casino slot."

Casino dealer. Figures. Probably wants to be a Spate dealer to swerve off his parents. I spot a clock next to the television: 4:59. Scoop and I have until 5:30 to get back to the boat. I'm almost at the door when the ratter-patter of hundreds of drums striking in unison, marching-band style, stops me in my tracks.

A baritone voice proclaims, "Next up on *Patriot Adventures*," and, of course, I turn back.

"Built over a century ago to house government records, Lim Tower is thought to be impenetrable. That's why the Drowned Landers made it their headquarters after taking over Krail. But what will happen when we send Seabert Oreganet in to destroy this vital building?"

"Kaboom!" a Real slumped on a couch crows. "I wish they were sending in the teen team, though."

"Teen team?" the woman next to him asks.

"Yeah, they've started transferring teenagers from *Days* to *Adventures*—they think they'll make better Patriots. More malleable."

"I hear they'll let Seabert opt out of his contract if he survives this one." *The show.* I bet this insane show, not *Blissful Days*, is what the Reals were referring to when I overheard the radio transmission. *Mom said it was frightening,* one had said, and then I remember being on the Tram, after the depot tunnel, when the man said that before they had a draft, *Before they do that, they should up the adventures.* He meant *Patriot Adventures.*

This is why Kat Deva knew my father was *tough*. Is tough. She's seen him in combat. What happens to Patriots has never been a mystery for the Audience. But if I thought they were heartless before, now I think they're a thousand times worse.

I remember how firmly my mother reprimanded me for mentioning my father on-mic and ruining our scenes for broadcast. All those reminders I threw out. Now I get that it was never about the Audience—it was how Media1 keeps *us* from questioning what happens to them.

A montage of destruction fills the screen—buildings toppling, flame storms, piles of fallen bodies. The drums start up again, and a Real claps in time on his knee.

Blood soaking through fatigues. Patriots racing through the jungle, fleeing gunfire. An agonized scream as someone falls to the ground. When I finally manage to tear my eyes away, I realize the Reals are rapt, unfazed by the carnage.

"Do you remember that time Starling blew up the bridge between the two rebel camps?" one of them asks nonchalantly. I look over. My father. They've seen him. I glance at the television. Maybe I can see him too.

"I miss him," a dry voice says. "What's it been, two years now?"

"Yup," the other one sighs. "Sad. But for the best cause. To Sectors reunification!" He lifts up his coffee up, and the others follow suit.

The carnage disappears, and the screen returns to the set with the commentators. I remain standing, in a trance. All these seasons, I thought he was in an office building in Zenta. Even after I began to question that, I never thought it out—never considered he could be . . . really gone. I thought I'd accepted that I'd never talk to him, never see him, never know him. But this is a finality I could never have conceived of before.

Patriot Adventures comes back on-screen with a sickening roar—a helicopter touching down on a ragged field—and I snap out of my trance and burst into the hall. Scoop is at the shooting gallery, watching Belle.

"Let's go," I say. He ignores me and keeps moving closer to the glass. A Real watches us curiously. I grab Scoop's hand, harder this time. "Let's *go*."

"We have to help her," he says, arms crossed resolutely, like he's ready to take the place down now.

"We will! I got it. I got the proof. It's worse than we thought. I'll tell you on the boat, but we have to get out of here."

I don't wait for him to agree, just turn and start walking down the hall. It's all I can do not to break into a run.

Chapter 23

Lia and I stand next to each other in the lunch line. She steps in front of the trays of noodles and spoons some into her bowl without dropping sauce on the counter like everyone else. *If nothing else, she's poised,* I think. I need her to be, since what I plan to show her will seriously test her ability to hold it together.

"How's it going with Callen?" she asks as I lean over the noodles. I nearly drop the ladle. We haven't talked about him since we were in the bathroom with Selwyn. We haven't been talking much at all, about anything.

"It's not really going," I say as we walk to the table. Media1 knows too—this morning I had received a Missive officially letting me out of the suggestion due to the breakup.

"Really?" Lia says, her voice an octave higher than usual. She bumps into a freshman, apologizes, then turns back to me. "What happened?"

I keep walking. "We had an argument," I say, not bothering to contort my body in any way for the cameras. "We sort of—" I swallow, still finding the words hard to get out. "We sort of broke up."

"Aw, Nettie." Lia pats me on the back as we reach the table. "Callen is such a nut," she sighs. As far as I can tell, she's actually sad for me, not just saying so. Good. I need her to be on my side today.

"I know." I don't want to talk about it anymore. "How's your mom doing?"

"Actually, the therapy seems to be helping," she says. She puts her napkin on her lap. "She's been doing these exercises about exploring her feelings, trying to figure out why she drinks. Her counselor said she's hiding something."

"Maybe she's really ready to change," I offer. I hope so—she was scary on the day of the Flower Festival.

"I'm ready for her to change too," she says. "I've missed you, Nettie." She digs into her noodles. That's it, and it's enough. I know we're good again, and at least there's a chance she'll listen to what I have to tell her.

Across from me, Lincoln wolfs down a hamburger, and I'm wondering how he'd fare as a Patriot. He can wound with words, but I can't imagine him using actual weapons. And Martin would wet his pants if faced with a gun. Henna, on Lia's other side, well . . . I've seen how she watches us, noticed the politic way she has of handling Lia's suggestions. I think she'd survive. There's something not quite so innocent about Henna's innocence.

"So, are you and Callen going out or not?" Mollie Silverine, who's taken Selwyn's place, is studying me with interest. Her reporter's notebook is on her tray.

"No comment, Mollie," I say, cringing and scooting my chair a few inches away from her.

"I need something, anything," she pleads to the table. "Any plus-ten gossip? My deadline is in four hours. There are, like, six other people competing for two slots at *Bliss Daily News*. I need a big scoop."

"Okay, okay." Lia puts down her fork. "Let me think. Do you want to write about my play? Auditions are done."

"I need something juicier, Lia. Do you feel like Nettie betrayed you?" Mollie flips her notebook open and uncaps her pen. Lincoln snickers. Lia doesn't respond, and Mollie begs again, "Please, please. I don't want to get anyassigned."

"Mollie, the Double A is tomorrow. They already delivered the lists to my house to put in the program tonight," Lia says, her tone calm but firm. She motions for Mollie to close the notebook. "It's *over*. You either have the apprenticeship or you don't."

After lunch, I pull Lia aside and say on-mic, "I think we should talk about Callen. But alone, so Mollie doesn't hear. Janitor's closet?" I cross my fingers, hoping they haven't gotten around to fixing it. We can't stay here. A team of crickets is nearby, filming the post-lunch hall.

"All right," she sighs.

"Good," I say, dragging her down the stairs. Worried that the crickets will chase after us, I sprint into the closet, and Lia keeps up with me, panting slightly as she closes and locks the door. I make my way to the clearing in the back, my legs colliding with buckets and mop handles. She follows more slowly.

I pause, listening for the buzz of the cameras and peering into the dark, trying to detect red lights. Nothing. Luz was frazzled and probably forgot to give the order. We only have a few seconds alone, but I explain everything in a rush, and she doesn't have a chance to respond before crickets charge in, breaking through the lock. Light from the hall blasts us. I untuck my mic automatically, and Lia does the same. A tall man stoops and tilts a camera up into our faces.

Lia says on-mic, "God, I hope I don't have puffy eyes from staying up so late, photocopying programs. But it'll be worth it. It's nice that Scoop can help me."

"Definitely worth it," I say. The bell rings, and we press past the crickets, walking up to our lockers. They follow us the whole way.

Now that I've talked to Lia, I don't have anything to take my mind off *Patriot Adventures*. Calculus is a strange kind of torture. The objects in the classroom, the Characters here, seem rigid and hard, yet I feel transparent. Terra props her elbows on Scoop's desk and prattles on about how she had to sit in on a tonsil-removal operation as part of her apprenticeship.

Scoop laughs at something she says, raking his hair back in a sort of *Bliss Teen* hunk cover pose. The natural glow of his hazel eyes is more obvious than ever. Maybe he figures he might as well give her what she wants, since she'll have real problems to handle after tomorrow. Every Character will.

Mr. Black calls on me to solve a problem on the whiteboard,

and I watch my arm move. I hear myself explain my calculations, but it all seems ephemeral. Like I'm a watercolor that used to be an oil painting. Maybe this feeling is like the final manifestation of never being at ease here, not in the way that Lia is.

That's it, I conclude at the end of class and the closing down of the day. *I've never been at ease.* It's been a secret inside me, but now it's sprung out, and it's confronting me everywhere.

I don't fit in, and I don't belong on *Blissful Days.*

At the end of school, I pass the athletic fields while going to get my bike. The Ants and Pigeons practice at separate ends, with the Pigeons closer to the high school. I decide to watch Callen from a distance—just a little. I miss him. I idle on the sidelines, hovering behind two sophomore boys with clipboards and whistles who occasionally refill water bottles and trot out to the field to pass them around.

Callen sees me and drops his head, kicking up dirt on the pitcher's mound. I should leave, but I stand in place, waiting for him to look up again. I want to make things right between us before tomorrow.

I wait until he looks at me again and jerk my head toward the bleachers behind me. He pauses, then nods quickly, and I climb until I'm on the highest row. I wait the entire practice, until the sun begins setting, shredding the sky. The breeze picks up, and I zip up my jacket and wrap my arms around my bent legs, resting my chin on my knees, inching my head down, like a turtle retreating into its shell.

The sounds of practice are melodic: yelps and yells, grunts and groans. The crack of the bat. The whistle of the ball flying through the air and the thump as it's caught.

Callen acknowledges me with another nod as he walks off the mound and into a swarm of players gathered around the coach, who's giving them a pep talk. At one point, there's a rousing cheer, hands clapping. Callen claps, but he's disengaged, not smiling or reacting to any individual line. He's going through the motions. Like I've been doing on the show ever since we learned about *Patriot Adventures*.

I get lost in thoughts, running through the details of our plan, hoping Lia and Scoop come through.

"Hey, Nettie." I look up, startled. Callen's standing next to me. No trace of a smile, but at least he's here.

"Oh, hi. Sit down." I pat the space next to me, trying to think of how to word what I want to say without bringing up the Initiative. He sits but maintains a distance between us.

"I feel bad about Wednesday," I say. "I think . . ." I quickly glance around, looking for cameras. They're all over the place, on railings and poles above us. Even though Media1 let me off the hook with the suggestion, I'm still hesitant to tell him the full truth. But why not? "I just wasn't feeling like myself." I lean over and whisper into his ear, "They made me push for the close-up for the Initiative. I'm in it. They made me do some other stuff too, about us." I tell him about the suggestions related to him. I fight the urge to close my eyes—I'm so scared of his reaction. I go back on-mic. "I want to be with you. I don't care about the close-up."

He shifts his gaze toward me, still not smiling, but his features more relaxed. Open. "I believe you," he says on-mic. "I'm not thrilled about—that other stuff." He touches behind his ear. The Initiative. "But it explains a lot." He clears his throat, choosing his next on-mic words with care. "Nettie, I was always a little worried—that you didn't really like me. The way Lia didn't. It seemed to take you so long to notice me."

"I was shy—and you were dating Lia," I protest.

"I know, but . . . ," he says doubtfully. "Even when we ended up on the rocks together, it almost didn't seem real. Too good to be true." He stumbles, sandy eyebrows knitting together as he tries to figure out how to not mention the Initiative.

"But it *was* real." I pick up his hands and interlink our fingers. "We have to start over and trust each other." I bring my mouth up to his ear and whisper, "Because after tomorrow, I won't be in the Initiative. No one will."

He turns his head sharply to me, mouthing, "What do you mean?"

I grab his hand. "Do you remember what you told me about the island being a trap?" I say on-mic, hoping it'll just pass as teenage angst. "You were right, but . . . that's going to change."

Chapter 24

Our Double A earrings are simple—*classy*, Lia had called them. Luminous single imitation pearl droplets at the end of braided wires. The morning of the Double A, I put them on clumsily, not used to earrings. I look quite demure with them on and my hair up in a bun. I turn around a couple of times, checking myself from all angles. Different expressions. Smile. No smile. My skin, the result of many days of diligent Skin Sequence, glows. Dr. Kanavan will be proud.

I didn't have time to buy a new dress, so I put on an old one. It's a white sleeveless silk shift, with some crystal beadwork at the bottom. Selwyn had picked it out for me a long time ago, so it's covertly in honor of her.

As soon as I step into the dining room, Mom rushes to the doorway, spatula in hand. "I'm not finished yet," she says. "I'm making pancakes." Underneath her apron, she's dressed up, too, in a gray skirt suit and black pumps.

"It's okay, Mom. I can wait." I sit at the table, glancing out the window. The sky is pure and cloudless, scripted. I heard the helicopters outside while I listened to the radio last night.

"I just want everything to be perfect," she says, returning to the kitchen. "You'll remember today for the rest of your life." She comes back with a glass of orange juice. "Here, the pancakes will be done in a minute."

"Thanks," I say, holding the glass in both hands as I sip, like I used to when I was a kid.

"You can turn on the radio," she calls from the kitchen. I turn on the radio behind me, battered-looking since our trip to the Sandcastle—I think it got knocked around a lot when Scoop was whipping the boat back and forth, trying to damage the cameras—but I don't think Mom has noticed. I twirl the dial to *voxless* music and tap my fingers on the table to its slow rhythm.

"Ready!" Mom comes back, bearing a stack of pancakes. She places them in front of me, then fetches syrup and fresh whipped cream.

I smother the pancakes in syrup and dig in. Mom eats too, but her eyes dart over to me and away, over and away, like I'm something so precious that I'll break if she disturbs me with a lingering look.

"Are you nervous?" she asks. "My legs were shaking when I walked up to the podium to get my assignment."

"A little." But not for the reasons she thinks.

"Well, that's natural. Nettie, you look *beautiful*. I'm so proud," she gushes. She puts down her silverware and settles back in her chair, gazing at me warmly.

I feel awkward, but it suddenly seems vital to say, "Thanks, Mom. That's nice to know."

I swallow the lump in my throat, imagining her seeing the pictures of my father and finding out how the company has been deceiving her. She trusts Media1.

"Nettie, Violet called. She said she got a message from you saying not to come to the Ceremony today."

"Yeah, I called last night, but she was asleep, so I spoke to Tula. Violet's been fragile lately. I think it'd be too much excitement for her."

"Okay," Mom says, confused. But she doesn't question me. The Double A has brought out a softer side to her. I'm glad that, at least for a few hours, I can live up to her hopes.

Lia and Henna are by the fountain, inspecting the seats for the chamber music group that sits near the mayor. Tinsel stars twinkle in the trees. I give my mother a hug and move to the front rows where the juniors sit in alphabetical order. I pick up the program waiting on my seat. *Seventy-Third Apprenticeship Announcement Ceremony.* Instead of the solar system Lia had described, there's just one magnificent sun on the cover, a golden orb wreathed in orange-gold flames.

Lia catches my eye from her spot by the fountain and nods, her earrings bobbing with the dip of her head. She's wearing a black chiffon dress, a red rose tucked behind her ear. She scans the plaza methodically, checking the tinsel stars, the mayor's podium, refreshment tables off at the side bearing bottles of wine and soda. Conor is sitting behind the podium, wan, folding and unfolding a battered piece of paper that must contain the poem.

Lincoln is a couple of rows in front of me—I recognize his curls, cropped closely to his head in a fresh cut. The boys have it easy. Suits and ties, all in the muted colors of *voxless*. I locate Callen and wave at him, but look away quickly after he waves back. I've been having trouble coming to grips with the fact that I might lose him after today, and seeing him in the flesh just makes it harder.

Navia Suchere, whom I've been lining up with my whole life, scoots into the row. Her dress is gray, with taffeta at the hips. She places the program in her lap, her hands on top of it, relaxed. She looks over at me. "What's up with your dress?" she says. "Seems . . . seriously out of date." We're not allowed to talk directly about motifs, but the conversation can easily be cloaked.

"A good friend chose it for me. A friend who's no longer with us, so I want to honor her by wearing it," I say on-mic. Navia pales at my reference to Selwyn and turns away just as Mayor Cardinal raps the microphone at the podium.

Henna and Lia run down the steps to their seats in the plaza while parents, relatives, representatives from the professions, and a host of other Characters settle into their seats. The chamber music quartet behind the mayor starts playing.

I take one last look behind me, trying to calculate how many Characters are here. At least five hundred, I estimate. The chairs are filled, and others sit on benches or stand. Plenty of crickets are around, too, but no Authority. The Double A is too perfect a scene to mar with edits. The chamber music group stops playing as the last stragglers take their seats. I turn and fix my eyes on the mayor, a pudgy man with thick black eyebrows and a mustache. He grips the top of the podium and clears his throat.

"Welcome to the Seventy-Third Annual Apprenticeship Announcement," he says. Applause erupts, and some of the football tracs stomp their feet and guffaw like it's the funniest thing in the world. Lia shoots them a murderous glare.

"Every year, we gather to celebrate one of the most memorable occasions in a Bliss Islander's life. What you learn today will set the course of your whole future. We understand that you're desperate to know, but please remember, you are not permitted to open the program until everyone has received their assignment."

Navia clutches her program tightly. "I'm dying," she whispers.

"Oh, you can hold out," I say, crossing my legs.

"I remember my first Apprenticeship Announcement," the mayor says. "I had no idea what I wanted to do, had left the line on my application blank, ready to be anyassigned."

The mayor goes on, but I stop listening, distracted by the sight of Navia's index finger slipping underneath the program cover. My stomach starts doing flip-flops.

The mayor landed a town council clerkship. Navia lifts her hand and joins the smattering of applause. I hear a few usual disgruntled rumblings. Some Characters hate that story because the chances of an anyassigned apprenticeship being good are slim. The mayor was lucky.

The mayor finishes up his prepared remarks, and Conor

shuffles up onstage. I remember how Selwyn was worried his poem will make everyone cry or something. But it's actually okay and incredibly short.

Today our lives begin.
As we sit among our friends,
Watching our childhoods end.

There's not even time to let the final lines of the poem sink in, because Mayor Cardinal springs from his seat, clapping, and we all clap while Conor walks away. An assistant brings a basket of scrolls to the mayor. The assignments are on scrolls stacked inside the basket like logs for a fireplace. The anxiety that's been right under the surface during the ceremony rises up and settles heavily over the audience. I glance over—Navia has her program open, but she still hasn't seen the insert, tucked between the third and fourth pages of apprenticeship listings.

"Pruelle Ash," the mayor calls out. Pruelle, a misfit who managed to scrub up pretty well for the occasion, runs up the podium stairs, pleated skirt swinging, a smile so nervous it almost looks like a grimace. The mayor hands her the scroll. "You have received a journalist apprenticeship."

Pruelle's smile grows, and she skips down the steps to her chair, holding the paper aloft. Someone calls out, "You deserve it, Pruelle!" from the back rows. I twist around with everyone else, trying to see who yelled. A girl sitting near Scoop. He's not part of the ceremony, of course, but he looks as nervous as any of us: hunched forward, elbows on his knees, hands knotted together.

The crowd quiets down as the mayor moves on to the next Character, Anders Batling—policeman. Two more Characters receive their assignments amid flurries of celebration. And then: "Lia Burnish!"

Lia rises and squeezes out of her row. Behind me, I hear whispering, and I resist the urge to turn around this time.

"Lia Burnish," the mayor repeats as he hands her a scroll. "A future Blisslet." She smiles graciously, showing none of Pruelle's or the others' open relief. As always, she has perfect poise, and pauses at the top of the steps to give Scoop's mother time to snap a picture for the newspaper before beginning her descent.

"What is this?" I hear someone whisper behind me. Lia walks down the stairs, gazing into the crowd, and our eyes meet. She knows it's out there. My heart thumps louder, about to break through my rib cage. Lia sits down in her chair, calm and collected.

"Look inside," someone whispers, and now Navia is turning the page in her program.

"*Patriot Adventures*?" Navia says, frowning. She takes out the insert and shows it to me. "Nettie, have you seen this?"

"Um, yeah." At last I open up the program. I flip to the insert that Lia photocopied and put in all the programs. The top has the ad for *Patriot Adventures* that I stole from the Center. I flip the paper over.

"Hey, check out the back," I whisper loudly to Navia. "There's a message."

Characters of Bliss Island: We have never been told what happens to our loved ones, the Patriots. We've taken solace in the Contract's promise that their needs will be met. Maybe you heard rumors of circumstances that were less than comfortable, but you had faith that Media1 had their best interests at heart. Perhaps others urged you not to ask questions. Ultimately, you decided it wasn't worth risking your life on Bliss to find a truth no one else seemed to care about.

But many of us do care, even though we've been told not to.

That's why we looked for, and found, the truth. This is what becomes of those of us who are cut. They join the cast of a show called Patriot Adventures. *On the back of this statement you'll find pictures and descriptions of the stars of* Patriot Adventures. *They're enlisted to help the Sectors government defeat the rebels in the Drowned Lands. To do so, they put their lives on the line—carrying guns and bombs, attacking Drowned Landers directly or going undercover among them. Read the show descriptions. They'll tell you everything you need to know. You'll also see references to the "Ultimate Sacrifice." That's death. Patriots get killed on* Patriot Adventures.

We also believe that Media1 has been deliberately cutting younger Characters because they make better—and more pliable—fighters on **Patriot Adventures.**

Media1 can no longer be trusted. We demand an end to the Contract.

The murmurs of the crowd grow louder and louder. The mayor is oblivious; he keeps calling out names, assuming the murmurs are just the usual sneak peeks. Characters go up and receive their assignments, but no one's paying attention to the stage anymore. When he gets to Shar Corone, however, Shar just sits there, shaking his head. The mayor repeats his name three or four times before saying into the microphone, "Is something going on?"

"Do you know about *Patriot Adventures*?" someone calls out.

"*Patriot Adventures*?" the mayor repeats, scratching his beard.

I hear a click and look down at my mic, put my ear down against it.

That high, nearly imperceptible buzz it usually emits is absent.

"Is your microphone off?" I ask Navia. She checks and nods, face solemn.

"Is that my uncle?" Caren Trosser asks behind me, puzzled. "He's *killing* people in the Drowned Lands?"

The mayor says again, voice tremulous, "Is something going on?"

"The cameras are off!" A boy points up at a dead red eye in a tree. Hundreds of heads turn up, scouring the camerapoles and the trees and the backs of chairs—anywhere a camera might be.

"He's right," a man shouts.

"Our mics are off too." I recognize Lia's voice. She's standing among a group of our classmates. "It must be true."

Her parents wade through the crowd over to her. "Lia, I think we should go home." Eleanora Burnish puts her long arm over Lia and, with a flick of her wrist, tosses the program into a nearby trash can. She pushes Lia forward, trying to usher her out of the plaza.

I put my hand over my eyes to block out the sun and see Characters leaving. I can't tell if they're scared or don't care.

"This is a prank." A new voice rings out over the crowd. A cricket is clattering onto the stage and has commandeered the podium, pushing the mayor to the side. He seizes the mic and starts talking, but he's too fast and no one can understand him. He takes a deep breath and slows down. "Ladies and gentlemen, this is a prank. There is no *Patriot Adventures.*"

"He's lying," I call out, pointing at him. Now people lift their heads from the programs and the dead cameras and turn to me, including the cricket at the podium. Uh-oh. I glance down at the insert in my hands and the faces on it, and I think of how Selwyn's going to be joining them soon.

"It's not a prank." I'm standing up now, but my voice is still shaky. "They're training the Patriots to kill people. Right here on the island." The words hang in the air as Characters around me quiet down. All eyes are on me, and my heartbeat accelerates as I realize what I've done. So much for anonymity.

A frantic woman with a long nose calls out, "Is my son there? Revere Yucann? Is he part of this?"

I hesitate, aware of crickets within listening range. Revere's mother looks up at me so plaintively, though, that I gulp and just plunge ahead. "He's still here, training. But he won't be safe for long; none of them will."

Characters start tossing out more questions now. I see the glint of Mom's glasses. Her mouth is pinched tight, and her fingers are clutched around the program as she watches me, petrified. I don't respond to her or anyone, distracted by the streaks of black I see—Authority running into the plaza. My breath comes faster as I whirl around, trying to find a path out of the crowd, but I'm blocked on all sides. Scoop manages to push through and takes my hand. Authority plow through the crowd, shoving Characters out of the way, coming after me.

A cricket with soft brown eyes reaches us before they do and puts her hand on my shoulder.

"Nettie. Did you write this?" She waves the insert in front of me.

"No, I did," Scoop says. He keeps his eyes fixed on the cricket's, daring her to contradict him. "I wrote it and slipped the flyers into the programs while I was helping Lia Burnish. Nettie and Lia know nothing about them."

"But that can't be true," the cricket says, voice gentle. "She just said she knows where Revere is." Scoop squeezes my hand harder, so I keep my mouth shut. Three Authority break out from the now-silent crowd and circle us. I try not to panic. It'll be okay, I recite to myself. It'll be okay.

"You'll have to come with us to the Center," the cricket says.

"No!" my mother wails.

Scoop and I exchange looks. I know we're thinking the same thing: we're going to be locked up in the Sandcastle. My mother lunges forward, and one of the Authority holds her back. His grip on her arm looks tight, and my mind is made up.

"Okay, we'll go," I say. I don't want to get any of the Characters in trouble. We did our part—they know the truth. "Okay?" I whisper to Scoop, and he nods.

An Authority approaches me, bearing handcuffs, and the nice cricket shakes her head adamantly. "Those aren't necessary." She walks up to the Authority, and I can read her lips as she murmurs in his ear, "We don't want to upset the cast." She turns back, smiling, like she's inviting us to a party. "Come with us. We have some questions." She coaxes us forward, and Scoop and I obey.

I search for Callen, but I don't see him, so I just follow the path the Authority clears for us, leading toward the white van on the side of the road.

Chapter 25

We're in a dark, cramped cell in the Sandcastle, with one slender window fronted by rusty bars and a rickety cot in the corner. We've been here for two hours. I can hear the ocean pounding the shore outside and gulls flapping and screeching nearby as I pace the floor. I'm worried they're abandoning us here. Letting us starve to death. The solution to traitorous Characters. Media1 killed my father, and now they'll kill me.

Scoop stands on his tiptoes and peeks through the bars. "The freighter's still docked," he reports. "I think we stopped them from shipping the Patriots out." A note of satisfaction is in his voice.

I try sitting on the rusty cot, scrambling up when my legs make contact with surprise moisture. I pace again. I knock on the walls. No echo. Thick. There's nothing behind there. In the joint where the ceiling meets the wall is a familiar sight. A camera, and it's on. I've never seen a camera in the Center before. I look around the cell for mics. None—and ours are still off.

"They're gonna come get us. Stop worrying," Scoop says,

turning away from the window. "Rest a little. You're putting grooves in the floor from all the walking."

"Fine." I stop in front of a thin crack in the wall and stare at it, as if it'll grow into a passageway we can slip through. And go where? Hijack the freighter? For a second, I think about it, letting my mind spin out a fantasy—grabbing a gun from an Authority, saving the Patriots, Scoop taking control at the helm and going . . . where? There must be places in the world that are free from Media1.

Scoop slides down and sits against the wall underneath the window, resting in the single pane of light stretching across the floor. The tick of his watch is amplified in the quiet cell.

"Some of the Characters were pretty mad," I say, sinking to the floor next to him. I don't mention the ones who seemed ready to pretend none of it ever happened. If there aren't enough Characters brave enough to stand up to Media1, it'll all have been for nothing.

Sensing my distress, Scoop reaches over and tousles my hair. "Let's play a game," he says. "I was thinking How Many Bugs? There's a beetle." He points toward a crevice in the floor, and I force myself to look, seeing the beetle toddle along. "One."

I shudder and draw my knees up to my chin, then point to the floor. "The spider."

The game goes on for at least fifteen minutes, and then we run out of bugs to count. We talk, trading stories of our earliest memories, then our favorite desserts and our worst teachers, our best teachers, our happiest spring days, our proudest moments.

Scoop is the one who keeps coming up with the new topics. Then we run out of things to say and sit in silence, me fading in and out of a restless sleep.

A rattle—key in the lock—and a screech as the bolt slides open. We jump up as the door opens and fluorescent lights from the hall invade the room. Two Authority march in, with Luz following behind them, wearing his purple jumpsuit for once.

"Come with me," he says tersely, turning and walking out of the room.

"That's my producer, the guy who came up with the Initiative," I whisper to Scoop as we follow him. Luz leads us through a labyrinth of halls, single file, one Authority in front of us, one behind. We pause at an unmarked door. The Authority unlocks the door, then Luz ushers us into the mostly empty, windowless room, gesturing for us to sit down at a round table. He sits, putting a megaphone I hadn't noticed before in his lap.

Scoop tries to act calm, but his jogging knee gives him away. "I want to see Belle," he blurts out.

"Not now," Luz says sternly. He's not looking at me. Is he mad? I guess I'm not one of his favorites anymore.

"Is she safe?" Scoop persists. "I have to know that she's not going to be on that show."

"I'll let you see Belle, but I need you two to do something for me. For us. The Characters have ignored our orders to return to their homes. They've gathered outside the gates, and they're refusing to leave," Luz tells us. "The board is deciding how they want to handle it. Some want to deploy tear gas. Others think less violent means may be more effective. I've proposed that you help us by talking to the crowd, urging them to go home."

"Are you kidding?" I break in. "I think you've forgotten whose side we're on."

"Nettie, if you don't cooperate, things could get much worse," Luz says, scratching his beard, agitated. "The board is furious."

"We'll do it if you stop *Patriot Adventures*," Scoop asserts.

Luz just laughs. "No. I shouldn't laugh," he says. "It's just that the board would throw you right back in that cell if I suggested that."

"Fine, have them do it," I retort. "We're not going to help."

"Wait." Scoop puts his hand on my arm. "We'll talk to them, but only if you stop the next shipment of Patriots. Belle, Revere, all of them."

"You can't bargain." I turn to him. "*Patriot Adventures* has to end. My father died on that show."

"We need to do what we can right now," Scoop says firmly. "What exactly do you want us to say?"

Part of me knows he's right. There are no Authority in sight, but it wouldn't take one long to barge in and make the same demand with a gun to our heads. Though we've shocked Media1 and scored a psychological blow, they still hold most of the power. "Okay," I nod. "We'll talk to the Characters if you free the next shipment."

"Just a second." Luz leaves the room, and I hear him whispering outside to someone.

Scoop yells after him, "And we need to *see* Revere, Belle, and Selwyn free before we say anything."

Luz comes back in after a few minutes, nodding. "Done. This batch of Patriots will be released to their families while Media1 decides how to handle the dangerous situation you've created on the island," he says, gesturing us to our feet. "Now it's time to hold up your end of the bargain."

"What do we say?" Scoop asks as we follow Luz through the winding subterranean Sandcastle halls, Authority trailing us.

"I'll tell you when we get outside," Luz says, standing and handing me the megaphone. "Nettie's going to do all the talking."

"I don't say anything?" Scoop frowns.

"Media1 wants Nettie," Luz says, leading us up the stairs and outside into the sunlight.

Luz moves close beside me as we climb the hill from the Sandcastle to the Center gates. "I feel so bad, Nettie," he says softly. "To have put you all through this. It's my worst nightmare. When I started the Initiative, I thought I was going to save you, get you off the E.L. forever, ensure that you made tons in ratings payments and could enjoy a good life on the island. But look what happened." His laughter is tinged with bitterness. "It couldn't have ended worse."

"A good life?" I snort. "You thought threatening to cut me if I didn't close up with Callen was part of a good life?"

Chastened, all he can do is mutter back, "I'm sorry. I did

my best—the board just kept demanding more and more. They want *Days* to be doing as well as *Adventures*."

"Scoop?" a voice cries in the distance before I can respond. Coming toward us, marching around the corner of Character Relations is a block of Authority surrounding three smaller figures in camouflage.

"Belle?" he calls out.

The Authority part, revealing Belle, Selwyn, and Revere, clinging tightly to one another as they stumble toward us dressed in Patriot fatigues and blinking as if they haven't seen the sun in a hundred seasons. Belle frees herself and quickens her pace. Scoop runs to meet her and crushes her into his arms, her face buried in his shoulder.

I approach Selwyn and Revere more slowly, the guilt from both their cuts weighing heavy on me. Revere's face lights up when he sees me, but before he can say anything, Selwyn recognizes me—she's squinting in the bright midafternoon sunlight—and squeals, sprinting forward the last few yards to reach me.

We hug, and her bristly hair scratches my cheek. "I should have stopped you from talking so much in the bathroom," I whisper into her ear.

She pulls back and says, "Nettie, it's not your fault." She notices my ears. "Your earrings! Our Double A earrings." She touches her own bare lobes wistfully. Her voice is hoarse and dry. "You look so plus ten in them. Are you okay? I was worried—I heard you told everyone about what they're doing to us.

It's all the Reals have been talking about all afternoon. How'd you do it?"

Before I can answer, Revere comes between us. "Nettie," he says.

He's thinner, and his weight loss makes his beaky nose stand out even more. When he looks at me, his brown eyes radiate pure gratitude. "I saw you that night," he says, "looking out from Character Relations, and I hoped . . ." His voice trails off. When he speaks again, it sounds like he's fighting down sobs. "Thank you."

Scoop and Belle come over to us, hand in hand. "Do you hear the Characters outside the gates?" Belle asks.

I hear the roar now, rising up and down, a rhythmic chanting. The sound is a tidal wave that might take me under.

We want the truth. We want the truth.

Belle drops Scoop's hand and runs ahead, toward the gates. Selwyn and Revere follow her. Their speed and tight coordination speak to their Patriot training. As they approach the gates, the chanting subsides, the crowd shocked out of their rage. No one's ever seen a Patriot before. I hear Selwyn squeal out to her parents. Scoop takes a step forward, like he's going to join them, but Luz yells, "Wait," as he comes over to us, the other Reals flanking him.

"All right, Nettie," he says. "You're up. I'll tell you what to say."

All of us—the released Patriots, the Authority, Luz, Scoop, and I—approach the fence separating the Center from the set.

Selwyn, Revere, and Belle are further ahead, standing right at the locked front gates, face-to-face with the crowd.

There are so many more Characters than I thought there would be. Word must have spread from the Double A, because it looks like almost the whole island knows and that, in the hours since we've told them, what's going on has sunk in—the initial shock is over, and the anger has begun.

"Do you think they could stop the Reals?" Scoop whispers. "The police might do something."

I shake my head. I hope they don't. We can't risk lives now. Ending *Patriot Adventures* is all about saving lives.

"Tell us the truth!" someone shouts from the other side of the fence, and something ripples in the air. Glass shatters against the pavement, and I hop back, narrowly dodging the shards. Someone hurled a bottle over the wall. Authority stand by the iron gates, impervious to the chants.

"It's Nettie Starling! Nettie Starling and Scoop Cannery! They've been taken prisoner," a man shouts, and the chants dissolve into epithets and curses at Media1 and unintelligible screams and cries. The gates creak under the weight of the crowd. The Authority watch, still as stones.

Luz steps close to me. "This is what I want you to say: We're unharmed, and we ask that you return to your homes and wait for a Missive from Media1 about how we will proceed in light of the day's events. Got it?"

"Say it again?" I whisper.

Luz repeats the words. I raise the megaphone to my lips, and sunlight bounces off it, slashing deep into the crowd, but when I open my mouth, no sound comes out.

Scoop strides up, reaching for the megaphone. "I'll do it," he says. I pull it back. "Nettie, c'mon," he pleads. "I want to make sure Belle stays safe. Let me speak," he demands, turning to Luz.

Luz shakes his head firmly. "It has to be Nettie."

"Why not Scoop?" I ask. "Why does it have to be me?"

"It just . . . does. The board says so." Luz fumbles with his answer, and I know exactly what he can't bring himself to say. I'm Lia's sidekick. Quieter than Scoop. More obedient.

I turn toward the crowd and bring the megaphone to my lips. "We're unharmed—"

The chants and cries begin to die down, and they watch me with the same awed reverence they gave to Belle, Selwyn, and Revere.

"We're safe, and—" I pause. Luz is watching me with steely eyes, and it's as if he knows what I'm about to say even before I do. I take a deep breath. Media1 isn't entirely wrong—I used to be more obedient, but I've changed.

"Scoop and I wrote the statement and put the ads in the programs. We saw *Patriot Adventures* with our own eyes. Media1 is sending our families to the Drowned Lands, where they kill people and get blown up and murdered. This isn't what the Originals intended when they signed the Contract. They wanted security, but instead—"

Luz lunges toward me. I break into a run, but slip on a can

someone threw over the fence, and my dress tears as I stumble to the ground. Scoop breaks free from the Authority and throws himself at Luz an instant before one of the Authority tackles both of them.

I scramble back to my feet. My knee is skinned, a bloodstain darkening my dress's ragged hem, but I bring the megaphone back up to my mouth.

"We need to . . ." I search frantically for the right words. "We need to show them we can't be ordered around. *Patriot Adventures* ends, or *Blissful Days* ends." The roar from the crowd is overwhelming.

"Nettie, behind you!" Selwyn shrieks, but it's too late. A sharp pain as a cricket rams into me, and I fall to the ground, the megaphone tumbling from my hands. The crowd's roar grows louder until sharp cracks peal in the air, and then the roar becomes deafening, punctuated with screams. All I can see is the gravel beneath my face; in my mouth I taste the dull metal of blood.

"Get them out of here," Luz yells from behind me.

Chapter 26

My head throbs. I rub my temple, trying to coax the pain away as we're escorted into Luz's office. Scoop is hovering next to me.

"Have a seat," an Authority growls, motioning toward the sofa. Scoop and I obey. Luz comes in a few minutes later and orders the Authority to leave.

"Did they hurt anyone?" I ask, rubbing my head. "Is my mother okay? Was anyone shot?"

"Your mother is fine," Luz says, resting back in the chair. "They used tear gas, but no one was injured. Those were just warning shots. The tear gas is what persuaded the Characters to return to their homes. We issued a Missive ordering them to stay inside while the board works out how to address today's events."

"They just . . . everyone went home?" I say, torn between happiness that no one's hurt and fear that nothing is going to change.

"For now," Luz says. He sighs and does the beard-scratching thing. "But I don't know how long it will last—Characters were ripping their mics off and destroying cameras. If you wanted to sow discord and discontent, Nettie, you've succeeded, and you have most likely cost me my job. The board's blaming me for your newfound, um, confidence. Which means the Initiative's over."

"Our hearts break for you." Scoop rolls his eyes.

"The Initiative was good for a lot of Characters," Luz says sharply. "You may not like to hear this, Nettie, but many Patriots thrive on *Adventures*. Your father was one. His popularity before his death was why some people in the producers' circle wanted to cut you, Nettie, instead of Belle."

"Do you expect me to thank you? No one should have to go on that show," I cry out. I lean my aching head back and close my eyes. "Did the Originals know about *Patriot Adventures*?"

"No, not unless they snuck around like you did. They only knew what was in the Contract," Luz says. "It wasn't always like this. Yes, part of the initial deal to get the island and the broadcasting rights from the Sectors was that Characters who were cut could be used by the government in some of their war efforts, but there was no broadcast, and it was much less dangerous. After all, the problems in the Drowned Lands weren't as severe when *Blissful Days* started. Then, their needs changed. It was the Sectors government that came to us with the idea for the show twenty-six seasons ago. They thought it might rally the Audience into supporting their efforts in the Drowned Lands, as well as pull a profit and help with combat itself."

Scoop fires questions at Luz. "Why have you brought us here? What are you going to do to us?"

"The board wants me to ask you some questions, to find out how this happened. Why you two disobeyed the Contract so thoroughly. After you answer my questions, well, you're going home. I mean your real home. The Sectors. Off the show."

"The Sectors?" My mind whirls. "Wait, what about our parents—what about—"

"Where exactly will we go?" Scoop interrupts. "Nettie said virtually all the Originals came from the Drowned Lands. We can't go there." He shakes his head. "That's too dangerous."

I knock his knee with mine. "Wait, this is okay with you? What about *Patriot Adventures*?" I turn back to Luz. "You can't keep killing Characters."

"We've decided you and your family members can no longer be trusted to perform. We'll resettle you in Zenta and provide work training so you can make lives there. The rest of both casts—everyone who is on the island or currently on *Patriot Adventures*—can leave. Or they can remain on their respective shows, with the Characters signing a new Contract that states that they're willing to perform Patriot duties in the event that they're cut. With the situation in the Drowned Lands being what it is, we're going to be pouring more of our resources into *Adventures*."

My jaw drops. "Wait—you think killing the cast is okay? Media1 still thinks this is an option after today?"

Luz starts playing around with papers on his desk. "That's the deal," he says. At least he doesn't say he's sorry. I'm getting sick of hearing that.

"This is the best we can do," Scoop whispers. "We can have a new life in the Sectors, with our families. Everyone can—it's up to them."

He's right, but it still feels like we've played into the company's hands somehow.

"Fine. But what about my grandmother?" I ask. "What's going to happen to her?"

"She'll be given the option to renew like everyone else. The phones are working, so you can call her up to discuss it," Luz says, relaxing. "The board wants this to be done in a civilized, orderly fashion.

"I'm going to take you two home now," he says. "We'll be distributing a revised Contract tonight, and tomorrow we'll be sending buses to pick up those Characters who don't wish to sign it. The freighter that was meant to transport the Patriots can take Characters to the mainland. The rest can stay in the Center until new freighters arrive. We should be ready to start filming again on Tuesday."

"How are you going to explain all this to the Audience?" I ask as we walk out into the hall. "And what about all the Characters who'll be missing? How will they explain them?"

"Most likely they'll put the show on hiatus for a week or two." He lowers his voice. "Show archived episodes until they come back with a campaign presenting an updated, superior version of the show. The truth is that they can say whatever they want, and the Audience won't question it. They're hooked."

• • •

Sobering sights at the edge of the Center as we pull away. The twisted fence. An upturned trash can, smashed bottles. We see a lot of the island as crickets drive us back home. Authority are everywhere, blurs of black. I don't see any Characters. The van pulls into Treasure Woods, and we stop at Scoop's house. All the lights are on, and I imagine the Cannerys having a lively discussion about the day's events. Scoop gives me a quick hug.

"See you on the earliest bus tomorrow," he whispers.

The van backs up and turns, headed toward the Arbor. I see the columns on Lia's house, and I realize I don't know if I'll see Lia tomorrow—I don't know if I'll ever see her again, except on television.

"Wait," I burst out. I'm shocked when the driver actually does stop the car.

"What is it?" Luz asks.

"I want to see Lia," I say. "I'm worried—I don't know what she's going to do."

Luz nods. "Fifteen minutes."

I scramble out of the van, run up the stairs, and press the doorbell. My heart thuds as I wait. Lia comes to the door, still in her black Double A gown, the rose wilting behind her ear. She envelops me in her arms.

"I was there outside the Center, but I didn't see you—I left before you came out. It was getting dangerous," she says. She reaches out and neatens up my hair. "You're a mess. There were all these rumors about what they did to you—oh, God. The company sent a Missive saying you were okay, but I wasn't sure."

"I'm all right," I say, in a choked voice because she's holding me so tightly. "Media1 is escorting me home tonight. But, Lia—I'm leaving tomorrow. For good. Will you come?" It's strange to say the word *Media1* aloud on-set.

She grabs my hand and tugs me inside. "I want to," she whispers. "But my parents are reviewing the new Contracts. My mother . . ." She picks up her dress at the waist as she leads me, to avoid tripping on it.

"Who is it?" her mother says from their dining room.

I approach the dining room table with trepidation. Eleanora looks up at me, smiling drunkenly. Lia's father sits across from her and has what must be the Contract spread out before him, muttering as he reads.

"We don't need to read this." Eleanora swipes the papers away from him. "I'm not going anywhere."

"Why not?" I drop Lia's arm and step forward. "Don't you get it? If you get cut, you'll *die*."

"*My* ratings are excellent," Eleanora says, pointing at herself. "I will never get cut, and I will not end up in the Sadtors." Eleanora grabs the pen from Mr. Burnish and signs the Contract while he glances up at Lia, helpless.

"I have to leave the show," I say to her quietly. "They're making me, not that I wouldn't go without them telling me to. But I wouldn't trust any piece of paper from Media1, no matter how good my ratings were."

"I know you're right, but . . ." Lia bites her lower lip. She goes over to her father at the table, kneeling next to him. "Dad, earlier we talked about trying a new life in the Sectors?" she says, low, almost whispering. "A sensible life, without—"

"Without what? Without *me* you mean?" Eleanora raises her voice grandly. No one says anything. We just watch as she fixes her mussed golden hair in the mirror behind her table. Then she reaches down and takes a swig from the wineglass at her elbow. Mr. Burnish watches her, then snatches up the pen and signs.

"I have to take care of her," he explains. "She's my wife, and your mother. Who knows what she might do to herself if we leave her alone, with only . . ." Lia stands up and backs away from them, her eyes growing glassy with tears.

"Lia, spend the night at my house," I say. She looks over at me, blinking, like she doesn't understand. "You can take the bus with us tomorrow."

She looks back at her parents. Her dad just keeps nervously rubbing at the paper of the new Contract. Her mom is silent too, swirling the wine in her glass. Lia blots out the tears in her eyes with the back of her hand and says to me, "I'll come. I just need to pack."

Chapter 27

The doorbell rings while I'm on the phone with Selwyn. She's having trouble figuring out how much clothing to bring to the Sectors. Lia, eating chips and perched on a stool by the counter, can hear her and keeps rolling her eyes. Her infinite vacillations over tops and gloves don't bother me at all. This conversation is a lot easier than the one Mom and I had earlier with Violet, who seemed nearly destroyed by the news of my father's death. I don't think I'll ever forget her sobs, and she'll never forgive Media1—the last words she managed to get out were that she'd see us at the Center tomorrow.

My mother answers the door, and when I hear Callen's voice, I nearly drop the phone. I've been deliberately not thinking about him. I'm terrified that he'll stay.

Lia begins bustling about the kitchen, and I avoid looking in her direction.

"Selwyn, I need to go."

I hang up the phone and run to the front door, where Callen is waiting for me. He grabs my hand and pulls me toward him, and we kiss for the first time since that doomed evening.

"You're okay," he says, and when we draw apart, I see relief in his face, but something else too—he seems more *present.* Has he ever looked at me like that before? "You're okay? Are you sure?" he insists, not letting go of my hand. "The plaza was terrifying, and then outside the Center, I was worried there was going to be a riot. I can't believe you're safe. I heard what you said on the megaphone, and I was so worried the company would hurt you."

"Yeah, I'm fine," I say, leading him to the living room. "I'm fine, except—have you made up your mind? Are you going to stay or go?"

"My whole family is leaving the island," he says.

Joy erupts inside me, and I smile. "Us too," I whisper, mindful of Lia in the next room. I take his hand and pull him down to the couch.

"It wasn't so easy." He raises his hand, considering it, like he's assessing its value. "Dad, I think, could have stayed, but Mom wanted out, and . . ."

"You weren't tempted, were you? If everyone had seen *Patriot Adventures,* like I did, there's no way they'd stay."

"I thought about staying for a second, because the Sectors are scary. Not as scary as *Patriot Adventures,* obviously, just unknown. But I kept looking at the pictures you and Scoop put into the program . . . and I thought about the Initiative and what they tried to make you do with the close-up. We can't stay."

"You're coming?" Lia says from the doorway. I stand up quickly, without thinking, guilty. "Your father's okay with that?"

"He's dealing with it," he says coolly. "Why are you here? Saying good-bye?"

"I'm going to the Sectors too," she says, staying in the doorway.

"And your parents?"

"Nope," she says blithely. "I'll be an orphan, but at least I won't end up on *Patriot Adventures*." She gives a harsh sort of laugh and crosses her arms. I can tell how hard she's trying to act casual.

She just stands there. No one says anything, and it's really uncomfortable. I want her to leave and give me more time alone with Callen. I think that's what he wants too, but she stays in place until he says, "Well, I'm leaving with you. I just came to let you know." He gets up and gives me a chaste peck on the cheek, mumbling good-bye to Lia as he passes her on his way out.

"So you two are back together? I hope he doesn't stay so awkward around me." She sighs.

I stare at my feet, touching the place on my cheek where he kissed me. "I'm sure it'll get easier," I say, but what I really want to say is that it's not about her.

Lia's legs are too long for my jester-patterned pajama pants. She lies on her back, the Diary lifted above her, biting her lower lip as she turns its pages, squinting when she can't decipher my handwriting.

"Oh, Nettie, look." She sits up. "Do you remember when we

did these Vows for Life during our freshman year? We were so ambitious."

"What'd we say?" I turn to my side and prop my head on my hand. Freshman year was so long ago. *Blueblood* motif, with, like, bodices and stuff, and string music constantly on the radio.

"I wanted to marry . . . oh, God, no," she says, groaning. "What a tragedy. Dennis Touray, that trac with the eye patch. Do you remember, Nettie? He said he had a scratch on his cornea, and he wore that filthy eye patch for thirty-four straight days."

"You counted?"

"He *announced* it, like, every opportunity he had," she exclaims. "And I wrote our kids' names down here. Cressida and Credulous. Twins. I must have been joking about Credulous, or delusional if I thought I could get a name like that approved by the company."

"We wrote that we'd get side-by-side houses in Treasure Woods." I giggle. "With my ratings? *That* was wishful thinking."

"You don't know that," she says thoughtfully, turning the page. "Your ratings might have changed if you stayed. You've been doing so well."

"Hmm" is the most I can summon up. In my mind, I'm already living a life without ratings. Ratings are irrelevant now that I've accepted a life without numbers. Without being measured.

"I'll have to give my kids stupid Real names now," Lia continues with a dramatic sigh. "I always hated my name because it's short and ugly, like a Real's. God, I guess I'll have to close up with a Real," Lia says, scowling. She gets up and puts the diary on my desk and returns to her place on the floor, snuggling down with the blankets.

"Are you sure you don't want to sleep somewhere more comfortable? There's not much room up here, but you know you can use the couch downstairs."

"I like it here," she says as I reach over and turn the lamp off. "On your lovely carpet. The way we used to."

I yawn, lying on my back. The ceiling is a swath of black space, impenetrable without the red lights from the cameras on.

"I'll end up with a Real, most likely," she says. "But who will you end up with? Callen looked like he was ready to follow you to the moon."

"You think?" I say.

"Yeah. And the way you've been acting, he better be careful. You just might drag him there."

The morning sunlight wakes me up. It starts as a sliver and widens until it covers my whole desk, bouncing off the mirror hanging behind my door. The camera lenses glitter with the light, but the cameras are still off.

I close my eyes and listen to the birds and suddenly realize that I'll never hear them again. I wish I could cut my connection to Bliss, but I think it's going to hurt a little. I'll miss the island.

I sit up and swing my legs over the bed. The floor beside me is empty: pillows, sheets, and the paisley comforter are stacked on the knobby chair in front of my desk. I listen for the sound of running water from my bathroom. Nothing. Lia's book bag is no longer by the door. I walk over to the desk. The Diary of Destiny is still there, lying open.

Good Things: Nettie is starting a new life off the island.

Bad Things: Lia can't. Sorry.

Vows: Don't forget me—I won't forget you. (And watch my episodes.)

I shut the notebook and put it back on the desk.

I open my bedroom door and see Mom dragging a hard-shelled suitcase out of her room. She's dressed—and formally too—in a gray lamb's wool skirt and a crisp white blouse.

"Lia left," I tell her, my voice quivering.

"Oh, Nettie." She comes over and hugs me. Her chin rests gently on the top of my head. "I know it hurts, but I think for Characters like Lia and Violet, Characters who have never worried much about ratings, the Sectors don't seem so appealing. They don't realize life can get better than it is on *Blissful Days*. They may be wrong, but we can't convince them. We just have to do what's right for us."

I'm about to protest but my voice catches in my throat. She's right. I pull away and blink back tears. I know if I cry in front of Mom, I might never stop. "Um, I need to shower."

I run into the bathroom, close the door, and go to the window. I look outside. Mrs. Herron's garden is covered in mist. She's watering her plants, and Callen's sitting on their old splintered picnic table, feet on the bench. "They'll take care of the flowers when you're gone, Mom," Callen says to her. "The garden's too camperf to let it go." I wish I could run to him now and tell him what's happened. I wish that he could just hold me.

I take my shower, forgoing the Skin Sequence, then put on some clothes, pick up my packed duffel bag, and go downstairs.

Mom jumps up from the dining room table. "I'll get you some cereal," she says.

"No, I'll get it." I go into the kitchen and fix myself a bowl, slicing a banana on top and wasting a few seconds wondering if I should throw in some propro before I remember that I'm done with that now.

"She might change her mind again," Mom says as we eat. "Maybe you should call her?"

"No. She's not worried about ending up on *Patriot Adventures,* and maybe she's right not to be." I shrug. "It doesn't matter—we should think about ourselves, our future. How much do you know about the Sectors?"

Not much, it turns out. She tells me a few things she's learned from some of the books Media1 let through. For example, there's an annual cough that goes around that they can't eradicate and cities where the train system runs all night. I tell her the names of the places I've seen on Dr. Kanavan's calendar.

"I think I'd like to see them," I say. "All of them."

"But, Nettie, it could be dangerous," Mom says as I gather our bowls. "I don't want you to—"

"End up in the grave, like Dad?" The response comes out sounding a lot colder than it had in my head.

She sweeps the crumbs off the table and into her napkin, then readjusts her glasses. "Yes, that's what I mean," she says. "You may not have to listen to Media1, but you'll still have to listen to me out there."

I rise from the table to bring my bowl back to the kitchen and hug her impulsively. "I will," I promise. I wasn't lying when I said I wanted to see all of the Sectors. I just want both: home and Mom and freedom and the outside.

A large motor growls down the street. Mom snatches up her suitcase. "That must be the bus."

The sky is cloudy, and it's drizzling lightly. No scripted sky today. I stand on our porch while Mom, maybe unnecessarily, locks up. I see people streaming from their houses to get on the bus, which stops every dozen or so feet to pick them up. Whole families and individuals. The bus is supposed to be making rounds all day, and it looks like it will need to—it's already filling up.

The bus arrives in front of our house just as Mom and I are still walking toward the street, and the Herrons beat us to it. I fall in line behind Callen, and Mom is behind me, and there are people behind her, but I don't look back to check who they are. Callen glances back quickly, once, just to smile.

We pile into the bus in silence. Even the kids seem to know that this is a sober event. A brother and sister around the same age—six or so—sit together without making a peep. Their father sits behind them, wearing a wedding ring, but without a wife. I wonder how many families have been torn apart.

Crickets are here too, in uniform. One stands at the back of the bus; others are scattered throughout, whispering to one another. Callen's parents sit together, his mom gazing forlornly out the window, while Callen sits across from them, alone. He gestures me over, and I look up at Mom.

"Go ahead," she says.

I slide in next to Callen. He puts his hand protectively over mine on the seat, but when I look in his eyes and see the worry there, I'm not sure who's protecting whom. I rest my head on his shoulder.

"Lia didn't come."

"I didn't think she would," he says. We pass the playground dividing Treasure Woods from the Arbor.

"She could change her mind," I say, but I know she won't.

We drive through Treasure Woods, and hardly anyone gets on. Life on the island is pretty good if you have strong ratings. We pass the Graysons' mansion, perched on a hill. None of them are waiting for us. Callen grips my hand tightly as we pass Lia's house.

Then Scoop, Belle, and their parents come aboard. Loudly. Mr. Cannery tips his hat to the Authority bus driver, and his mother puts her hand above her eyes as she scouts out the seats, mock-complaining, "I have to go all the way to the back?" and the mood on the bus lifts, coinciding with the sun breaking out from behind gray clouds. Scoop and I exchange nods as he goes to the back of the bus. Two partners finally at the end of a project.

I press my face up against the glass, and I try to watch without thinking, wanting to remember the way the hedges run along the sidewalk, how weeping willows kiss the ground. Details that *Blissful Days* might miss.

"We're never coming back," Callen says, rubbing the back of my hand with his thumb.

I'm leaving. I can carry the island in my head for a while. But bit by bit, the sense of it will fade, like a gradual changing of seasons, and it will all just be images on a screen. I think that I can live with that distance. Distance from Lia, from the familiar places flying by, from the certainty that my world ended at the ocean.

The Reals treat all the departing Characters like royalty at the Center. As soon as we step off the bus, it's all "Welcome," "Right this way," and "Glad you're here," as they break us up into separate groups, directing us to different Center buildings. I think they're worried about a repeat of yesterday's hostility. With at least three hundred of us here, serious damage could be done if the group got angry. A nervous energy runs through the crowd, but it's excitement all aimed at our futures as normal citizens of the Sectors, not hostility toward the company.

All the Characters traveling with the rescued Patriots end up in Character Relations. There are about thirty of us—I think Mom, Violet, and I are the only ones who weren't connected to the Patriots. There's a table with some snacks. Children run around, testing the limits of their new freedom by chasing one another throughout the entire building and talking to Reals directly. Adults are more cautious. Some even still have their turned-off microphones clipped to their collars.

We're only there for a few hours, until the sun begins setting. Then the Reals take us outside and lead us down the road to Eden Beach. The black freighter waits in the water for us, long and low, with colored storage containers stacked on top. Reals in purple jumpsuits lead us up the gangplank. We're at the end of the line, Violet hobbling slowly. She hasn't been saying much and refused the grapes I brought her from the food stand. I'm grateful when she jabs me with her elbow and lifts her cane up, aiming it at Callen's back. "That's him, right?" she says, the ghost of a smile on her lips. I nod, glad she's showing some life.

A brown-eyed female Real with chipped nail polish shows us to our cabins. "You'll understand we weren't prepared for your voyage," she says as she struggles to unlock the door with a big iron key. "Please forgive us." Scoop rolls his eyes at me. He's not impressed. He's right. *Puppets,* I remind myself. Any friendly attitude is just today's company policy. As if I need more of a reminder not to trust them, the last thing she says to us—with a big smile—is, "Remember, don't leave your cabin until 8 a.m. tomorrow."

The cabin is small, with only one real bed, which Violet takes, and a cot for Mom. I get a sleeping bag on the floor. There's a tiny bathroom adjacent to the room, thankfully. Settling down, I think about Lia, who slept on my floor last night. I replay our conversations in my mind, grasping for clues that I failed to pick up on. Was it seeing Callen with me? Maybe it was the thought of having Real kids, maybe . . . but then the freighter's engines kick up, and there's a long screeching noise—the anchor?—and the foghorn bellows, a familiar sound. I close my eyes and I can see it: the black shadow moving away from the island. Me, moving away from the show.

The trip is supposed to last three days, and, yes, for some of that time, we're confined below deck. But during daylight hours, we're allowed to roam free. We learn all this during a quick morning meeting led by the ship's captain. We're each given diagrams of the freighter's interior with emergency escape routes. As soon as the meeting is over, everyone heads up to the deck. Selwyn and I break off from our families and walk together.

Selwyn is overdressed, a cardigan over her short turquoise summer dress. I think she's still shy about showing the tattoo. She takes one step on deck, sniffs the salty air, shakes her head, and points at her diagram. "I'm going to the game room," she says. "I think I'm seasick—it started last night. Watching some games might get my mind off of it. Maybe there will be some cute Real sailors," she speculates.

"All right, have fun." I find my mother and Violet strolling around the deck, using one of Violet's frilly parasols to block the sun. Ever since the captain finished his lecturing, they've been caught up in an endless dialogue about my father. That's why I paired up with Selwyn, not ready to listen.

Scoop is up here too. He and his family seem to operate as

one seamless unit, even if Belle still stands out—quiet, without a gleaming Cannery smile. She's happy, though, and her face looks fuller. Scoop points to the ocean, maybe spotting a dolphin or something, and they all chatter about it. I look away, content to let them have their family moment.

The freighter's so huge, you almost can't feel it moving. I don't know how Selwyn got seasick. I watch the waves. Something feels different, and I think it's the absence of fear. The future's so unknown that I can't begin to worry about it.

"I found you." Callen comes up from behind and puts his arm around me. I rest my head on his shoulder, resisting the urge to kiss his neck; Violet and Mom might see us. He watches the ocean with me for a bit. "This is it. We're out of the trap. The great beyond."

"The great beyond," I echo. We're out of earshot of anyone who might accuse him of being cynical. But who could really deny it? Leaving the island is a death of some kind. Death of my old self. What Luz always wanted.

"Nettie, Nettie!" Selwyn jogs up the stairs. "Oh, hi, Callen. Nettie, you've got to come downstairs. Guess what's in the game room? A television, and they're running all these old episodes of *Blissful Days*. There's one on now about Lia's seventh grade birthday party. Do you remember, with the bad magician who let the rabbit loose?"

"Yeah, I remember."

"Well?" she urges, raking her hand through her short hair.

I pause. I'm sort of curious. I could see my younger self. Could see us the way everyone else saw us. Watch Lia's episodes.

"Let's go, it'll be fun."

Callen stays silent next to me, but grabs my hand. I look over my shoulder, like someone's calling me from the ocean. No, just the waves. Still, they're enough of a reason to miss *Blissful Days*, for now.

"No, thanks," I say, looking out at the ocean and the freighter and Callen. "I'll stay up here."

Acknowledgments

Many thanks to Michelle Andelman, my kind, sensitive, and brilliant agent, and to Arianne Lewin, my funny, tough, and smart editor, who has taught me so much about how to craft a novel. Also thanks to Eveline Chao, Chantal Clarke, Lara Ehrlich, Trish MacGregor, Katherine Perkins, Paula Sadler, and Heather Wagner for their editorial input. Last, I am eternally grateful to Pat Willard and Al Zuckerman, my wonderful mentors and inspirations.